I0563250

Redemption on the Run

by

Donnette Smith

Love and Law Series

Cover Art by *Kristian Norris*

The Wild Rose Press, Inc.
PO Box 708
Adams Basin, NY 14410-0708
Visit us at www.thewildrosepress.com

Publishing History
First Edition, 2024
Trade Paperback ISBN 978-1-5092-5669-3
Digital ISBN 978-1-5092-5670-9

Love and Law Series
Published in the United States of America

Dedication

I dedicate this book to my beautiful mother who instilled in me the love of reading at a young age. This love led me to write stories, and later to pursue publishing for all the world to enjoy them. Mom is the first to read every manuscript I write, and her guidance over the years pushed me to write the next story even better until I gained her approval. Now it seems, that each new adventure I create serves as new reading material for a woman who devours books like a kid binging on candy at Halloween. Don't worry, Ma. The next book is coming.

Chapter One

If they planned to execute him tonight, Lucas Kade would pulverize as many of them as he could on his way out. But when the savages kicked the living crap out of him and his partner, Dominick Barlow—because they had no weapons—then bashed their skulls in, they'd probably get creative with their methods of torture, then stuff their dead carcasses in five-gallon drums.

He had to ask himself if the DEA would be able to recover their corpses.

"Do you think they'll cut us into little pieces when they blow our cover?" Lucas spat on the ground, then glanced at Dominick, damn well knowing his expression gave away the fact he wasn't completely joking this time.

It took Dom longer to answer than it should have. "They're not going to find out who we are."

A muscle tightened in his partner's jaw, and his Adam's apple bobbed in a deep swallow, telling Lucas the guy didn't buy a word that came out of his mouth. Infiltrating the *Infierno* Cartel was like playing Russian Roulette every day. He couldn't be sure from one moment to the next which one of the hot-tempered members would be the first to blow a hole right through their secret identities and take them out.

"Listen," his buddy said, "We've been working this

operation for what, three months now? If these bastards were going to make us, they'd have already done it."

They should have stayed in Texas. After all, that's where the sting operation originated. But because of a drug lord's invitation to meet them for the first time at his mansion in New York, they found themselves in unfamiliar territory. Lucas didn't like it one bit.

"They could be waiting for the perfect opportunity." What made him think that? Probably the fact these animals had no conscience and got off on the element of surprise.

Dom shook his head, slipped a menthol cigarette out of his shirt pocket, placed it between his lips, and lit it. "Everything's going according to plan. We've put in some serious work to get this meeting with Victor. We stick to the script, and everything will fall into place."

The *clink* of his partner's butane lighter as it snapped shut had a way of steadying his nerves. Sometimes when tension ran high, all it took was a familiar sound to offset the anxiety.

An airplane rumbled overhead, and Lucas glimpsed back at the airport beyond the metal fence where they stood waiting for their ride. Puffs of cold smoke billowed from his mouth, and he settled the collar of his trench coat tighter around his neck. His rattled confidence wasn't the only thing that sent shivers slithering down his spine. "Did I mention the weather here sucks?"

Dom let out a *ha.* "Welcome to New York, Texas boy."

Headlights approached in the distance, casting a yellow glow on the falling snow coming down like confetti through the darkness.

His partner straightened, took one more pull from his cigarette, and flicked it into the night. "Put your game face on. Here comes Draco."

The *Infierno's* main drug distributor, Draco Vargas, wasn't Lucas' biggest worry. Even though the guy's violent reputation turned a lot of heads and kept many of the lower-level members towing the cartel line, he'd worked with him enough to have developed a kind of comradeship. But meeting Victor Craven for the first time, at his home and on his turf, caused the same level of anxiety as a soccer mom stumbling into a rodeo arena for a picnic. According to his briefing with the DEA last week, the drug lord had the tolerance of a gorilla for anyone who double-crossed him.

Breathe for God's sake. The fact Draco trusted him enough to introduce him to the boss proved he'd won their confidence. That had been the goal all along. Keep playing the game as if you knew what you were doing, and the takedown would come. Just like Dominick said.

The crunch of tires as the limo rolled to a stop attacked Lucas' nervous system, causing him to swallow the lump rising in his throat. If he didn't pull it together, he'd blow his cover. These guys kept a constant eye out for signs of edginess. They had the talent to sniff out an undercover agent like a hound dog on steroids. The DEA put far too many resources into Operation Snowflakes to have it all end in tragedy. The moment of truth stared him in the face like a prophecy waiting to unfold. He'd not only need to step up to the plate, but he'd also have to tiptoe around it as if he feared waking the dead.

Lucas' reflection in the passenger's window disappeared as it slid down the track. Draco grinned from inside the cab. "What's up, *mi hombres*? Y'all look like you're freezing your asses off."

Bain Delgado lowered his head and peered at Lucas from the driver's seat, saying, "What? Not in the mood to make snow angels tonight, gentlemen?"

Slipping into his role as Scott Conner became as comfortable as sliding into a pair of worn jeans, even if his nerves bounced around like a ping-pong ball tonight. Lucas grabbed the window frame and leaned in. "I'm thinking a warm house and a cold beer sounds much more appealing."

Draco nodded in agreement. "Well, jump in, and let's get out of here."

After throwing his travel bag into the trunk, Lucas and Dom climbed into the back seat. Draco said, "We got one stop to make and then we'll be on our way."

"A stop?" Lucas gave Dom a quick glance. The expression on his face didn't set off alarm bells, but he sensed tension rolling off him. When you were working undercover infiltrating one of the most dangerous drug cartels in existence, and one of its members mentioned making a stop, there was reason to worry.

Draco tossed a stare over the passenger's seat. "You all right, man? You seem a little on edge."

Through the adrenaline lighting him up, Lucas managed to calm his nerves and offer a passing smile. "It's called jet lag, my friend. That was one long flight."

"Oh, I know. Ours got in yesterday and I still haven't recovered."

Dom piped up. "So, what's so important we need to make a stop?"

"Since it's on the way, the boss asked if we could

swing by and pick up his woman."

The second Draco swung back around to face the windshield, Lucas closed his eyes. His heartbeat slowed, and he allowed himself a moment to calm the storm that impaled him. He had to be out of his mind to have thrown his name in the hat regarding this undercover sting. Eight years of working as a DEA special agent did nothing to prepare for a raid as massive as this one. Christ, what made him think he could cut his teeth on a case like this? He should have started out with some local drug bust before jumping into the fire. But his ridiculous need for an adrenaline fix led him down this path.

At least he could rest assured knowing Dominick had some previous experience working undercover before taking on his role as Dante Thatcher in this investigation. The man's knowledge sure came in handy in a pinch. At any rate, rethinking his involvement now was a bit too late. He'd already stepped knee-deep in shit. Might as well wade out as far as he could and pray to God someone didn't take him out before he could stumble out of it.

Bain adjusted the rearview mirror, and his attention zeroed in on Lucas. The informant's black-brown eyes cut through to his soul, reminding him the only person in this vehicle who had no part in the undercover sting was the cartel member sitting in the passenger's seat.

All three of them could take Draco down if the unexpected occurred right now. But once they arrived at Victor's place, surrounded by hardened criminals who would cut their heads off just as easy as look at them, the odds would no longer be in their favor. He had to admit this wasn't like Texas, where a vanload of

DEA agents sat around the corner ready for action if something went down. They were in shark-infested waters now, with no help in sight other than a prayer and some fast thinking. Without his favorite weapon, he wouldn't have a chance of defending himself.

As Bain winked, Lucas took notice of the confidence in his eyes. The man had flown here with Draco; they'd spent yesterday together. If something seemed suspicious, surely the guy would have sensed it. He wouldn't be staring at him now as if everything was under control.

Before Lucas could invent another reason to panic, the limo swung into an apartment complex and rolled to a stop. He took a deep breath. Throughout this whole undercover operation, he'd kept his cool—for the most part. Even though there were a few close calls, nothing shook him as badly as this approaching meeting. He could blame being in unfamiliar territory as the culprit for his uneasiness. It made perfect sense.

So why did he sense the night was about to take a turn for the worst?

The door across from him swung open. The face that peered into the cab answered his question with heart-stopping accuracy. *Jesus Christ. Remi Shaw.*

As her gaze fell over him, her mouth opened. From her appearance, what she witnessed sitting in the seat next to Dom, stole her train of thought.

Lucas' brain was still reeling when she snugged into the seat and said, "Hey, Draco. Who's the new guy?"

Did he misread her initial reaction? No way. She had to recognize him. You don't sleep with someone for as long as they had and forget their face. He offered a nervous grin and tugged the Fedora hat over his forehead to hide his eyes. "I'm Scott."

She stuck out her hand, smiling as if she'd encountered the biggest stranger in the world. "I'm Remi. Victor's girl."

After shaking her hand, he looked away even as fire engulfed him. Then he focused his attention on his reflection in the dark-tinted window. The shock of the situation came in waves. Of all people, what was Remi Shaw doing here? Victor's girl? Did someone hit him over the head and knock him unconscious? He'd been dreaming. And right now, somebody damn well needed to pinch him.

"You're not from around here, are you?"

That voice belonged to her, all right, even though he hadn't heard it in more than a decade. He couldn't put his finger on the game she was playing. She was no longer in law enforcement, hadn't been on the force since that day thirteen years ago when she ran out on him and left her life behind as if it was a bad novel she'd tossed into the trash. So, she couldn't be here on police business.

Which meant she'd turned to a life of crime.

He took care not to allow his gaze to collide with hers. He had no idea why she didn't announce his identity to her friends but he was in no position to question her motives. "How can you tell?" he said, referring to her question. Ignoring her would only draw unwanted attention.

"You don't have that New York accent."

Neither do you and we both know why.

Even though he refused to glance at her face, and kept his focus trained on the floorboard, he had a clear

7

view of her tan, slender legs. The silver stilettos with the diamond straps showed off her pink, manicured toenails, and it sparked a memory. The image played across his mind as smoothly as a shot of whiskey going down after a long day. They had spent the summer sneaking away every chance they could to his parent's cottage, lounging in the hammock in the backyard, her feet resting over his legs, her pink toenails shining in the sunlight. He found it hard to believe she still painted her nails the same color as she did back when they couldn't keep their hands off each other.

You're in a shitload of trouble and all you can think about is nail polish?

He shook the recollection from his head like clearing away old cobwebs. Even after all this time, there were days when some woman passed by him—in a store, or on a sidewalk—wearing the same perfume she wore. It always took him back to that place, trapped in that glorious time with her, and he'd have to fight his way to the surface where the cold reality of his miserable life waited.

"If you're not from here, where are you from?"

Why she dug for answers she already knew, baffled him. Perhaps, this way she'd get him to say too much, and let Draco figure out the important parts. Or she was playing it cool in an effort to act as if she wanted to make pleasant conversation with someone she'd just met.

"Texas," he said, working to regain his voice.

This time he let his gaze travel to her hands folded in her lap. Keep it short and to the point. No need to say too much and open himself up to the possibility she'd decide to reveal his identity.

"Ah, yes," she said, her voice taking on a poignant tone. "I lived in Texas for a long time. Which part are you from?"

For a fleeting minute, he considered telling a fib but decided he couldn't bring himself to cheapen those memories with her by uttering a lie. It wouldn't have mattered anyhow. She knew the answer. "Dallas."

Now, she slid her hands to her knees and gripped them. Silence filled the cab. Perhaps, she was preparing to make that dreaded announcement, giving away his identity to Draco.

"Dallas, huh?" she finally said.

The second round of silence sent an ounce of relief tumbling over him. He never wanted to get out of a vehicle and away from a beautiful woman more than he did right now. He couldn't predict what she'd do next. And the fact he'd once been the guy she vowed her undying love to may not have stopped her from committing an act that would bring certain death. Surely, she wouldn't do that, would she?

"You don't talk a lot, do you?"

The limo braked, and once more, relief settled into his bones that he'd be saved from further conversation with her. Once he stepped out of the limo, he'd be free to move about, and he planned to keep as much distance from the woman as possible.

Armed guards took up posts outside the entrance of the mansion. He noticed the heavy security first thing after shuffling out of the limo.

"Damn, dude. This place is massive," Dom said, coming up beside him.

The place had to be a good fifteen-thousand square feet. Golden lights emanated from damn near every window setting the residence aglow like a magical kingdom. He marveled at the bankroll a person must have in order to live in a pad like this. But the palace belonged to Victor Craven, one of the wealthiest drug lords of his time.

The front door opened, and the figure lumbering out appeared tall and slim. As the man got closer, Lucas figured based on his formal attire he had to be one of the staff.

"The bags are in the trunk," Draco said and then led the way up the wide steps toward the house.

The employee simply nodded and headed toward the back of the limo. Lucas could tell it was a do as you're told around here and don't ask questions rote response.

Another guard stood just inside the door, a machine gun across one arm and nodded curtly as they filed in. The stone expression on his face never flinched as he stepped back, allowing them passage.

"So, I assume the flight went without incident. You two look like you're in one piece."

Lucas glanced in the direction of the voice. A tall, handsome man dressed in a black tuxedo, and a red vest strolled toward them.

Victor Craven appeared larger than life, like more of a celebrity than a kingpin. The callous manifestation Lucas expected to see shrouding his dark, brown eyes didn't exist. He displayed a rather surprisingly gentle expression that strangely put him at ease. "It's an honor to have you in my home, Mr. Conner," The man extended a hand with long fingers that appeared as if they never experienced a day of hard labor.

Lucas grinned with warmth and shook his hand,

surprised even more by the soft contact. "I cannot express what a thrill it is to finally meet you."

Craven's hand lingered before letting go. Then he drew back, the light in his eyes dancing with intrigue. "Somehow, I imagined you much different. In my mind, you were this shrimpy nerd with glasses. You know, the bookish type. With the massive business opportunities your mortgage firm has brought to our enterprise, I couldn't help but picture you that way. Excuse my frankness."

Lucas laughed, even though he wasn't the least bit charmed by the guy's humor. "I hope I haven't disappointed."

"It's a pleasant surprise to see you're just an ordinary guy like us." He put his hand out to the men standing around him. "But I will say, your work has been impressive, to say the least." After a moment, he shook off his train of thought with a nod of his head. "But we're not here to talk about business. Tonight," he said, holding out his arm, beckoning for Remi to join him, "we're here to celebrate new friendships and prosperous business. And enough wealth to make all of us stinking rich. Isn't that right, baby?"

The moment Remi responded by burying herself in his arms and running her fingers through the back of his blond hair while brushing her lips against his, Lucas wanted to vomit. That used to be his hair she threaded her fingers through, his mouth she ravaged. He could still picture her naked in his bed, reacting to his every touch, and the small sounds of pleasure softening her voice to the point he wanted to explode.

Christ. As much as he wanted to, he couldn't look away. More than anything, he wished the intimate display of her touching another man would just vanish, not burn a repulsive snapshot in his mind.

Victor drew her away. "You look positively radiant, my love. And I have a special surprise planned for us tonight."

"I can never get used to the way you spoil me, Victor," she said, planting a kiss on his cheek.

She ate up his affection like a female dog in heat. It sickened him how Remi Shaw went from being a respected officer with the Dallas PD to the groveling girlfriend of a drug kingpin. Sure, Craven had the kind of money that would support the lavish lifestyle of any woman who became a fixture in his life, but the Remi he once knew would have spat in the face of a man like that. She always served the PD with the highest integrity. Then again, she'd quit the force and run as far as she could, didn't she?

"Is that okay?"

While Lucas' brain wrapped around the voice talking to him, Victor swiveled on one heel to glance back at him. "I was asking if you'd like to follow me to the ballroom. I have special seating arrangements for us."

"Of course," he answered, getting a move on even as his legs turned to rubber. The sight of a known criminal's arm wrapped possessively around Remi caused far more discomfort than it should have. She'd disappeared from his life; he shouldn't give a damn where she went or what she'd been doing. So, why did jealousy rage through him at seeing her cozying up to another man?

"You good?" Dom asked, catching up with him.

Lucas swallowed what could've only been pride

and adopted a collected front. What would his buddy say if he spilled Remi's identity? He could only hope she'd go on pretending she didn't know him. Jesus, if she blabbed his identity to a single person here, he wouldn't live to see another day. Acknowledging her comfort level with these people and in this environment, he wouldn't put it past her to blow his cover.

"I'm fine," he told his partner, even though irritation and anger gnawed at him with the force of an axe splitting into wood.

After stepping out of the elevator and trudging down a narrow corridor. They stood in front of a large set of mahogany doors and Lucas picked up the hint of music.

"This, gentlemen." Craven glanced back as his hand curled around the doorknob. "Is what a party is supposed to look like." He threw open the doors, and the sounds that spilled out were a mixture of music, laughter, and loud chatter.

Lucas stepped into the room, unable to deny its breathtaking appearance. Gold-colored molding encased the cathedral ceiling, and large, crystal chandeliers hung from several places above their heads. At least fifty guests filled the room. Couples danced to the slow beat of the music; others lined the walls socializing while some were seated at the few tables set sporadically throughout. In his navy-blue, Cashmere suit, Lucas was thankful he fit right in with the lavishly dressed guests.

Victor showed them to a horseshoe booth toward the back of the room, complete with black velvet seats, and a bottle of champagne protruding from a silver bucket placed in the center of the table.

Draco and Bain followed. Craven swept out his hand, gesturing for him and Dom to take a seat. Lucas stepped aside for his partner to slide in, and then took his place at the end of the booth. He never sat in the middle. Especially tonight, given where they were, and the company surrounding them. If things went south, he'd need to get on his feet as quickly as possible.

The kingpin and Remi settled in on the opposite side from him.

Victor removed his suit jacket, loosened the knot of his necktie, and tugged it off, then released the first few buttons of his shirt. He worked his head from side to side, easing the kinks in his neck.

A slim redhead in a little black dress stepped forward. The bright red lipstick she wore complimented the oval features of her face. A dusting of light freckles dotted her complexion, giving her the appearance of innocence. It struck him she was anything but. "May I take your jacket for you, Mr. Craven?" She put out her hand.

He handed it over. "Thank you, Lucy. Let me introduce you to our new guests. This is Dante Thatcher and Scott Conner."

She swept her attention in his direction, and Lucas found himself immediately taken in by her stunning, aqua-colored eyes. She beamed. "It's nice to meet the illusive Mr. Conner. You have quite the reputation around here. And I mean that in a good way."

"Good, because if you meant it in a bad way, then I'd be forced to live up to it."

"Well, who would I be to stand in the way of a man and all the naughty things he must do?" The direct eye contact when she said that kicked his testosterone into overdrive. "Perhaps, I can take your jacket too, Mr. Conner."

"Please, call me Scott. And that's okay. I'm quite comfortable."

She leaned over him, and her tantalizing cleavage blocked out the view of everything else. "Then would you allow me to get you something to drink?"

He cleared his throat, his attention discreetly roaming to Remi. To his surprise, she sat there uncomfortable, staring at Lucy as if the sight of the woman disgusted her. That egged him on. "Only if you'll have one with me."

She pursed her lips, and the sparkle that lit her eyes told him such an invitation would please her. "If it's okay with Mr. Craven. I'd love nothing more than to share a drink with you."

Victor spoke up. "Lucy, you know the satisfaction of our guests is always one of my top priorities. If you didn't join Mr. Conner for a drink as he wishes, I'd be offended."

"Then it's settled," Lucas said. "I would love the company of such a beautiful woman." He gently took her hand, placed it to his lips, and kissed her palm.

She closed her eyes, and when he released her hand, she gave such a slight sigh he barely detected it. "Give me a moment," she said, breathlessly, "and I'll be right back with a round of drinks."

Victor appeared as pleased as a king sitting on his throne, and he grabbed Remi's hand, giving it a kiss of his own. "God, I've missed you, baby." He leaned in and took her lips.

It gnawed at Lucas that Victor Craven was such a

handsome, suave son-of-a-bitch. He could totally see how Remi could be attracted to him, when he, himself was just some rough, unsophisticated guy from her past.

Remi Shaw could go straight to hell. At his beck and call was a stunning redhead who he sensed would be willing to live out just about any fantasy with him he desired. He damn well intended to bury himself deep inside of her. Perhaps, he'd never resurface, and his old flame could be fooled into thinking she could run off into the sunset with her drug-dealing lover. In the end, he'd blow her plans to smithereens when he carted Mr. Debonair off to prison.

And she'd get caught up in the web.

Christ. He didn't think of the repercussions of that.

"She's beautiful, isn't she?" Lucas peered over to find Victor smiling slyly. "Lucy," Craven clarified. "That woman will rock your world, brother."

As gorgeous as she was, and as hot in bed as he assumed she'd be, he somehow realized sex with her wouldn't be as intense as with the woman sitting across from him. Even after all these years, he had yet to chase the memories of their lovemaking from his mind. She knew just the right way to thrust her body beneath him to send him crashing over the edge of madness. God, how he missed her. But tonight, he had nothing but loathing for her.

"Well," Victor said under his breath, leaning across the table, "Lucy is yours. My gift to you. It's the least I can do after all you've done for us."

Lucas acted the part, smiled gracefully, and said, "Thank you."

It was all a component of the game he played. And right now, he ought to be on top of the world to have the opportunity to spend the night with such a lovely creature. One-night stands were right up his alley. Lord knew he'd participated in enough of them over the last thirteen years. Yet not one of them managed to drive Remi Shaw from his mind.

But this would be different, wouldn't it? She shacked up with the biggest kingpin in existence, even though she once swore she'd never leave him. And seeing the way she fit right into her role as Craven's woman, should be just the thing to free the shackles around his heart.

And he'd be damned if he would allow the memories of that woman to sabotage a long night of pleasure with the redhead in the black dress. Screw her. After tonight he'd be done with Remi once and for all.

Speaking of the beautiful woman in question, she sashayed over right now with a drink tray in her hand. She strutted like a panther, smooth and effortless. How exquisite would those legs be wrapped around his hips?

"I brought you a brandy if you don't mind." She set the tray down and stared at him as if she knew a dirty little secret she planned to reveal later in the night.

He stood up and stepped aside to allow her to scoot in and sit beside him. "That's perfect. Thank you, Lucy." He gave her a seductive wink.

The gesture made her blush, and she cleared her throat, sliding into the booth.

He sat down next to her, and the warmth of her thigh brushing against his, penetrated through the thin material of his slacks. It gave him a clear indication of how warm her body was going to be under his roving hands when he had a chance to explore every sensual inch of her tonight.

Victor popped the cork on the champagne and poured a helping into the empty glasses sitting on the table. Then he placed a glass in front of each person. He stood up, saying, "I have an announcement to make. I was going to wait until later, but the excitement is just too much. And seeing as we're all together." He put his hand out for Remi, and she took it. Then he helped her out of the booth.

Remi stood there appearing as puzzled as Lucas was when Victor closed in on her, got down on his knee, and produced a red velvet box from his pocket.

The full brunt of Victor's intentions slammed into Lucas like a sucker punch. Craven's voice sliced through his brain, "Remi, I have never loved a woman as deeply as I love you. And I'd like to know if you would do me the honor of being my wife."

Lucas couldn't help the direction of his stare. Though shock hit Remi's face, she rebounded quickly with a smile. Yet, embedded deeply in the hollows of those blue eyes existed a fleeting emotion of dread. She didn't appear to be a blissfully happy girl who waited for a marriage proposal from the guy she'd fallen head-over-heels in love with.

Was she disappointed he proposed to her? It sure as hell seemed like it.

Then, as if she'd never shown a sign of hesitation, she threw back her head and laughed with delight. "Oh my God, yes, Victor. I will marry you."

As he slipped the diamond ring on her finger, stood, and folded her in his arms, Lucas wanted to crawl into the crevice of a wall and disappear.

Applause stirred around him as everyone at the table stood up and cheered.

It took everything he had to join them in celebrating this new vow of marriage. A smile spread across his face for show as he clapped along with all of them, but inside a storm brewed, and it ticked like a time bomb.

Glasses clanged together, and the guests took a sip of wine in a toast. When he stared at Lucy, he noticed an expression of jealousy etched on her face. And then Victor's earlier words struck him. *That woman will rock your world.* It couldn't have been more apparent at that moment Craven had been sleeping with Lucy. How many women did he sleep with while he strolled around with Remi on his arm?

He didn't feel sorry for her. She'd allowed herself to get tangled up with these people. He considered it par for the course. At any rate, he wondered if she remained oblivious to lover boy's infidelities.

The moment Lucy noticed him staring at her, her attention darted away, and she cleared her throat. "How romantic, isn't it?" she said, flashing her aqua eyes on him again. This time with a controlled reaction.

Suddenly, Victor's sloppy seconds didn't seem so appealing anymore. He grinned as smoothly as a man who grew accustomed to playing the part of Scott Conner. "Excuse me," he said, setting his flute on the table, "do you know where the restroom is?"

"Sure thing." She ran her hand up and down his arm in a show of seduction. "You'll have to go out the doors you came in. At the end of the hall, it's to your right. But hurry back."

Before he knew what hit him, she had the back of his head cradled in her hand, and she tugged him toward her. She covered his mouth with her lips, and he closed his eyes, imagining Remi in her place as the kiss deepened. She slid her tongue into his mouth, and he ravaged her, yanking her against him and molding his hands around her slender bottom. His erection throbbed against her belly, and her soft sighs echoed in his ears. Jesus, no matter how much he wanted it to be, it wasn't Remi.

He broke the intimacy, breathing heavily to get his pounding heart under control. Lucy backed away and licked her lips. "I'll be waiting right here when you get back."

What did he get himself into?

He threw open the ballroom doors and stomped down the hallway. His bladder didn't need relieving like the hot anger welling inside him did. This fantasy Remi Shaw would somehow tell Victor Craven to go to hell, and then fall into his arms was not only foolish, but it had the potential to get him killed.

He stormed past the bathroom and kept going toward the terrace he'd spotted while making his way to the ballroom earlier. He sought fresh air like a moth drawn to light. His hand curled around the silver knob of the French door, and he jerked it open. Cold air hit him instantly; he stepped out into the snow swirls caused by his heavy breathing. God, he longed to be home in Texas where at least the weather was much less brutal this time of year.

Lucas stepped over to the iron railing and gazed down at the circular drive, then his attention swept across the grounds with its snow-covered grass and manicured hedge bushes. He could never give Remi anything close to this. Victor could offer her a life of lavishness, full of expensive jewelry, designer clothing, new cars with all the latest features, and extravagant vacations.

And the man spent his time fucking Lucy and God knew how many other women on the side while he pledged his love to Remi. Why was that any business of his? Like his father used to tell him. The way you make your bed is the way you sleep in it.

She made her choice about which bed she'd occupy. And it wasn't his.

He shouldn't concentrate his energy on worrying about who she'd been sleeping with. He needed to watch his back. It had become more important now than ever, to bring Victor Craven down. That meant continuing to conceal his identity and taking the role of Scott Conner to a whole new level. Until now, thanks to Remi crashing the party and screwing with his mind, he'd been standoffish with the guy. But the time came to snatch his head out of his ass and cozy up to him.

The door opened, and he straightened, preparing to launch into a fine rendition of Scott Conner. But before he could glance over his shoulder, the words, "Lucas Kade," combined with the familiar voice uttering them, caused his heart to drop to his feet. Remi slowly stepped toward him. Snowflakes landed on her mink shawl and stuck to her long lashes. And those memorable blue eyes bore into him. She snapped open her evening bag, drew out a gold cigarette case, slipped a cigarette between her lips, dug for a lighter, and cupped her hand over the flame to light it. She took a long pull of her smoke and dropped the items back into her bag.

"Since when do you smoke?" Jesus, did he just say that out loud? She shouldn't know he even cared.

"When I'm stressed. Congratulations. You've succeeded in doing that quite effectively."

"I'm the cause of your stress?"

"What are you doing here, Luc?"

He faced the driveway again, closing his eyes and allowing the heatstroke that accosted him to pass. No one ever called him by that name except her. And when she did, it had always been in the heat of passion.

"If Victor finds out you're undercover for the DEA, I won't be able to stop him from killing you in ways you could never imagine."

He spun around to stare at her. His eyes burned into her. "How do you know about that?"

She took another puff, blew out a stream of smoke, and lowered her head. "I heard you were working for the DEA a few years ago."

He threw out his hands. "Jesus Christ, Remi. Who else knows?"

"Relax. No one here."

"Then how do you know about this covert mission?" He couldn't believe his ears. How long did she know he had been working undercover?

"I figured it out on my own tonight. When I saw you. I put two and two together. I figured you had to be working undercover since I knew you'd never run in the same circles with these guys."

His hands tightened into fists, and he wanted to punch the brick wall. "But you are?"

She shook her head, and when she set her eyes on him again, the temptation to haul her into his arms and kiss her until all rationalization fled ripped through him like an earthquake. "It's not what you think," she said, her voice melting into a mere whisper.

His hand wrapped around the banister to keep from seizing her around the wrist and drawing her against his hardened body that craved her nearness for far more years than he could count. Instead, he said, "Bullshit, Remi. Lying to me is beneath you. We promised honesty would be the only thing between us. Remember?"

The unembellished proof she'd well remembered was written all over her face. "We made that promise thirteen years ago."

"Do you love him?" Why that question flew out of his mouth with total disregard for what he should and shouldn't give away, was beyond him. He might as well have announced his jealousy of drug peddler boy and how his hands were all over her.

"No…yes…That's none of your business."

"Professing your love for someone was never that difficult when your legs were wrapped around my hips. Or were those empty words in the height of getting off?"

She raised a hand as if to slap him. "How dare you."

He caught her wrist a few inches from its intended target, and the cigarette dropped from between her fingers. He leaned into her face. "You never answered my question. At least not with any honesty."

The reflection in her eyes, although filled with anger, also appeared haunted by weakness, a sign of faltering resistance to his suffocating nearness. He leaned in swiftly and took her lips.

She didn't fight him as his hand slid to the back of her neck and he gathered a fistful of long, silky tresses. His heart throbbed with an adrenaline rush unlike any undercover mission could have triggered. And the sweet scent of her perfume drenched his soul and left him lightheaded. The nights he'd spent thinking about how she would feel in his arms again, could not compare to the reality of touching her this way. The woman's reaction to his caress beat any expectation he could have ever drummed up in his wildest dreams.

He christened her neck with wet, slow burning-kisses, and the soft moans emitting from her sent him over the edge. He whispered, "You have no idea how much I want to bury myself inside of you, and never let you come up for air until my name is the only one pouring out of your mouth when you're coming."

She wrestled out of his hold, and stared at him as if his words sent her reeling into another dimension. "Oh my God. What are we doing?" She scrambled away from him.

And he stood there, the taste of her still burning on his lips, his breaths coming in heavy rasps, and his body stiff with wanting her.

"This is not a game. What we just did could get us killed."

It didn't matter he realized she spoke the truth. In one reckless moment, he was willing to risk it all just to have her in his arms again.

She swallowed and straightened her shawl. "I'm going to head back in there." She pointed toward the door. "And we're going to act like this never happened. Draco told me you're catching a flight back to Texas tomorrow. Go home and tell the special agent in charge at the DEA this mission is far too dangerous. Victor has ways of uncovering your identity. And when he does, you won't see him coming."

She circled toward the door and put her hand on the knob when he said, "Are you going to marry him?"

She slouched, not moving a muscle. "That's none of your business." Then she glanced back one last time. "Go home, Lucas."

When she slipped through the door a knife twisted in his gut.

Chapter Two

Lucas strolled across the ballroom floor with purposeful strides. Screw Remi Shaw and her kingpin fiancé. A certain redhead waited who would let him take out his sexual frustrations any way he pleased. And it no longer mattered she'd been sleeping with the enemy. After that heated exchange on the terrace, he needed release more than he desired righteousness. Lucy peered up as he approached. He didn't bother with formalities, simply put out his hand. When she took it, he drew her out of the seat. The woman blushed when he leaned into her ear and whispered, "Do you have a room where we can go?"

She nodded, and he glanced at Victor, who cradled Remi in his arms. The man smiled like a Cheshire cat, and Lucas bit back the harsh words on his tongue, saying, "I want to thank you for such a warm welcome. But if you have no objection, I'd love to spend some time with Lucy."

Victor said, "I understand completely. I'll have one of the employees move your travel bag to Lucy's room in the morning. You kids have fun."

His glance cut to Remi, and that go-to-hell expression was all the satisfaction he needed.

"Shall we," he said, placing his hand on Lucy's back.

She drew her eyes away timidly, and he led her

across the floor to the door.

Once they approached the hallway, she stared at him and winked. "I like that you're direct, Scott. That's a big turn on for me."

He wrapped his arm around her waist and tugged her closer. "Well, in that case, we should get along just fine, sweetheart."

As they arrived at the elevator, she halted. "My room is on the first level." They stepped into the car and rode it down.

It occurred to him as the ding—indicating they'd arrived at their floor—rang out and the doors slid along the metal track, he should feel much differently than he did right now. Any normal guy about to get laid by a beautiful sex goddess would be in heaven. But standing in the bowels of hell would have been a more fitting description of what he'd been going through since Remi crawled into the limousine.

What were the odds he'd run into his ex-lover while infiltrating drug traffickers? And what likelihood could have existed she'd be the girlfriend, now fiancée of the very drug lord he intended to take down?

When he stumbled out of bed this morning, he'd never dreamed events could spiral out of control with this kind of magnitude. Everything hinged on Remi's decision to keep quiet, yet he continued to piss her off. He couldn't help himself. Jealousy outweighed his good sense to keep his distance and remain indifferent.

"You still with me?"

When the fog cleared from his head, he realized his stare focused directly on Lucy, without seeing her at all. He frowned, giving a half nod. They stepped off the elevator together, and he found her still gazing at him, her expressive eyes telling him she suspected something was amiss. She stopped advancing, and he halted alongside her. "Are you sure this is what you want?"

The uncertainty written on her face made him regret he was the cause of her feeling this way. After all, he extended the invitation to share the night together, not her. She didn't do anything wrong and only went along with this because she thought he wanted it.

He clasped her chin in between his fingers, leaned in, and gave her a gentle kiss just before a slow smile crept over her face. "You are a beautiful woman. Any man would be insane not to want you."

After a minute, she peered away, and stared in the direction of the hall. "My room is right around the corner."

This is what you wanted, isn't it? He stepped aside so she could open the door, and they strolled in together.

"Let me take your hat and jacket," she offered.

He slipped off both, handed them over, and then loosened his tie, laying it over a designer chair sitting a few feet from the bed.

When she sashayed back, she had two rock glasses in her hands filled with a few ice cubes and brown liquid. "Here," she said, "This brandy should relax you."

He cocked an eyebrow. "Do I need relaxing?"

"No offense. But you seem a little on edge."

He took the drink and put it to his lips. It was gone in one swallow.

She frowned as if not expecting him to down it in

one gulp but took the glass from him either way. "Should I fix another?"

In leu of an answer, he grabbed both glasses from her, strolled over to the nightstand, set them down, then sauntered back. He slipped his hands around her neck, cradled the back of her head, and then tugged her to him, taking her mouth in a heated kiss.

She responded by moving with him, issuing small sounds of pleasure that drove him on.

At that moment, an image of Victor Craven on one knee proposing to Remi crashed through his brain. Jesus, he despised the fact that creep took her to his bed tonight. Not his Remi. She belonged to him and no one else. The way she responded to his kiss on the terrace proved she still wanted him after all this time. She damn well enjoyed the intimacy every bit as much as him.

He dropped soft kisses across her collarbone, his fingers working to unsnap the buttons on the back of her dress when an image of Remi in Victor's bed struck again.

He broke the contact, and stepped away, cursing.

Lucy's breathy voice snapped him back to reality when she whispered, "What's wrong?"

He stared into her confused eyes knowing what he had to do. If he didn't sleep with her, Victor would suspect something below the surface was going on with him. And he'd dig until he found the answer. The evening had already taken an unexpected turn with the arrival of Remi, throwing him off his game. Turning down a hot tryst with a gorgeous redhead would only raise eyebrows. He didn't need that kind of attention.

He took her by the hand, led her to the side of the

bed, and switched off the lamp. Remi left him wanting the moment she stepped away from him and fled the terrace. Finding sweet release even in the arms of another woman would serve its purpose. But if he must do this, immersing himself in darkness would be the only way to get through it. He'd pretend Remi's body writhed beneath him instead of another woman.

****

Lucas opened his eyes to bright sunlight. He stirred in bed and sat up. The curtain once covering the window on the west side of the room was tied back, letting in the morning light.

Lucy didn't lie beside him. Thank God. He'd be saved the awkwardness of day after sex conversation with her.

He glanced at the clock on the bedside table. The infrared digits told him the time. Eight-thirty a.m. His eyes brushed across his travel bag sitting in the designer chair by the bed. He couldn't remember anyone coming into the room to deliver the bag, but he imagined at some point early this morning one of the employees, as Craven told him last night, brought the luggage in.

He shuffled out of bed and headed for the shower. He brushed past a small collection of perfumes sitting on the counter, as well as a pink makeup bag and a curling iron with the cord unplugged and hanging down the front of the cabinet. The sight of the shower lightened his spirit, and he headed toward a wicker basket tucked in the corner of the room with neatly rolled towels and plucked one out.

His mind wandered to the escapades with Lucy last night as he twisted the shower knob and tested the temperature of the water. After Remi left him burning for more on the terrace, it didn't take long to reach the conclusion of their love making. The redhead must have thought his performance a wash since he orgasmed so quickly. She had no idea Victor's fiancée revved his engine to the point of a blowout.

Remi spent the night in Craven's bed, no doubt. He gritted his teeth and slung the towel over the glass partition. He wondered if the little lovefest between him and Remi got her as hot and bothered and ready for sex as it did him. And if it did, that meant the kingpin would have been on the receiving end of her preparedness. He wanted to drive his fist through the tiled wall.

He had to stop this, or he'd drive himself crazy. Thank God he had a flight booked that would take him the hell out of here this morning. There'd be no telling what another day in proximity with Remi under the watchful eyes of her lover would cause him to do. He needed to escape these walls closing in on him and take a moment to regroup. He couldn't do that here, in the palace belonging to the man who was screwing his girl.

Is that what she was? His girl? He slipped into the warmth of the shower, and placed his hand against the wall, letting the water cascade over his body. She used to be his. And she made a promise long ago she could never love anyone else.

But thirteen years came and went. And the tragic day they found his brother hanging from his belt in the back room of that church, everything he knew ripped out from under him.

Dwelling on the past would only bring on the nightmares all over again. He couldn't go back there. He'd made as much peace with what happened as he could ever hope to make.

After washing up, he slipped out of the shower, dried off, and wrapped the towel around his waist. Then he roamed into the room to fetch his travel bag.

Remi stood at the foot of the bed when he entered. His heart instantly dropped to his feet.

The commotion caused her to swing her attention his way. She took a step back and stared at him. Her pensive gaze seared his flesh as she slowly swept it over every inch of him. She kept her stare trained on him, and damn well took her time getting her money's worth.

He leaned against the casing of the bathroom door, letting her have her fill. "Do you like what you see?"

The spell broke, and she finally cleared her throat and glanced away. "Get dressed. Victor is expecting you in the dining room for breakfast."

Lucas wasn't deterred. He remained in his position, and cocked his head, staring intensely at her. "And he sent you to get me? Or did you offer?"

"We're experiencing a staff changeover. So, he asked if I'd come and get you. It's not that complicated, Lucas."

"Oh, now I'm Lucas. But I was Luc last night." He leveled her with a knowing grin. "Do you remember what you were doing all those times you called me Luc, or better yet, what I was doing to you?"

She snorted, as if she refused to let him drag her down memory lane. "You're going to get yourself killed if you keep this up. Victor isn't stupid. The first sign something isn't right, he's going to be on you like a junkyard dog."

He winked. "I think I can handle lover boy."

She strolled over to him and got in his face. "When did you become so smug?"

Anger coiled inside him. He matched her contemptuous glower. "Perhaps, it was the result of you running off and leaving the way you did."

She snapped her attention away, putting distance between them. "I'm not doing this with you."

"Maybe another time then," he said.

She spun and headed toward the door but stopped the minute she encountered a pair of women's underwear curled up on the floor. She threw a disgusted glance in his direction. "I hope Lucy satisfied your needs."

"You were too busy fucking Victor to care, sweetheart."

She stood ramrod straight for a moment, then shook her head and continued on her way.

When the door shut, he let out the air trapped in his lungs. How big of an idiot could he possibly be? Why did he insist on treating her with such contempt?

Because she was sleeping with another man, and he ached to have her in his bed. *You stupid fool. You might have gone on with living after she made a break for it, but you never moved on from the past.*

Standing there reliving it now, wouldn't get him through the next hour with Victor. He needed to put this behind him, ignore the storm of emotions that ripped through him every time his attention collided with Remi, and play it cool to keep from blowing his cover.

He only had a little more time before he'd be climbing on that plane bound for Texas. Although leaving this place sent a wave of relief cascading over him, it also disheartened him, because departing New

York also meant he'd probably never see Remi again.

At least now he knew where she was. It sure as hell beat spending the next several years wondering where she'd ended up when she left him without a word so long ago.

****

He strode into the dining room, noticing the crew gathered around eating breakfast. Victor sat at the head of the table, and when he realized someone had entered the room, he folded the top corner of his newspaper and grinned. "Good morning, Mr. Conner." He snapped his fingers to beckon one of the maids who was leaning over the table and placing a glass picture of fresh orange juice in the center.

The young woman stood at attention, and he gestured for her to fetch Lucas a plate.

She departed to do his bidding, and Lucas sank down into the chair closest to him.

"I hope your evening with Lucy was satisfactory," the kingpin said, folding his paper and setting it to the side.

"Where is she this morning?" Lucas wanted to know, as he hadn't seen a hint of her since last night.

"Why?" Dominick asked, that familiar, pestering expression hugging his face. "Do you want to go back to her room and say goodbye?"

Draco let out a laugh, and a tisk tisk. "I can't say I'd blame him."

The glow in Victor's eyes told Lucas it pleased him to have made his stay more interesting. "She had to run a few errands for me. But I'll tell her you said goodbye when she gets back."

"Not in the way he wants to tell her," Dom piped

up and added.

As laughter spilled out around the table, Lucas wanted to comment, that's exactly the way he'll tell her since he's already been sleeping with her. Instead, he pasted on a good-humored smile as if accepting he was the butt of the joke. "That's okay, gentlemen. I'll take the jabs, just like I took the lovin' last night."

"Ooh," Draco said, flitting his eyebrows. "I bet she was hotter out of that dress than she was in it. And she was a scorcher with it on."

"A gentleman never tells," Lucas shot back.

"But you're not a gentleman," Dom ribbed.

The maid carried a plate over brimming with food and laid it in front of him. He nodded his appreciation as she filled his glass with orange juice and asked if he'd like a cup of coffee as well. "That would be great," he told her. She departed and he dug in.

He noticed Remi wasn't anywhere to be seen. And even though part of him suffered from disappointment, the other half admitted, at least he wouldn't have to put up the façade of not acknowledging her existence when that'd be all he'd end up doing the entire time. It would have resulted in as big of a distraction as last night, while he sat across the table and watched Craven paw all over her.

How pathetic was that proposal anyhow? If it had been him vying to marry Remi, he would have spilled his heart, laying it all on the line, and she would have been left with no doubt concerning his love.

But it wasn't him. It was the asshole sitting at the head of the table with a grin as large as a king, while everyone groveled at his feet like peasants.

The maid returned with his coffee, and he rubbed

the back of his neck to work out the kinks caused by the colossal stress he'd been under, before picking up the brew and taking a sip. God, he needed to get the hell out of here, leave this frigid state and return home to warmer weather and familiar surroundings. He couldn't think clearly between Remi crashing through the thin wall of his resistance, and the pressure of keeping up his persona as Scott Conner.

Victor said, "I know you have a plane to catch, but Dominick is going to stay behind. We need his help with a small matter. I was hoping if it wasn't too much trouble, you could drop Remi by her apartment on your way out. You can take the Viper and I'll have one of the guys swing by the airport to retrieve it."

Just perfect. More close quarters with a woman he could never have, but one he was sure he wouldn't be able to resist stealing away with if she would allow him to break through her barriers. How could his sanity survive this?

He pursed his lips and nodded as if Victor didn't just ask him to strap a detonator to the tiny shreds left of his fortitude. He took another swallow of his coffee, and rose, staring across the table at Victor, and doing his best not to let the revulsion he had for the man show. "I appreciate your hospitality, and the next time you're in Texas, look me up. We'll go have a drink."

And maybe I'll bust a beer bottle over your head.

"I have a business meeting in Dallas next week. I might just take you up on that."

"I'll look forward to it then." He nodded at Dom and left the room to gather the few things he'd brought with him. The time to put this shitshow behind him couldn't come any sooner.

****

Despite the freezing temperatures, a cold sweat broke out over Remi's forehead as she approached Victor's sports car. Lucas climbed out of the driver's seat and jogged around to open her door. Her heart stopped just the way she knew it would, and her steps faltered.

Staring at that face was like a flash from the past; every time her attention swept over him, heat pulsated through her like a warm rush of water. The same as when she'd caught him coming out of the shower this morning—and she was rewarded with a full view of his shoulder-length, blond hair.

He replaced the business suit he wore last night with a pair of jeans and a dark polo shirt that accented the lean outline of his torso. From his appearance, he had no idea his sex appeal drove her crazy while he stood there, waiting. He stared at her expectantly, the door open, and his arm braced across the top of the window frame.

She took a much-needed breath and forged forward on legs that morphed into rubber.

After climbing into the passenger's seat, he shut her in and strode to the driver's side, folding himself behind the wheel, and closing them off from the world with the shutting of his door.

The quiet between them seemed to stretch on forever. The only sound ringing throughout the cab was the revving of the motor when he threw the gearshift in drive and tore out of the driveway. His muscular arm fiddled with the rearview mirror, and it sent a memory spiraling through her of his strong hand caressing her thigh, her cheek, and a thousand body parts the way it had done on many occasions. He had the warmest hands of anyone she knew, and she could always feel their incredible heat penetrating through her clothes whenever he placed them on her. Sometimes late at night, when all the ghosts of her mistakes came calling, the only thing that could comfort her was the memory of those hands stroking her.

"Are you going to tell me why you're doing this?"

His hoarse voice caught her attention, and she glanced at him. "What do you mean?"

He raised his hand above the steering wheel. "Why this? Why Victor Craven?"

Before she could open her mouth, he said, "Don't tell me it's none of my business. It's just you and me right here, right now. Honesty, remember?"

The way he cut that, putting all bullshit aside, glance in her direction, she realized she'd never get away with lying. Besides, he'd see right through it. He always had. "I'll tell you this," she said, in a kind of admission though she wasn't about to spill all the beans. "I met Victor through Draco Vargas. He showed up at the bar one night where we were celebrating Draco's birthday."

"You realize Vargas works for Craven as his distributor, right? What possessed you to get involved with someone like him?"

"I had my reasons. Besides, when I met Draco, he wasn't that high up in Victor's enterprise."

"That makes it so much better."

"Judgmental much?"

Now he tightened his grip on the steering wheel and his jaw muscle flexed. "Jesus Christ, Remi?" He jerked in the seat and stared at her as if she'd just pissed in his corn flakes. "You were a police officer. How in fuck do you go from working in law enforcement, to sleeping with a drug lord?"

Anger settled in her gut, while fire crept up her cheeks. She swung her attention straight ahead and shot daggers at the windshield. "Take it whatever way you want. I'm used to people thinking the worst of me."

He became silent for a moment, and then, "Shit. I wasn't referring to that."

That old pain snuck up on her, and wrapped around her heart before she had time to brace for it. She closed her eyes, steadying her nerves, and swallowed the tears that threatened to tear down the wall of resolution she worked years to construct. Being confronted by Lucas Kade again after so long brought it tumbling down.

If she chose to be logical, she could understand his confusion. But he didn't have a clue what brought her to Craven's doorstep. He automatically assumed what everyone at the Dallas PD did long ago. Somehow, it came down to her unethical morals again.

"I'm sorry. I never meant to imply that—"

"It's fine."

"You didn't deserve the way they treated you."

She snorted, wringing her hands in her lap. "I probably did. If it wasn't for what I did, Gavin would still be alive."

He pounded his fist against the steering wheel. "Are we back there again after all this time?" he said, gritting his teeth.

A shiver ran through her. God knows she didn't want to be. She had run far away from it. Funny how it found its way back to her.

"My brother was selfish. What he did was on him,

not you. All you tried to do was come clean with him. If you didn't tell him the truth, I was going to."

If he meant for his confession to magically relieve her from the responsibility of Gavin's death, he needed to try another tactic. "I was sleeping with you while I was engaged to him."

He jerked his head in annoyance. "You say that as if I wasn't there. You can't control who you fall in love with. You tried to keep him from making the biggest mistake of his life and marrying someone who didn't love him. If you went through with the wedding, it would have just ended in a painful divorce. You and I both know that."

Is this what he told himself to get through the days? "I can't have this conversation with you."

"Then when? At what point can we discuss the elephant in the room? This is exactly what drove you to pick up and leave without a word. And I'm not supposed to talk to you about it. Just great."

On the verge of tears, she blurted, "I'm sorry. "I just can't."

The silence that filled the car told her, for whatever reason, he was willing to drop further conversation regarding the tragedy with his brother, at least for now. She blew out a sigh of relief and calmed her pounding heart.

Once she recovered from her mini breakdown, she decided to ask what had hounded her since the moment she saw him in the limo. "What exactly is Scott Conner's role in the *Infierno* Cartel?"

He threw an incredulous glance in her direction. "You're engaged to the man running the show, and you don't know."

"Victor doesn't share that kind of information with me. He says the less I know the safer I am. Sometimes I overhear things. But he does his best not to let that happen."

"I guess if your fiancé thinks you don't need to know, then you probably shouldn't."

"I'm being serious, Lucas."

He chuckled. "So am I. Just because we used to sleep together, doesn't mean I can trust you. Especially now that I know you're with them."

She caught the overtones of disgust in his voice. She wasn't *with* them the way he assumed. She could easily dispel his suspicions and tell him the truth, but that might compromise her position. At all costs, she could not let that happen. And what the hell did he mean by, *just because we used to sleep together?* Apparently, their relationship didn't run much deeper than that.

"You realize what's going to happen when the DEA busts this thing wide open, right? You're guilty by association, and Craven won't be able to protect you from a cell."

"It boggles the mind you think he'll go down like that. I once worked in law enforcement, so I get the misguided conception you can just sweep in and take out the bad guys. But not someone like Victor. I'd bet he's got half the Dallas PD in his pocket right now, as well as New York's finest. A guy like that is untouchable."

"You say that as if you're rooting for him."

He infuriated the hell out of her. "I mention it because you're going to get yourself killed thinking you can cart him off to jail."

He hung a left onto Springs Drive. They were only ten minutes from her apartment when he said, "Now you're worried about me?" When his attention drifted over her, she swore she detected a hint of softness in his eyes. But in a flash the sentiment was gone. He continued. "You should be worried about yourself. This is going down whether you think it is or not. You need to get out while you can."

He munched on his lip and wormed uncomfortably in the seat. "You're really going to marry him?"

"He proposed to me."

"That's not what I asked."

"He's not as bad as you think."

"Still not what I asked."

She let out a sigh, stealing a glance at him. The side profile of his face sent a flashback tumbling through her mind. It had been Easter Sunday, and he rented a sailboat for the two of them to enjoy a day on the lake. She'd studied him closely as he let down the sails, his face directed to the side as he tugged on the ropes, just the way he appeared right now. At that moment she fell hopelessly in love with him.

That day might as well have been a lifetime ago. Their futures didn't include each other anymore. He worked in law enforcement, and she stood on the opposite side of the fence. At least she'd try to keep him alive. Her attention focused on the floorboard when she said, "I'm going to marry him."

He worked his jaw again. And she could almost feel his muscles tensing when he replied, "Tell me you love him."

"Does it matter?"

"Christ." He stabbed her with an expression of

impatience and annoyance. "You can't answer the damn question, can you?"

She couldn't. She'd made a promise long ago they would never lie to each other. Out of all the dishonest things she had to do over the years to get where she was, and all the phony relationships she had to establish, she couldn't bring herself to dishonor this one special connection she'd had with him that meant something.

The car swung into the parking lot of the apartment complex, and her hand wrapped around the door latch. "Remi, wait."

She couldn't look at him for fear she'd confess everything in one impetuous moment and throw herself into his arms. She held back the tears welling in her chest and stared at the floor. "It was really nice seeing you again." And she slipped out of the car.

Chapter Three

It was really nice seeing you again.

Those words churned around in his mind for the past hour like a song on repeat. He'd dissected them as many ways as he could and still couldn't unlock their meaning. Why couldn't women just come out and say what they thought? And why wouldn't she answer his question about whether she loved Craven? She wouldn't lie to him, which meant either she loved him and didn't want to tell him, or she didn't love him and didn't want him to know.

Either way still left him guessing how she felt about him. He shot out of his seat in the terminal—too restless to remain still—and marched to the large window overlooking airplanes preparing to load and unload passengers. Meeting with Victor Craven was supposed to be the highlight of the operation. It meant he'd earned the trust of the *Infierno* Cartel and could move to the next level. Then he'd bond with the man. Once he became like a brother, he'd get Victor to share details, bringing him closer to the intel he needed to take them down.

Then Remi Shaw came along and brought a shitstorm the size of Texas with her.

He checked his watch and realized he only had ten more minutes before they would announce his flight. The thing he regretted most after today, was he'd never see her again.

"You need to come with me."

Lucas peered over his shoulder at Draco standing a few feet behind him, and fear instantly converged on him. Did they somehow find out his identity? It became difficult to read the guy's body language when he stood there with no expression, only one hand buried in his pocket, and the other perched on his hip.

"I'm about to board," he said, swallowing the slightest hint of panic, and putting forth a casual stance to the best of his ability. How much longer could he keep up this charade?

"It can wait," Draco said. "Victor got word a banker he's been negotiating with is in town. He wants to meet us at the packing plant. The guy has a shit ton of contacts, and Craven thinks it could be beneficial for you to meet with him."

Lucas allowed that information to sink in. He couldn't see a trace of bullshit in Draco's eyes. Such an opportunity wouldn't be out of the ordinary for the cartel. But the agents involved in Operation Snowflakes expected him to touch down in Texas in a little more than four hours from now. They'd sound the alarm when he didn't show, and he had no way to get in contact with them to let them know of this change in plans.

No matter which way he spun it, this impromptu deviation posed a risk. If not for the confusion and chaos it would cause for the agents expecting him, it was a huge gamble that Draco was telling the truth, and they didn't intend to lead him into a trap. If he learned one thing from working undercover, you always stuck to the plan, and never veered off course. That's how good agents got themselves killed. Then again, if he refused Draco's request, it would throw up a red flag because he played the role of a broker on the lookout for new ways to move money into offshore accounts, yet he'd be willing to pass up a meeting with a promising banker who could assist them in that.

"Okay. But I need to catch this flight today. Do you see that as a problem?"

Draco shrugged. He grinned that familiar grin Lucas became accustomed to the better he'd gotten to know him. Nothing stood out as strange behavior. "I'm sure Victor can arrange that," the guy said, then grabbed Lucas' duffle bag off the floor, and waited for him.

Lucas strolled out of the airport, following behind Draco.

Once they arrived at the parking garage, Lucas noticed the Viper no longer sat where he parked it, and it struck him as odd they would have retrieved the car so quickly after his arrival. He had only been sitting in the airport ten minutes before Draco showed up.

The guy wandered past a few parking spaces, and the limousine they'd used to pick him up outside the airport last night sat between the yellow lines. Why did Draco bring the limo? Who else hid in waiting, behind the darkly tinted windows?

Draco clicked the unlock button, and Lucas' hand molded around the latch, even though a clammy sweat broke out all over.

When he swung open the door and peered inside, examining the back of the limo as well, he found no one waiting. He closed his eyes and took a deep breath. Perhaps Draco told the truth, and no one intended to drag him off to some isolated location, torture him, cut him into little pieces, and feed him to the fish.

"You hungry?" Draco said, climbing into the driver's seat. "We can swing by and grab a bite on the way."

"I think I'm good." His stomach recovered from doing flips. He just wanted to get this meeting over with and book another flight home in one piece.

"So, what did you think of Victor's girl?" Draco asked, reversing out of the parking spot, and heading toward the exit.

He worked to keep his expression neutral. "She seems nice."

Draco rolled out of the parking garage into the light of day and hung a left onto the adjoining street. "She used to be a cop. Worked for the Dallas PD if you can believe that."

Lucas acted as if that news blew him away. "You're serious?"

Draco grinned and shook his head. "No bullshit, bro. I met her in a bar. A little joint me and my buddies used to haunt. She put her money down on a game of pool we were playing. She ran the damn table on our asses. I couldn't believe it."

This surprised Lucas. He figured he knew everything about Remi. But being a pool shark never entered into any of their conversations.

"After she took our money, I had to buy her a drink. I knew she was something special. I kept bumping into her at the same dive, running the table on every guy in there. We had some deep discussions and became friends over time."

As the guy braked at a red light, Lucas recalled

Remi mentioning she met Victor at a bar while celebrating Draco's birthday. "Victor trusts her, huh? Even though she used to work for the DPD like you said."

"Naw, man. It wasn't like that. The department did that girl dirty. She was supposed to marry some cop. But when she finally told the guy she didn't love him, he committed suicide or some shit. And the people they used to work with inside the department treated her like a leper. You wouldn't believe some of the cruel shit they did to her. When she couldn't take it anymore, she turned in her badge, left, and never went back. Fucking cops, man. They're worse than criminals."

The light switched to green, and Draco leaned on the gas pedal.

Lucas' mind wandered back to that time when practically everyone in the department had it out for Remi. They hated her for what happened to Gavin, and she became the target of their retribution. He couldn't count the arguments and fights he'd gotten into defending her. His fellow officers were creative in their efforts to make life hell for the woman engaged to his brother, and who they considered responsible for his suicide. He'd just wanted to be there for her but eventually, she pushed him away as well. She cleared out all her belongings in her apartment and left. That was the day his world fell apart.

"To be honest," Draco said, throwing on his blinker, and swerving into the turning lane. "I was a little pissed Victor swooped in and swept her off her feet. I had my eye on her, you know. I was working on getting past the friendship stage."

"Ah, that's a bitch of a place to be with the woman

you like."

"Tell me about it. The boss wanted her. And that was that."

The nagging question of why she got tangled up with these people resurfaced. She kept skating around the question every time he asked her. She'd said she had her reasons. That wasn't good enough. But since he would probably never see her again, it would have to do. He could only hope she would take his advice and get out before hell rained down on the cartel like Armageddon.

Lucas noticed the landscape changing as they drove beyond the city limits. Draco veered down a dirt road with nothing on either side but snow-covered trees. After about a three-minute trip, they approached what appeared to be an old, abandoned warehouse sitting a good distance off the road.

They swerved onto a white-rock road, and Lucas got a clear view of the metal building. Most of the windows were boarded up, and the ones that weren't, were either so cloudy you couldn't see through them, or covered with newspaper. Someone took pains to make sure nobody saw inside the structure. Before he let the fact a cartel member drove him to what appeared to be an abandoned building closed off from the rest of the world unnerve him, he reminded himself the joint served as a packing plant after all. Of course, they wouldn't want anyone to notice what went on inside.

The limo rolled up next to the Viper and parked. And Lucas wondered why the fancy automobile appeared here at the plant, when he'd used it just this morning. The question again popped into his mind of why Victor had someone fetch it from the airport so soon after he'd driven it? More importantly, when Lucas scoped out his surroundings, he couldn't see another vehicle in sight. How did the banker get to the warehouse?

Before climbing out of the limo, Lucas—hoping to drag information out of Draco— mentioned, "Victor must have a thing for the Viper."

"He likes to show it off. He drove the banker here."

That would explain why he had someone return the muscle car so soon after he arrived at the airport. *Calm down already. No one is on to you.*

They both exited the vehicle, and Lucas fell in step behind Draco as they approached the steel door of the warehouse. The guy fished a key out of his pocket, slid it into the deadbolt, and opened the door. An entrance as dark as a haunted house stared him in the face, so Lucas waited outside for Draco to locate the light switch and flip it on.

Once light spilled from the doorway, Draco reappeared just before the threshold. "The boardroom is in the back. When we don't have anyone working here, we always keep the light out to prevent peeping Tom's from getting curious, if you know what I mean."

"Shit, man," Lucas said. "This place is in the middle of nowhere. I doubt anyone would come out this far."

Draco frowned and shoved the key into the front pocket of his pants. "You'd be surprised. Kids ride their bikes out here sometimes on the weekend. We have surveillance cameras out front to make sure no one gets too close. Have to keep an eye on the product, you know."

"Oh, hey, man," Draco said, before Lucas had a

chance to step inside, "Would you grab the gas can sitting outside the door and bring it in here?" The expression on the guy's face dropped clues as to his irritation. "The idiots who work here can't seem to keep shit where it belongs. I don't know what's so difficult about simple, fuckin directions. Don't leave anything outside. Damn, dude."

Lucas did as he asked, and when he stepped through the doorway, several rows of stainless-steel countertops lined side by side got his attention. A cluster of boxes filled the space at the end of the counters, and cans of vegetables sat willy-nilly in front of the boxes. He pointed at the small metal bars and bags of sand. "What are these for?"

Draco chuckled, and strolled over, handling one of the bags. "I forgot, you've never been in one of our packing plants before, have you?"

Lucas shook his head.

These," he said, holding out a small bag of sand, "are used to make the empty cans with the product weigh as much as the cans with vegetables in them." He dropped the item on the counter and headed over to the small metal bars. "The ingots are used for the same purpose as the sand." He then grabbed a can sitting next to him, held it up, and showed Lucas it was hollow. "This is where the product and fillers go. These others," he said pointing at a few more, "are cans with vegetables in them. We pack both. When the boxes get loaded into the cargo, we usually keep the ones with the product in the back, and the ones with the vegetables in the front. This way—"

"They're harder for the highway patrol to spot at weigh stations."

"Bingo, my man." Draco appeared proud of himself. "And they all weigh the same and have the same labels."

The clever strategy impressed Lucas. But the drug distributor had just unintentionally explained their operation to an undercover agent.

"C'mon," Draco said, waving his hand for Lucas to follow. "They're waiting for us, and I'd like to get this over with and go have a beer." He opened the door at the end of a long hallway. Lucas followed him into the room.

What waited beyond the threshold caused the blood to drain from his face.

The door shut, and the click of the lock spun him around to stare at the person behind him. The armed guard with the machine gun posted by the front door of Victor's house the night of the party, stood in position, the same assault weapon held against his chest, nozzle up. His attention swiveled back toward the scene in front of him. There, seated around the conference table were Victor, a few of the men Lucas recognized from Craven's house, and his partner, Dominick Barlow.

They'd strapped the poor guy to a chair. Black and blue abrasions covered most of his face. His left eye was swollen shut, and his lip split, with dried blook caked to his chin. Lucas' breath abandoned him.

Victor Craven smiled. The malice flourishing in his eyes made his expression appear freakishly malevolent. He put his hand out to the chair at his side. "Won't you join us Mr. Conner…or should I say, Kade."

Lucas' limbs locked in place. Machine Gun Kelly blocked the only exit out of there; everyone else in the room packed enough heat to take down a small army.

His chances of escape were one in a million. A hard blow struck the back of his legs, buckling his knees, and spiraling him onto the floor. When he glanced back at his attacker, the gunman at the door held his weapon like a bat. Now that the guy moved away from the exit, instinct told Lucas he should make a run for it, but the click of a gun hammer ensured he wouldn't get far.

Draco pointed the barrel of his firearm at Lucas's head. And the sound of Victor's voice boomed in his ears. "I insist you join us. I have something to show you, and I think you'll be very interested."

With a hand clamped on his shoulder, Draco muscled him into the chair. Dominick sat silently, his chin now resting on his chest with his one good eye open to a mere slit.

Craven stretched his arm across the table and opened the laptop sitting there. He stroked the keypad a few times, then apparently satisfied with what he saw, slowly rotated the display to face Lucas, and struck a key.

Horror settled into his gut as Remi's face filled the screen. The red, leather headrest she leaned against as she spoke, was a dead giveaway the video had been taken while he and Remi took the Viper to her apartment. Hearing his own voice on the audio clip filled him with dread. *"You realize what's going to happen when the DEA busts this thing wide open, right? You're guilty by association, and Craven won't be able to protect you from a cell."*

The drug lord rotated the laptop back around, slid his fingers across the touchpad, then spun it back toward Lucas and clicked a button. Remi asked, *What exactly is Scott Conner's role in the Infierno Cartel?"*

The son of a bitch rigged the car with a recording device. Had something made him suspicious—or did he know about the undercover operation long before Lucas stepped foot in his house?

Victor shut the computer and folded his arms against his chest. "You see, I knew something was going on between you and Remi. The body language between the two of you was impossible to ignore." He got up from his chair, and slowly circled the room. "You left the ballroom, and it wasn't ten minutes before Remi took a cigarette break. The last time she lit one up was at least seven months ago. She only smokes when she's nervous. And you," he emphasized, pointing a well-manicured finger at him, "made her nervous."

Now Craven approached him, crouched to his level, and cocked his head with those dark, baleful eyes zeroing in on him, and driving home the point he had Lucas cornered with nowhere to run. "Why didn't my fiancée tell me you used to be her fuck buddy? Why wouldn't she warn me about who you are, knowing you were here to raid our operation?"

He stood, flicking a finger against his skull. "These are the kinds of thoughts that run around my brain, making me question her loyalty from the very beginning. I gave her everything a woman could possibly want. What more could a guy do? You feel me?"

Lucas sat there without saying a word, while Craven knelt on the floor once again, staring unabashedly into his eyes. "Fuckin' women, right? No matter what we do, it's never enough. I mean look at you. Apparently, you gave her everything too and she left you anyway."

He took a deep breath, as if in a quandary, hauled himself to his feet, and clucked his tongue. "And Gavin, that poor son of a bitch never saw it coming."

"Mention my brother again and I'll kill you," Lucas said. They were going to murder him anyway before this ended. He'd be damned if he'd sit here and listen to the bastard talk shit about his dead brother.

Victor laughed, nodding at everyone in attendance as if Lucas' outburst was the funniest joke he'd heard all day. Chortles from the cartel members drifted around the room. When the amusement melted away, Craven glared at Draco and said, "He's a brave motherfucker. I'll give him that."

"Go ahead and kill me, you fuck," Lucas stabbed a gaze in Victor's direction that could have sliced metal, even though fear for the ways they were going to torture him ran through his blood like ice. "We all have to die sometime."

"Who said anything about killing you?" the kingpin countered, moseying over to the chair they'd strapped Dom to, and gripping the back of it with both hands. "I have much bigger plans for you, *amigo.*"

Tears racked Dom's body, and when he gained control of himself, he raised his head, staring at Lucas with the one eye still open. "I'm sorry, man. They beat the living shit out of me and I...I...folded like a coward". He lowered his head again. "I deserve whatever they do to me."

He found himself in this situation because of Dominick's traitorous actions, and he ought to be pissed as hell at his partner's inability to keep his mouth shut, even under threat of torture and death, but Lucas knew going into this Dom was the more vulnerable of the two. At least he had his experience in the Iraq war to fall back on before joining the police force, which conditioned him to deal with situations under pressure. But his partner signed up for the academy straight out of high school.

More than anything, it sucked to see the man breaking down this way, and knowing he had no remedy at his disposal to help him. But before he could open his mouth and utter a word, Victor backed up, whipped out a pistol, pointed it at Dom's chest, and squeezed the trigger. A rush of staggering emotions hit Lucas all at once, and when he regained his bearings, he lunged out of the chair. "No!"

He charged straight for Craven—pistol be damned—and clobbered him so hard the bastard flew backwards, and the weapon jarred loose from his grip. Blood poured from the drug lord's nose, and Lucas clamped his hands around his throat, shoving both thumbs into his windpipe. The pressure on his back mounted, as he imagined one goon after another piled on. They tugged and tugged, swinging hard blows to his side and head.

Just as Victor's face took on a white hue, and his lips swelled, turning purple, something crashed down on Lucas' head with such force his vision swirled.

He fell away from Craven, rolled on the floor, and struggled to make out the blurry figures standing over him. The next strike hit him in the gut, bawling him over, as another one thundered into the side of his face.

He was going to die this way. Then the darkness closed in on him.

****

Remi Shaw's heart hammered like a drum as she

staggered through the door of the cabin with the majority of Lucas' weight sagging against her. She picked her way through the darkness, colliding with a few pieces of furniture, and practically tripping up the single step leading to the master bedroom. After shuffling into the room, she plopped him down on the side of the bed, and he fell against the mattress. Then she painstakingly wrestled the cover out from under him, grunted with exertion as she twisted his body around, and positioned his head against the pillow. She nestled the blanket tightly around his shivering form, then made her way to the living room straight for the fireplace.

She rummaged across the top of the mantle in the darkness for the matches she'd left the last time she was here. Cobwebs tangled around her fingers, but she finally found the small box. Her hands shook so badly from the freezing cold, it posed a challenge to slip out a match and slide it across the striker. A ball of flame lit a path across the room to the nearest light switch. She flipped it on, and relief flooded over her at the realization the owner kept to his word by leaving the electricity turned on.

"Ouch," she cried, and tossed the match that burned down to her fingers onto the hardwood floor, stamping it out. Except for the cobwebs, it appeared as though everything remained exactly the way she'd left it a year ago when she packed her things and walked away from this place.

She lumbered over to the firewood heaped against the hearth, knelt, grabbed the first stack of newspaper sitting on top, crinkled it, and placed it on top of the grate. Luckily, she'd left some kindling from the last time, and she arranged the small slivers of wood over top of the paper. She steadied her hand that still trembled from the extreme cold, so she'd be able to strike the match. She dotted the newspaper with flames.

The smell of the tinder as it burned awakened her senses, causing her to reflect on what the hell she was doing. When the call came in from Draco, warning her Victor knew the truth and she needed to get the hell out of town, there'd been no time to think. She realized everything had fallen apart and that Lucas was made. Common sense told her if they dragged him anywhere to finish him off, it would be the packing plant.

The only individuals inside the warehouse when she busted through the door of the conference room was a dead guy strapped in a chair, and Lucas laying on the floor not moving. Pinpricks of horror twisted her gut. She wondered if she'd ever get the gruesome image out of her mind. But in all her life she would never forget the gratitude that flooded her after she checked Lucas for a pulse and discovered it still beat strong.

Shaking off the memory, she stacked a few logs on top of the burning kindling and looked around. Thank God Stan Emerson kept his second promise—to leave a key to the cabin under the same rock by the front door—in the event she ever needed to come back. The last time she left the remote Putnam County cabin, she'd hoped she'd never have to return. But here she was once again, coming back to the very place she'd run to after hightailing it out of Texas, hoping to outrun the tragic suicide of her fiancé, and how she was to blame for it.

When she heard moans coming from the master bedroom, she got to her feet, held her hands in front of the fire for another few seconds to warm them before heading to check on Lucas.

He shivered under the blanket and mumbled incoherently. She didn't want to turn the lights on and stun him, so she stepped over to the bedside table, grabbed the box of matches laying there, and lit the candle that sat next to them.

She situated the flame close enough to his face to better examine him. His cheek and chin were bruised, and the dried blood could be traced to the side of his head, directly above his ear. She set the candle down in such a way the light reflected on his injury, and she parted his hair to inspect the wound. Even with the crimson/black color of blood shrouding her view, she could still see the cut for the most part, and it had to be at least three inches in length.

What could have caused it? The butt of a gun, a blunt object, the pointed tip of a boot? That bastard Jimmy—the one who always roamed Victor's castle with the machine gun—wore a pair of pointed snakeskin boots. She couldn't imagine what they'd done to him before she got there. But why didn't they kill him like they did the guy in the chair? They wouldn't have left him lying there thinking he was dead. Victor didn't make sloppy mistakes like that. He would have checked to make sure.

"You killed him."

Lucas' rambling prompted her into action, and she ran her fingers through his hair to calm him. "Shush, now. It's okay. You're here with me."

Sympathy tugged at her heartstrings for what he must have gone through. Although she couldn't be sure what tipped Victor off to his identity, she regretted climbing out of the car when he dropped her by her apartment. She should have done more to convince him how dangerous Victor was and refused to leave until he completely understood.

Craven asked her to marry him, and she'd agreed. That made her want to vomit. Over the last several months she learned to get by as his girlfriend, but only because she knew the imperative nature of that connection to her mission. She never dreamed he would ask for her hand in marriage. He put her on the spot, and she had no choice but to accept. But the hurt in Lucas' eyes when she said yes was like a knife twisting in her stomach.

"Remi," he muttered in a hoarse whisper, not opening his eyes.

"It's me. And I promise I'm not going to leave you."

She settled in beside him, draped the cover over her body, and snuggled against him. They both lay there, shivering together.

Chapter Four

Lucas' eyes snapped open. He stared at an antique lamp sitting on a black end table, then the wall behind it made from old wood, log cabin wood. He sat up and winced in pain, forcing him to lay back against the pillow. The source of the aching came from his abdomen, and his hand roamed in that direction. The smooth surface his fingers encountered had to be a bandage, and the discovery made him peer down at his stomach. The white, cotton patch was eight inches or better, and he peeled away the tape to examine the injury. A nice sized cut stretched across his skin, and the area surrounding the contusion appeared purplish and black. That's when he noticed the bruise on his right side was as large as the sole of a shoe.

What the hell happened? As he gingerly swung his legs over the side of the bed and planted his feet on the ground, it all came tumbling back. The warehouse. The laptop and the recording of him and Remi. The gunshot to Dom's chest.

Shit! He shot out of bed and paid for it instantly. Pain seized him, and his head became woozy. He staggered to the wall and braced his hand against the rough wood to steady himself. The cartel found out they were DEA agents and killed Dominick Barlow in retaliation. He needed to contact his SAC. Once he got hold of the Special Agent in Charge, they could get him

61

on a plane to Texas, and sort this out.

Where was he? Once he regained his balance, he stumbled into the bathroom—his bladder near to exploding—and relieved himself. He stepped to the mirror and ran his fingers across the bruises and scrapes on his face, and the cut on the side of his noggin. Then he glanced down at the vanity, and his attention brushed across a pair of sapphire earrings he recognized as the ones Remi wore that night at Victor's house.

A recollection so ambiguous it seemed like déjà vu splashed across his mind. His body had been so cold he couldn't stop trembling. He had called Remi's name, and a warmth he could only describe as comforting enveloped his entire body.

She was here. But how had she found him?

He stepped lightly into the bedroom and found his clothes folded in a neat stack on the dresser. Sitting on the edge of the bed, he carefully dressed, though it took time and repetition. His chest hurt like a sonofabitch. After he was able to get his shoes on, he wandered into the living room.

Logs crackled and popped in the firebox. And the place smelled of freshly burning wood and coffee. A white glow brought his attention to the storm door, and he lumbered toward it, realizing on closer inspection, the brightness appeared to be a landscape of nothing but snow-covered ground.

"How are you feeling?"

Lucas spun toward the voice to find Remi standing behind him dressed in a sweater and jeans, clutching a cup of coffee. "Like I've had the shit kicked out of me."

"Here." She held out the mug. "I heard you get up and thought you'd like coffee."

He took the steaming brew, nodding his appreciation.

"Before you ask—because I know you will," she said, while he took a sip, "I hauled you out of the warehouse by putting together a makeshift gurney from materials Victor and his pals left behind at the warehouse and brought you here two nights ago. No one knows about this place. And I made sure I wasn't followed."

So, he'd been asleep that long. Since he woke up naked, and found his clothes stacked on the dresser, freshly laundered, he assumed she'd taken them off and bandaged him up, too. Well, she'd seen him naked before, although it had been too long since he'd seen her in her birthday suit.

"First question," he said, staring out at the endless snow beyond the storm door, "Where is *here*?"

"Putnam County, just north of New York City. You remember me talking about my sister, Jacqueline?"

"Go on."

She cleared her throat. "She dated a guy who worked in the real estate business. He bought this cabin for him and his wife as a little vacation home. Of course, she died before he met my sister. Anyway, I needed a place to stay when I left Texas. Jacqueline contacted him, and he hooked me up here in New York. He doesn't come out here anymore, and when I was able to get on my feet and move into an apartment, he told me this place would be here if I ever needed to come back."

"So, this is where you went to get away from me, huh?"

When he continued to stare at her, she stepped

away. "To answer your second question, Draco tipped me off that Victor discovered you were an undercover agent. He said Craven would come looking for me since he found out I knew about it all along and didn't tell him."

She made a beeline for the couch, sat down and took a deep breath. "I figured Craven would take you to the packing plant. And that's where I found you. I brought you here because it was the only place Victor doesn't know about."

"Number one," he said, zeroing in on her, "I didn't ask that question, and—"

"You would have."

"Number two," he continued undeterred, "why would Draco warn you Victor was aware you knew me, and that I was working undercover? He's on Craven's payroll. It makes no sense he would have undermined his boss like that."

"What are you saying?" She lunged off the couch, got in his face. "That I'm in cahoots with them, and me bringing you here is all part of some devious plan we all concocted together?"

He pursed his lips, stepped over to the coffee table, put his mug down, and leveled her with a shrewd grin. Even though he figured she'd had nothing to do with this, he said, "You're the one who said it, not me. Besides, you're sleeping with the enemy."

"Not anymore, I'm not." The wounded expression in her eyes told him the idea she would somehow be involved in a plan to take him down was farfetched. "If I was working with Victor and his men," she continued, "I'd have left you in that warehouse. I damn sure wouldn't have risked my neck to get you out."

"They killed Dominick." The words sounded unreal even as they left his mouth.

She lowered her head and shrank back down onto the couch. "I know. I saw him."

"Why didn't they kill me, too?"

"I wondered the same thing myself."

"I'm sorry you had to see that." Even though she'd only just met his partner, encountering a dead body had to be disturbing. He sat down in the chair across from her.

"I used to be a police officer. I've seen worse."

"Something isn't right here." There'd be no way they would have left him there alive unless they intended to. And then he had the fact Draco tipped off Remi to consider. They wanted her to find him. Victor's words hit him anew. *Who said anything about killing you? I have much bigger plans for you.*

"I think Draco made that call to you on purpose. And I'm guessing they wanted you to find me."

She threw out her hands. "But he didn't tell me where you were, only Craven knew the truth and he would come looking for me. I have no idea how they even found out you were working undercover for the DEA."

"When I listened to that recording of us, judging from our conversation, it would have been apparent to them you would have come looking for me if you knew my cover was blown. You yourself said earlier, the first place you would have searched was the packing plant. They knew you'd think that."

She looked dumb founded. "What recording?"

Then it occurred to him she didn't know. "Victor planted a surveillance device in the Viper. The whole conversation we had on the way to drop you off was recorded. He showed it to me after Draco lured me to the warehouse. He questioned Dominick, and he spilled the beans about the covert operation. That's how he knew we were there as undercover agents."

"But why would he record us? I never said a word to him I knew you."

"You didn't have to. He could sense the tension between us, and it raised his suspicions."

She covered her face with her hands and shook her head. "Shit. I never should have followed you to the terrace. That had to have been what raised his suspicions."

"It's not your fault."

She didn't answer, only sat there with her face buried in her hands.

"Listen to me." He got up from the chair, stepped over to the couch, and shrank down beside her. "You didn't cause this to happen." He gently grabbed her hands to remove them from her face, and the contact sent a cascade of warmth rushing over his body. It reminded him of the softness of her mouth when he drew her against him on the terrace and kissed her.

When she finally let him pluck her fingers away, the glistening of fresh tears on her cheek tugged at his heart. Then his attention dropped to her mouth, and it became a life and death battle to keep from moving in on her again.

She scooted away, and he directed his stare in the opposite direction. "I was the agent in this situation. It was my responsibility to keep my feelings completely hidden. I was reckless. It's my fault Dom got killed. Nobody else's."

"Don't be an ass." She shuffled off the couch and stepped to the window. "You act like I didn't have police training. I knew the way I was acting was dangerous. But I was so mad at you I didn't care."

Why were you mad at me? "You're right. You were a cop, and a damn good one. What caused you to choose this path...with these people?" Anger brought him to his feet, although slower than he would have liked. The last time he asked this question, she didn't answer. Now he refused to give her that luxury.

She continued to stare out the window. Not saying a word.

He would have stomped across the floor and twirled her around, forcing her to acknowledge him if his injuries would have allowed it. Instead, he slowly approached, leaned into her ear, and said, "I deserve an answer, and you're going to give it to me."

She spun, her eyes drilling right through him. She stood so close her breath skimmed across his face. "I was there for my nephew, okay?" she said tightly.

Her words baffled him. "Are you talking about Nathaniel?"

Now she backed away, wandered over to the fireplace, picked up the poker, and stabbed the logs. "He's my only nephew. I couldn't be talking about anyone else."

He slogged over to the sofa, planted himself down, and folded his arms over his chest, wincing in pain as he'd forgotten about the bruises covering his abdomen. "I'm listening."

When she finished stoking the flames, she leaned the poker against the hearth, took a deep breath, and a few steps back, staring at the mantle. "I don't know if you know this, but my sister died two years ago. Nathaniel had no place to go, so he came to live with me. He got in with some bad people and started selling drugs on the street."

"I didn't know your sister died. I'm sorry about that."

"She had bone cancer. After five months, she lost the battle."

He remembered Jackie who lived in New York but occasionally flew out to Texas. As Remi's only sibling, the two had been very close. The tragedy of losing her sister had to be especially troubling because Remi's parents died in a car accident within a few months of her meeting Gavin. Jacqueline and her son Natty were the only family she had left.

Remi shook her head, as if casting aside the bleak memories, and said, "Anyhow, I found out what Nathaniel was doing. I tried everything in my power to get him to stop. But it finally took one of his buddy's dying in a drug raid gone bad to convince him if he didn't get out, he was going to end up the same way."

"So, he got out."

She glanced at him, nodding. Then turned her back to him again and busied herself with dusting off the mantle. As far as he could tell, a layer of dust covered damn near every surface in the place. Why did she continue cleaning the mantle when it seemed like a lost cause? Because it gave her something to focus on while delving into a tale she obviously didn't want to tell.

"Things were going great for a month or two. Then he started getting threatening phone calls and messages."

"From the cartel? From a lower-level drug dealer?"

Lucas knew whoever supplied Natty with the narcotic, probably harassed him as well. They wouldn't have been happy if one of their avenues to make a profit dried up.

"He parted ways amicably with his supplier. Natty was just a small-time dealer. The guy wanted a payoff to let him go without incident. My nephew worked two jobs to pay him off. That was supposed to be that."

"But it wasn't." That information didn't surprise Lucas. Those who worked in the drug trade couldn't be trusted. They would cut your head off if doing so served some kind of purpose. In some instances, breaking away from dealing drugs was just as challenging as escaping the clutches of being initiated into a gang. Once a person enters a dark world such as that, it could cost their life to get out.

She finally relinquished her activities and plopped down in the chair he occupied earlier. "It was the dirty cops that wouldn't leave him alone. He knew some of the names of those in the Dallas PD who either headed up drug deals or had been paid off by the cartel to look the other way while drugs were being sold on the streets. Many of the shipments he dealt with came from Texas."

"What were the names of the cops?"

"He wouldn't tell me. He was afraid if I knew it could get me killed."

At least Natty realized that much. That kind of information would've gotten her killed. "Where is Nathaniel now?"

"He came up missing over a year ago."

The truth hit Lucas like a freight train. He lunged off the couch, and the pain in his body sent him reeling back down again. "Shit. It feels like a broken rib, I swear."

"I was afraid of that." She rushed over, lifted his shirt, and peeled back the bandage. "You've opened the cut again with the way you're moving around. The gauze is soaked with blood." She grabbed a throw pillow and situated it flat on the coach. "Here," she said, "lay down and I'll go get a fresh bandage."

"It's fine," he argued, wanting to finish their conversation, but she already made her way to the bathroom.

After a little clanging around in there, she strolled back with fresh gauze, medical tape, and a bottle of peroxide. She knelt on the floor and leaned over him. Her long hair brushed across his chest, giving off the sensation of a feather tickling his skin. It also hardened another part of his body.

He closed his eyes as she doctored him up. Her hands all over his chest and abdomen were making it downright painful, and not in the way that hurt. When he opened his eyes, she was staring directly at his hard on.

Their attention connected and she shot up. "Jesus, Lucas. Some things never change."

"What?" He painstakingly propped himself on his elbow and stared at her.

"That." She gestured toward his penis. "I could blow on it and it would spring up."

He couldn't help the laugh that escaped him. "I haven't forgotten how well you used to blow on it."

"God." She took a few steps back, her face flaming red.

"Well, you walked right into that."

She shook her head in exasperation and headed into the kitchen.

"I'm sorry," he yelled out. "It's been a while."

"The hell it has," she hollered back. "Have you forgotten about Miss Black Dress so soon?"

Actually, he had. That's how memorable that experience was. "Jealous?"

Silence, and then footfalls came into the living room. She stood at the end of the sofa, hands on her hips, and leveling him with a stone-cold stare. "You can fuck whoever you want. You don't need my permission."

He slowly sat up and braced his arm over the back of the couch, giving her a lazy grin. "Good, then I'd like to fuck you."

The shock of his words lit up her expression. "Not a chance."

He pursed his lips and nodded curtly. "Okay. I'll accept that for now."

"For now, my ass."

"Since you're offering."

"You are the biggest asshole I know."

He tugged his shirt over his stomach. "Let's get back to the discussion we were having earlier. You had to be out of your mind to infiltrate the *Infiernos* to try to find your nephew."

Her mouth hung open, then she shut it.

"Why didn't you tell me the truth when we were on our way to drop you by your apartment?"

"Because I hadn't seen you in years. I honestly didn't know if I could trust you, and I couldn't risk word getting out."

"Who was I going to tell? Victor? Draco? Do you

think I would have blown my cover to tell lover boy you were sleeping with him just to get intel on the whereabouts of your nephew?"

Fire shot from her eyes. "That's not fair."

He could relate. Anger bubbled up in him too. "It's true, isn't it? Or did you fuck him for the pleasure?"

"You son of a bitch." She stormed out of the room, and a door slammed in the distance.

Ah, shit. Real clever, pal. Why couldn't he keep his head straight and his temper in check where it concerned Remi Shaw? She had him flying off the handle ever since he laid eyes on her a few days ago. She'd been in another man's bed, and that realization ripped through him like an earthquake. She hit the nail on the head though. He was guilty of sleeping with Miss Black Dress. But in his defense, he thought about Remi the whole time.

He struggled off the couch knowing what he had to do.

He drummed his knuckles against the door of the guest bedroom. She didn't respond, and he tested the knob. She'd left it unlocked.

When he flung open the door, she sat there perched on the edge of the bed, staring straight at the wall. The tension visible from the profile of her face told him she wasn't going to forgive him easily. He stepped over, stared down at her, and said, "Jesus, Remi. I'm sorry. I'm a real bastard and I have no excuse for my behavior. I'd be pissed at me too."

Although she blinked a few times, and glanced down once, she still refused to acknowledge him.

He sank down beside her. "I'm grateful for you and all you've done for me. You thought enough to come and drag me out of that warehouse when you knew Victor was after you and you could have run the other way instead. Hell, you doctored me up when I was in such a bad way, I couldn't help myself. And you wrapped your body around me to keep me from freezing to death."

She finally glanced at him. "You remember that? I thought you were out of it."

He grinned. "Believe me, anytime you've touched me, I've remembered it."

She half smiled and lowered her head. "For the record, I didn't sleep with Victor because I liked it. The only thing I wanted to do was find my nephew. When he started showing interest in me, my back was against the wall. I had to make a choice. Either I went along with it, or he would have moved on, and I would have been stuck with no way to save Natty. Victor was my ticket in."

He understood that. He'd had to do things as Scott Conner he wouldn't have otherwise done if he wasn't bound by his duty to infiltrate the cartel. "Draco told me he met you at a bar he frequented."

She snorted. "That was no happenstance. Draco Vargas was Nathaniel's supplier. I found out where he hung out, and I made a point to be there when I knew he would be. I suspected it was a dirty cop who was responsible for my nephew's disappearance. My bad reputation with the DPD destroyed any chance of me going back to Texas and infiltrating them. So, my next best option was the cartel itself. Victor spends a lot of time at his mansion here in New York, even though his main drug distribution is in Texas. I was hoping he knew what happened to Natty."

"But Craven kept you out of the loop."

She sighed. "It was frustrating as hell. I felt like I was giving it my all and getting nowhere in return."

He knew exactly how that felt. He'd been hanging out with these guys for months, living like one of them, and now he had a whole lot of nothing to show for it. He wrapped his arms around her shoulders and tugged her close. "We're going to find Nathaniel. I promise I'm going to do everything in my power to make that happen."

"Thank you," she whispered, as he rested his chin on top of her head.

His stomach growled, and with her head against his chest, she said, "You haven't had anything to eat in two days."

"I'll go into the kitchen and rustle up something for us," he said, making a move to rise, and then recoiling in pain.

She jumped up before he could. "You're going to stay right here. I can take care of that." She lifted the right side of his shirt and ran her hand down the large bruise marring his side and some of his abdomen. "I'm really worried you have broken ribs. We should get you to the hospital.

He covered her hand with his and stared into her eyes. "No hospital. It's too risky with Victor and his men out there."

"But what if you have internal bleeding caused by a tear in one of your organs. I don't think we can afford to take that chance."

"I'll be fine. We'll just keep an eye on it."

She shook her head. "Lucas, we shouldn't—"

He put his finger to her lips to shush her and caught

that little swallow she made along with the softening in her eyes.

They both stared at each other in the silence of the room, then she broke the trance and stepped away. She cleared her throat and strode to the door. "I'll go make us something to eat. You relax."

****

The digital clock on the microwave made him aware of the time. Fifteen minutes past nine a.m. Remi placed the last of the breakfast items on the table and took a seat across from Lucas.

He stuck a fork in two of the pancakes sitting on a serving dish and slapped them on his plate. Then he helped himself to a few slices of bacon and grabbed the syrup.

She poured them both a glass of juice and set his in front of him. Monitoring his actions as he sliced into his pancake, dipped it in syrup, and slid it into his mouth, forced her to admit even with bruises and small cuts on his face, he was still a brutally handsome man. She'd never seen him with shoulder length hair before, but it suited him.

A flash of him standing beside the Viper with his arm braced across the top of the car door waiting for her to get in, blossomed in her mind. She recalled studying his attractive face, and how difficult keeping her attention off him during the ride to her apartment would prove to be. She couldn't remember ever wanting anyone as much as she wanted him. And it didn't start with that kiss on the terrace—although it stopped her heart—neither did it start the moment she climbed into the limo and recognized his face. The desire she had for him began thirteen years ago, the very moment she saw him standing at the airport waiting to pick her up.

Ironically, Gavin had sent his brother to get her that day as she returned from a trip to visit her sister in New York. Although he'd been introduced to her as her fiancée's sibling, and she'd seen him from time to time at the PD, they'd never spent any real time together. But that day at the airport changed everything.

Now, the reminder of Lucas' brother caused her attention to drop to the table. Loving Lucas Kade was always taboo because she'd been engaged to his brother. And even now, the guilt of what they'd done would forever prevent her from giving in to her need to have him.

"I assume you have a car here," he said between bites.

His voice interrupted her present train of thought as she filled her plate with food, topping it off with syrup. "There's an old Pontiac that's stayed here with the property. It belongs to Stan, the owner of the cabin. The keys are hanging there," she said, pointing toward the key peg affixed to the wall. "I started it up yesterday while you slept, and it runs, thank God." She took a sip of juice and continued. "Stan pays a guy to come out once every month and check on everything here. He keeps up with the maintenance of the car."

"He's not much for dusting and keeping the cobwebs under control, is he?"

"There's usually a maid that comes out on a trimonthly basis. I'm not sure what happened with that. But depending on how long we need to be here, I'll take care of the dusting when I get a chance."

"I wasn't implying—"

"I know you weren't."

He grinned, as if a memory surfaced in his mind. "I could never forget how much of a clean freak you always were."

She took a bite of pancake, and it melted in her mouth. "And still am. It's been driving me crazy to sit in the middle of this dust, but I did the best I could to try to at least clean off the regularly used surfaces. I've been a bit busy looking after you, chopping wood, and—"

"Wait. Is there a wood splitter in the barn?"

She shook her head.

"You've been chopping logs with an axe?" He appeared incredulous, as if the thought of a woman wielding an axe to split wood seemed like a foreign concept.

"I lived here for a while. I had to chop my own wood. Sometimes I had to cut down a tree when I ran out of logs."

"What?"

"Don't look so surprised. It's called surviving. I've learned how to do it well."

"You cut down a tree with an axe?"

"They make chainsaws for that. There's one in the barn."

"Oh."

She could tell by his expression he was impressed. "Is there a reason you asked about the car?"

He bit into a slice of bacon, chasing it down with a gulp of juice. "It appears there's no landline here. I guess Victor took my cellphone. The DEA gave me one strictly to use for my persona, so he won't find anything incriminating on it, but I need to get to a phone and call my SAC. I didn't see your phone here, so I assumed you left it behind at your apartment."

"My phone can be tracked, and I didn't want to take the chance." Then she slid another forkful of pancakes into her mouth, chewed and swallowed. "I don't think it's a good idea for you to call the special agent in charge. We know there's dirty cops involved, and we can't tell how far up the chain it goes."

He frowned, appearing as if she spoke in a foreign language. "That wouldn't involve the DEA."

"You don't know that."

"Look, there's not a lot of agents who know about the sting operation. I trust the people I work with."

"Like you trusted Dominick?"

The sudden change in his expression, going from casual to deadly serious, told her she'd gone too far. She lowered her head and sighed. "Damn, I'm sorry. I didn't mean it like that. I'm just trying to get you to understand we don't know who's involved, and we can't afford to tip off the wrong person to our whereabouts."

"I know what I'm doing," he said, contempt in his tone. "We can't very well sit around here for the next year, hoping no one will find us. There's a dead DEA agent in that warehouse. I can't just walk away and forget about that. I have to report it. It's my duty."

"I just think we need to discuss this before we make a rash decision and risk doing the wrong thing."

"There's nothing to discuss." She could tell by the stern expression in his eyes he would not be dissuaded.

"I need to pick up supplies anyhow." She decided giving in would be easier than clashing with his impenetrable stubbornness. Dealing with him in the past assured her there'd be no winning. "There's not much food in the freezer, and the axe outside is dull. I had a helluva time chopping the little bit of wood I managed to split yesterday."

"How much money have you got? Those bastards emptied my pockets. I don't have a dime."

"Since we can't use any cards, it's a good thing I kept a stash of cash here. I never knew if I'd need it someday."

He furrowed his brows. "How much cash?"

"Should be at least a thousand."

"That'll be more than enough to get us through. And we should be able to put some aside as well. We'll have to change our appearance."

She broke off a piece of bacon and popped it into her mouth. "I'll pick up some hair dye and a pair of sharp scissors." Then she leveled him with an expression of jest. "Sorry, cowboy. But we're going to have to whack that gorgeous hair off."

"Gorgeous, huh? You like it?"

"I didn't say that."

"You literally did."

He sat across the table staring at her with that playboy grin she always found so incredibly sexy. And he didn't even realize the effect it had on her. Her cheeks must be as red as his coffee cup. It took her more than a minute to rebound.

"Why did you give up on us so easily?"

With those unexpected words, her feeling of euphoria came crashing down. Why did he continue to push her on this? Why couldn't he just let it go? And why must he make her say the words? She stood from the table, taking a few seconds to gather her wits. "I'm sure you'll want to jump in the shower before we leave. I had one this morning."

"Remi, stop it." The wounded expression in his eyes mixed with frustration and anger made her cut her gaze away. "Just talk to me."

She straightened and gathered her plate. "I'll pick you up some clothes while we're out. I have more than enough here, but you only have what you're wearing." She stepped toward the sink, wanting to crawl in a hole and disappear.

His hot breath skimmed across her neck, and his fingers entwined around her wrist. If she glanced over her shoulder and gazed into his chocolate eyes, she would be forever lost in their glorious depths. She held on to control by a string when he whispered, "I don't want the damn clothes. I want you."

Her mind scattered into a thousand pieces, and she broke free, hurrying out of the room as fast as her trembling legs would take her.

Chapter Five

As Lucas sat in the driver's seat of the junker left at the cabin, hunched over the wheel, his attention drifted to her from time to time. She stared out the window in a trance, her hair pinned up inside of a sunhat with a wide brim, and a pair of sunglasses laying in her lap. She had continued to give him the silent treatment and kept her distance from him as much as possible until they climbed in the car together.

He tugged on the rim of the baseball cap to make it fit more comfortably. It was the only disguise available in the cabin to wear, and they needed to hide their identities as much as possible. The hat belonged to Remi, and it fit way too snug. But the headgear wasn't the only thing making him as uncomfortable as a hen locked in a cage with seven horny roosters. He imagined he came on too strong when he approached her while she stood by the sink. He'd only uttered the truth of the matter in her ear. But it caused her to scurry away from him again. She had a bad habit of fleeing the scene where it concerned him. Was she running from him, or from her feelings for him? Her body language, and the deep expression of hunger in her eyes every time he got too close, told him she wanted him every bit as much as he did her. So, what was the bloody problem?

Don't kid yourself. You know exactly what the issue

is.

Gavin Kade was laid to rest thirteen years ago, yet she couldn't get past the guilt of his death long enough to allow herself to live again. Self-punishment had become such a way of life she'd forgotten how to be happy. He couldn't compete with the hold a dead man had on her, and he'd been driving his head through a brick wall trying to. He'd be wise to give up, stop fighting to convince her what she took as a way of living, wasn't living at all. But she'd taken the easy way out years ago and look where that got them?

"Take a left here," she finally said, pointing in the direction of the crossroad coming up.

"I was beginning to think you weren't ever going to speak to me again. I'm glad you changed your mind."

"This isn't changing my mind, it's giving directions," she said in a matter-of-fact tone as she continued to stare at the windshield.

He threw on the blinker, yielded to traffic, and took the turn. "Well, I guess I'll take it any way I can get it."

He tossed a quick glance at her, and it became clear she'd clammed up again. There existed nothing on the face of the planet that managed to push his buttons like she did. Why God created women for the sole purpose of tormenting men was beyond him. But here he was, nonetheless.

He rolled into the parking lot of the small strip mall, found an empty space and killed the engine. She slipped on her sunglasses and curled her hand around the latch. He stopped her by grabbing her arm. "Hey," he said, as she spun around to confront him.

"I don't want to argue with you," she snapped, then

struggled against the hold he had on her.

And there she went again, pushing his buttons. He flung her arm away. "That wasn't my intention. All I wanted to do was coordinate and see if you wanted to head into the super center for groceries, while I go into the hardware store to get another axe."

She glanced away and sat straight as an arrow. "That's fine."

He shook his head at her childish behavior, snatched the sunglasses hanging from the rearview mirror, and slid them on his face. "We meet back here in thirty minutes." Then he opened the car door, stepped out, and slammed it for good measure.

It pissed him off even more, his injuries slowed him down. He'd much rather have the satisfaction of pouncing across the parking lot, flinging open the door to the hardware store, and storming inside. But he'd have to settle for grumbling to himself like an idiot as he approached the establishment. He ought to ignore her the way she did him and let her stew in her pity party all alone. Her ridiculous, unreasonable behavior grated on his nerves. She insisted on ignoring the attraction between them. How long could someone hide from the truth? Hell, she'd kept it up for thirteen years, what's another few days, a week, a month? And what did it matter? As far as he could see, she had no intention of ever confronting her feelings for him. It reminded him of the pointless effort to save a drowning man just to watch him wade back out into the water.

He stepped into the hardware store, and carefully made his way to the aisle where he located the axes. After settling on one that seemed sturdy enough, he carried it to the cash register and placed it on the conveyer belt. The short, stubby woman standing in line in front of him glanced over her shoulder, staring at him a little too long. *Yeah, that's right, lady. I'm wearing sunglasses in twenty-five-degree weather, and I have a ballcap over my head that fits like it was made for a Smurf. Thanks for noticing.*

She finally spun back around, and he worked his jaw, impatience curling around every nerve ending for the guy ahead of her who argued with the cashier about a two-dollar difference in the price of a leaf blower on clearance. Who the hell buys a leaf blower when snow covers everything in sight? Checking his watch, he realized he'd already been in the store for fifteen minutes. He didn't have time for this shit.

After plucking the wade of bills out of his pocket, and counting out two dollars, he shuffled around the lady in front of him to handle the problem. She stared at him, a stunned expression etched into her face as if he'd broken some kind of sacred shopper's rule by trying to scoot around her. He approached the cashier, smiled at the unhappy customer, and laid the money on the counter.

When he stepped away to reclaim his spot in line, the man trained an evil eye on Lucas, and said, "Hey, buddy. That's not the point."

The pudgy lady faced him again. This time a toothy smile was his reward. Then she told the disagreeable man still arguing about the price of the item, "Can you move it along. The nice gentleman behind you took care of the problem. We all have places we need to be."

The guy paid the rest of what he owed, threw one last disgruntled stare in Lucas' direction, and stormed away from the cash register.

After his pleasant experience in the hardware store, he dropped the axe off at the car, and then headed toward a small Mexican cantina a few doors down from the retailer he'd just visited. There were a few small crowds gathered around a handful of tables, and a horseshoe bar stood toward the back wall of the establishment. As he advanced in that direction, his eyes brushed across an old-style rotary phone sitting close to the bartender. He was in luck.

Lucas sat down at an empty bar. The barkeep with the man bun and bushy eyebrows got up from his stool and nodded in his direction. "What can I get for you?"

Even though he only wanted to use the phone, Lucas figured if he ordered a drink the guy would be more inclined to let him take care of business. "How about a draft beer. Lite if you have it."

"Sure thing." The fellow snatched a tall mug from the shelf and strolled over to the tap.

While the bartender filled his order, Lucas glanced at the television mounted in the corner of the ceiling. A commercial for auto insurance played across the screen.

The man strode over and set the beer in front of him, and Lucas said, "Do you think I can use that phone back there?" He pointed toward the telephone.

Without saying a word, the guy retrieved it, sat the bulky item in front of Lucas before wandering back to his stool. Lucas waited for a few seconds before he put the receiver against his ear and rolled out the digits for the DEA's Special Unit Division. Before he could complete the number, his attention connected with the television—and he almost dropped the receiver.

He asked the bartender to increase the volume, and

the man picked up the remote, pressing his fat thumb on the button.

A picture of Remi in her police uniform that must have been taken at least thirteen years ago, sat next to an older photo of him decked out in his policeman garb. The shock of witnessing their faces splashed all over the eleven o'clock news sent a tidal wave of utter disbelief winding through him. And it only got worse.

"Former police officer for the Dallas PD, Remi Shaw, and Lucas Kade, an agent for the DEA Special Operations Team, are wanted in connection with the murder of an undercover DEA agent, Dominick Barlow."

The screen switched to a grainy video of Lucas picking up a gas can outside the warehouse Draco drove him to and strolling through the door with the container in his hand. The newscaster continued. *"Kade's fingerprints were lifted from this gas can discovered at the scene of the burning warehouse. Barlow's body was found inside."*

Burning warehouse? Fingerprints? Son of a bitch. Victor and Draco set him up.

The reporter continued to bring his worst nightmare to life with the remainder of her report which contained more than the usual amount of information. Another clear sign of a setup. *"An informant by the name of Bain Delgado, now under police protection, came forward and claimed he saw Agent Kade shoot Dominick Barlow in the chest. Former Texas officer Remi Shaw was also present at the scene and believed to be aiding Kade in the murder."*

During his time at the warehouse, Delgado never showed his face. *What the fuck was going on?*

Informant's names were never *ever* released to the press, mainly because it was the best way to get someone killed.

The newscaster added a few more logs to the fire. *"Our information has it Lucas Kade has been working undercover to bring down the Infierno Cartel. Officials believe he became so embedded in the cartel he went rogue. He was last seen with Remi Shaw who no one has heard from in the last thirteen years."*

The news station again flashed a picture of him and Remi. The reporter told viewers Lucas Kade had shoulder length, blond hair, a goatee, and would be dressed in civilian clothing.

He peered down at his hand only to realize he'd never hung up the phone. He dropped the receiver into the cradle, knowing he couldn't make that call now. He needed to get out of here before someone recognized him.

He forced himself to focus on the simple task of plunging his hand into his pocket and retrieving the wad of folded cash. He managed to count out the dough and tossed the money onto the bar to pay for his beer. He tugged his ballcap down and strolled out of the joint as fast as his injuries, and rubbery legs would allow.

****

Remi loaded the last bag of groceries into the trunk, when she peered up to witness Lucas headed straight for her, hobbling along like an invalid being chased by an axe murderer. The stark expression on his face as he got closer, on top of the erratic hand gestures for her to get into the car, alerted her something had taken a turn.

Was one of Victor's men in the store? Did they

recognize him?

"We need to go. Now," he said, slamming the trunk and tottering over to the driver's side.

The minute Remi shut herself inside, she asked, "What happened?"

He slid the key in the ignition and threw the gearshift in reverse. Judging by the hurried way he backed out of the space, and the squealing of the tires as he sped away, whatever took place in there rattled the hell out of him. "What happened back there?"

Lucas swerved onto the highway and pointed the Pontiac in the direction of the cabin. "It appears we are wanted for murder."

"What are you talking about?"

Once he got good and settled into the seat, he tore the sunglasses off his face, and tossed them in the backseat along with the ballcap. His attention cut toward her, and he said, "I went into the cantina to use the phone like we'd discussed at the house, and the television was on the news. Our pictures were plastered all over the damn thing. They are saying I burned down the warehouse—after you helped me murder Dominick."

"What?" It was as if somebody splashed freezing water on her. "That's not possible. When I got you out of there, the warehouse was not on fire. There was nobody else there." She could tell by the expression on his face she was preaching to the choir.

"Evidently, they burned the damn thing down after you left with me. When I first got there, Draco asked me to bring a gas can into the packing plant that was sitting outside by the door. He acted like he was pissed at the guys that work there for neglecting to bring it inside. There was video surveillance outside the warehouse. The news station has the footage of me carrying the gas can inside, and the authorities have lifted my prints from the can."

Her mind reeled. This couldn't be happening. "How do I fit into this?"

"Bain Delgado, that's how."

She remembered Delgado being introduced to her as the finance guy for Victor. An image of the shrimpy man with big teeth and curly black hair formed in her mind. He appeared so harmless. "What's he got to do with this?"

"He's their witness. Claims he was present, and saw me shoot Dom in the chest, and you were there aiding in the murder."

"Are you shitting me?"

"The thing is," he continued, "Bain was never even there. Or at least before they beat me into unconsciousness, he wasn't."

Now he stared dead at her, frowning and waging a finger. "I told you something wasn't right. Victor wouldn't have left me alive unless he had a motive for doing so. And that call you received from Draco…that was intended to get you to the warehouse and drag me out of there before they burned the place down with Dom's dead corpse inside." He slammed his fist against the steering wheel. "I fucking knew it."

"Where's Delgado now?"

"They have him in protective custody." He glanced at her for a moment too long, and she could tell he had more on his mind. He sighed and said, "Bain isn't who you thought he was. He wasn't working for Victor. He was working for us as an informant."

Did he purposely hide that information from her, or just didn't have time to tell her with everything going on?

"Before you think the worst," he said, "It's not that I didn't want to tell you, it's just I honestly didn't even think to tell you until now."

"What now?"

"Now that we know he set things up to go down this way, we don't have to worry about being hunted down by Victor and his army. The bad news is, we are wanted criminals, and our faces will be plastered all over every police bulletin from here to Texas. So, to answer your question, I'll need a minute to think."

He swung onto the long driveway leading to the cabin and rolled the Pontiac into the garage. He clicked a button on the remote, and the metal garage door clanged as it slid down the track. After he killed the engine, they both sat in silence for a moment before he said, "I didn't see a television inside." He pointed toward the entrance into the cabin. "I'm assuming there's no Internet?"

"Stan bought this cabin as a getaway for his family. He didn't want the distractions of the outside world."

He frowned. "That may have been well intentioned, but it leaves us in a jam."

"Wait," she said, snapping her fingers. "There's a transistor radio in the closet. I ran across it one day when I was cleaning off the shelves to store my belongings."

"That could work." He opened the door and slid out from behind the wheel. She joined him around the back of the trunk to help unload groceries.

Once inside the house, she busied herself with

putting away the purchases when she noticed Lucas carrying in the last of the bags. His attention swept to the neat stack of garments folded on the table with a Braves cap sitting on top. His eyes filled with warmth and a tentative grin spread across his face.

"You didn't have to buy me clothes. I would have been fine with what I have."

"What," she remarked, placing a gallon of milk in the fridge, then her attention following his swagger as he approached the table, "and do laundry every day? No thanks."

"I would have washed my own clothes."

"Well, now you don't have to."

"Thank you." He slipped the cap on his head, and she could tell he was satisfied with the way it fit. Then he picked up the first pair of jeans and eyed them, saying, "How did you know what size to get?"

She grabbed a few items out of the bag at her feet and placed them on the shelf. "I remembered your pant size. And it appears as if that hasn't changed over the years. And I figured you'd like that cap since it's your favorite baseball team. Hopefully they still are."

The way he stared at her made her feel more appreciated in that moment than anyone made her feel in a long time. "Thank you," he said again. "You didn't have to do that."

There he went, bringing out emotions she couldn't allow herself to experience. Not with him. Not ever again. She cleared her throat. "Why don't you take the clothes to the master bedroom and put them away in the dresser? And I'll finish unpacking the groceries. I have to cut and dye your hair. The sooner we get that behind us, the sooner we can have lunch. I'm starving."

He didn't say a word, simply scooped up the stack of garments, and strode out of the kitchen.

When he returned, Remi was ready. "Have a seat," she said, gesturing toward the chair she'd planted in front of the sink. He shrank down and she wrapped a cape around his chest, snaping it snugly around his neck. She took a lock of his hair in between her fingers, and he held up his hand when she picked up the scissors. "Wait," he said. "How short are we talking here?"

"At least a few inches."

"Like, how short is that?"

"I'm not going to butcher your hair, although I'm tempted."

"Now I feel so much better."

"Need I remind you I went to cosmetology school before I joined the force."

"I remember."

"And I've cut your hair before."

"I know."

"The hair's got to go, cowboy. And you know it."

He sighed and dropped his shoulders. "Fine."

A few minutes into the cut, the tension in his shoulders eased a little. She could sense him relaxing in the chair and he closed his eyes as if he enjoyed the way she ran her fingers through his hair. If she dared to be honest with herself, she didn't know who enjoyed the contact more, him or her. He had a full head of thick hair, and she always considered it one of his sexiest traits. And sliding her fingers through his tresses now conjured the kind of sultry emotions that had her biting her lip to keep from hopelessly losing herself in them. The man was heart stopping beautiful. And so many times she'd ended up with a fistful of his hair while he drove himself so deep inside of her, she struggled to come up for air.

Stop it, she told herself, doing everything in her power to quiet the eruption of desire that ripped through her. This powerful connection between them could never be permitted to blossom again. *You damn well know that.*

"Ouch," he said, drawing back a little.

She realized she had a tight grip on his mane. "Oh, God. I'm sorry." What the hell was she thinking?

Before she could let go of his hair, he slipped his arm behind his head and wrapped his hand around her wrist. "You okay?"

She let out her breath, closed her eyes, and straightened. "I'm fine. Just got a little carried away." She took a few seconds to gather her wits and settle her pounding heart. Why did the man's touch stir up an earthquake every time it came into contact with her?

When she finished the last few cuts, she damn near needed resuscitation.

"Okay," she finally said, dusting off the hair clippings from his shoulders, and then holding the handheld mirror in front of him. "What do you think?"

As he took the mirror from her, the way his skin brushed against hers sent an explosion of heat snaking through her body…again. She jerked back her hand as if she'd been electrocuted. And he made a point to stare directly at her through the reflection. In his eyes didn't exist the question of why she yanked her hand back so quickly, but how much longer she planned to deny the sexual tension building like a tsunami between them.

Her attention immediately darted away. God help

her, she became so weak in that moment if he touched her again, she'd have melted like a snowball spinning round in the microwave.

He didn't answer her previous question about what he thought of the new cut, and she busied herself with mixing the color and developer together.

She noted the hoarseness in his voice when he said, "Am I going black?"

Her lips stretched across her teeth, indicating her displeasure at delivering the news. "We need to get you as far away from blond as possible."

"Let's go for it then." He held the mirror until their gazes locked again. He winked, and her heart hurled into a fit of palpitations she couldn't, for the life of her, control.

****

Lucas stepped out of the shower, dried himself, and wrapped the towel around his waist. He stepped over to the mirror, cleared away a circle of fog, and studied his reflection. Examining the new color Remi applied to his hair from every angle, he had to admit the jet-black hue didn't shock him as much as he assumed it would. If he stared at it long enough, he might even conclude the dark shade gave him an edge. She did a decent job on the cut. The hair style matched the way he normally kept it, until he'd been forced to change his appearance due to his undercover assignment, letting his mane grow much longer.

He picked up the shaving cream Remi bought and smeared it on his face. Then he got to work running the blade over the stubble, eventually doing away with the goatee. He'd become accustomed to seeing it in the mirror every day. But he considered losing the beard another sacrifice he had to make as a fugitive.

And, like it or not, he was a fugitive.

He slipped into his new clothes and made his way to the kitchen. Remi stood over the sink, the handheld mirror propped against the windowsill, and she put the finishing touches on her new haircut. Her attention collided with his, and her blue eyes appeared even more prominent with the shorter 'do'.

She frowned, uncertainty hugging her face. "Well, what do you think?"

She always struck him as beautiful no matter what style she chose, but she was like a brand-new woman. He'd never seen her with short hair before. It certainly suited her. "You're beautiful, Remi." He couldn't hide the rawness in his tone.

For a moment, a shadow of weakness passed through her eyes, then she lowered her head, rebounded, and took the mirror from the windowsill. "I guess it'll do."

He crept up behind her like a thief in the night. She stood as still as a statue, and the lingering of that familiar perfume she used to wear filled his nostrils. He closed his eyes, allowing the flowery scent to take him back in time, to a place where she eagerly awaited his touch, and a time when she shivered with wanting every time he trailed the tips of fingers from her throat to that spot between her thighs.

"Why do you do that?" he whispered, running his hands over her arms as if molding her skin like potter's clay.

"What?" she said, her voice catching on a gasp.

"Look away when I give you a compliment."

A tremor ran through her, and her reaction to his

nearness told him all he needed to know about how nervous he made her. "I...I..." she stammered.

He closed in on her, slid her hair out of the way, dropped tender kisses from the base of her neck to the center, and skimmed his bottom lip the rest of the way. "I want you naked and beneath me, Remi. I want to look deep in your eyes as I slide all the way inside you. Do you understand?"

Before he knew what hit him, she slithered out of his hold, putting enough distance between them to send a train chugging through the gap. "You," she said, wagging a trembling finger, "are making this so hard on me. All I want to do is give in."

"I'm standing right here," he said, frustration and desire coursing through him like flood waters pouring over a dam. "All you have to do is take my hand."

She stood there, appearing as distraught as a suicide jumper staring down the cliff.

He slowly approached, being careful not to make any hasty moves and send her scurrying away. "When I saw you climb into that limo, it was damn near impossible to keep my hands off you. And later that night on the terrace, you don't know how hard it was for me to keep from laying you down right there in the snow and giving you just a fraction of what I've been holding back for God knows how long. You want this too. It's the right thing. It's always been the right thing between me and you." He put out his hand in the hope she'd see the truth in his words and mold her fingers around his.

But she averted her gaze at the last minute and hurried off, ripping another chunk out of his heart, and leaving him wondering how much longer he could tolerate her rejection.

Chapter Six

Lucas splintered off small pieces of wood from some of the smaller logs with the handheld axe he'd rounded up from the barn. Chopping kindling. That's what his abilities dwindled down to because his blasted injuries prevented him from swinging a full-sized axe to split firewood like a real man.

And his lack of strength made him every bit as pissed as Remi's persistence in spurning his advances. The mindset she'd eventually come around and admit her attraction toward him and give in to the craving building like a storm between them faded as quickly as the sun going down over the horizon.

He'd been out here performing mundane chores since her latest episode of fleeing from him. He didn't even mind the cold. Hell, it wasn't as frigid out here as it would have been in there dealing with her aloofness. But time slipped past him, and it melted into the evening. He didn't have a damn thing to eat all day—thanks to the head games Remi insisted on playing—and his stomach growled.

He gathered an armful of kindling, worked his way inside, and lumbered over to the fireplace, dropping the load into the basket. The aroma of fried food filled the air. Although she'd been toying with his resistance like a puppeteer, at least she'd cooked dinner. If nothing else, his appetite for a good meal would get satisfied.

After wrangling out of his coat, he washed his hands in the bathroom, and then made his way into the kitchen. She stood over the stove heaping the last piece of fried chicken onto the serving dish. He noticed right away she dyed her hair red. The color perfectly matched the flowery blouse she'd slipped into.

She'd already set the table, complete with a basket of rolls, tray of butter, bowl of vegetables, and a picture of tea. He shrank down in front of the closest plate and filled his empty glass with the brown liquid. She spun around, the tray of fried meat in her hand, and gasped when she saw him.

"I didn't mean to startle you."

She placed the food in the center of the table and sat down. "I thought you might be hungry."

"Starved," he said, filling his plate with a helping of everything.

Doing the same, she pointed her fork at him. "That belonged to your father."

He peered down in the direction of her stare, then glanced back up, waiting for an explanation. "The flannel shirt you have on. I'm not sure how it got packed with my stuff when I brought my clothes here. But it was in my suitcase."

"I probably wore it to your apartment and forgot it." It hit him he had a habit of unintentionally leaving garments scattered all over her place. When they were together, the need for clothes hardly existed. He could tell by the reddening in her cheeks, and the way she averted her attention, the same thought occurred to her.

She smiled when her eyes met his again. "What?" Did he detect humor on her face? It was hard to tell with her lately.

Donnette Smith

"Isn't that the same shirt your Aunt Luna went to fetch out of your parent's closet when she got a chill, and discovered your mother's dildo in the front pocket?"

The memory of that day hit him anew and he chuckled. "I think you're right." Now he shuffled out of the garment and tossed it into a nearby chair. "You just ruined any chance I'll ever wear that shirt again."

She laughed and poured herself a glass of tea. "I'm sure it's been washed since then. It was a long time ago."

"You've just imprinted that specific memory on my brain forever. Thanks." He picked up a chicken drum and bit into it. God, it tasted delicious.

"I'll never forget your mother's face when your aunt came bounding into the living room and asking if she could borrow it. The dildo, not the shirt."

"That dildo was more information than I needed to know about my parents. And why would they keep it in the front pocket of Dad's flannel shirt anyhow?"

"They probably didn't want to risk anyone finding it."

"That didn't seem to work out too well for them, did it?"

She scooped up a forkful of vegetables and slid it into her mouth. After chewing she said, "Your mother was horrified. Standing there speechless, until your dad grabbed the dildo out of her sister's hand and made a beeline for the bedroom."

Lucas sunk his teeth into a roll and chased it down with a swallow of tea. "I remember. My folks invited the whole family over for Christmas dinner. Aunt Luna was always on the lookout for new ways to torment my

100

mother."

He continued to devour his meal, when Remi said, "How are your parents?"

He swallowed the food in his mouth and set the second chicken drum on his plate. He cleared his throat, doing his best to ignore the discomfort that crept up on him. "Mom passed away three years ago. A severe case of pneumonia. Dad doesn't talk to me."

"I'm sorry about your mom. I had no idea."

You would have if you stuck around.

Then the sympathetic expression on her face morphed into suspicion. "Why doesn't your father talk to you?"

He could tell it wasn't so much a question, as an accusation. He stared at her, realizing she read between the lines.

"You told them about us, didn't you?"

"So what if I did?"

She let her fork fall to the plate. The loud clang warned him of the cross reaction to come. "Why did you do that?" she said, a hint of distress reflecting in her eyes.

"Because I was involved, too. That's why."

"They didn't know that."

He laid his utensil aside, propped his elbows along both sides of his plate, and leaned across the table as far as he could. "It was enough I knew it. Did you really think I was going to let you take the fall all alone?"

"Oh my God." She peered at her plate, as if she couldn't stomach another bite. "Your family already cut me out of their lives for good because of what happened with Gavin. What made you think it was a good idea to tell them you were the reason I called off the wedding?

They didn't need to know we were together. Me, I was just some girl who came along and ripped their world apart."

He stood, zeroing in on her like a laser. "Are you going to fault me for telling the truth? They had a right to know."

"That must have torn your mother apart. Losing both of her sons like that. She already blamed me. I wasn't family, you see. Believe me, it's a lot different to shut someone out of your life who doesn't share a bloodline. But being forced to turn away from your only other child because he was sleeping with the girl who was supposed to marry Gavin…It was unnecessary."

"That's the thing," he shot back, anger pumping through him like a jackhammer. "You didn't stick around long enough to find out my mother never held what happened against me or you for that matter."

She appeared aghast. "What are you talking about? She told me—"

"I know what she told you. She'd just found out you told Gavin you couldn't marry him the day of your wedding because you were in love with someone else. She was reacting to what she had just learned. If you gave her a little time, you would have seen she didn't blame you. She understood we fell in love, and we didn't set out to hurt anyone. It just happened."

"But your dad, he doesn't talk to you because he blames you for what we did."

"My father uses that as an excuse to continue to mourn my brother. He was always locked away in his own little world, working overtime in the homicide division as much as possible, resulting in very little time spent with his family. When Gavin died, the guilt of that ate him up. He had to place the blame somewhere. Me telling him the truth just gave him another person for whom to fault besides you."

He took a deep breath, and carried his plate, still half filled with food, to the trash, emptying it. Although his stomach growled when he entered the house, the turn of events caused him to lose his appetite. "After my mother passed away," he said, putting the plate in the sink and running water over it. "My father's resentment toward me became an obsession. The last time I spoke to him was at her funeral. We got into an explosive argument back at the house. He insisted I was not only to blame for Gavin's death, but I killed Mom. I broke her heart, and she didn't have the strength to fight off the pneumonia after what I did to the family. It took away her will to live. In other words, she wanted to die because of me."

"He was wrong. You weren't responsible for your mother's death."

The sound of Remi's soft voice behind him forced him to close his eyes. He wanted nothing more than to go to her right in this moment, and take her in his arms, just the way he'd wanted to when this whole tragedy took place. But she wasn't there for him then, and she'd only shrug away from him now. He lowered his head and braced his hands against the counter. "I know I wasn't the cause of her passing. It took a good two years of therapy for me to figure that out."

"I wish I would have known you told them. All these years I had no idea."

He drew his full attention toward her. "Would it have made a difference if you'd known? Would you still have run away from me like you did?"

Now her eyes narrowed with a slow burning thought he could see churning around in her mind. "Is that why you told them? Because you thought it would bring me running back to you?"

"Is that the kind of person you think I am? That I would intentionally rip my family apart simply to keep you from leaving?"

"Your bother committed suicide because of what we did. That's the kind of people we are if that tells you anything."

He snorted and peered away, stabbing his gaze at the window overlooking the snow-covered ground. "Don't flatter yourself, lady. I didn't come clean with my folks on the hopes it would keep you in my bed."

"This conversation is over," she said, storming out of the room.

He hurried to the entrance leading into the living area where she fled. When he didn't find her there, he hollered into the empty space, "That's right, run away, sweetheart! You've been doing it for years. At least you're good at something."

"Go to hell!" Her voice floated through the air.

"I've been there since the day I saw my brother hanging by his belt from the rafters of that church!"

****

Remi stood alone in the guest bedroom with tears streaming down her face. She stepped over to her purse sitting on the nightstand, unsnapped the latch, and dug inside. When she retrieved what she wanted, she held it to the lamp, staring at the way the light bounced off the prism of the diamond. She slipped the engagement ring Gavin gave her on her finger. It fit tighter now than it once did.

She should have boxed the thing up and mailed it to his family a long time ago. She didn't deserve to keep it. Yet his face faded from her memory over the years, and the token gave her something to remember him by. But she couldn't be sure if she kept the ring as a way to reminisce or to punish herself for the ultimate betrayal she committed against him, and against his whole family.

If she'd just married him, the tragedy of his untimely death could have been prevented. Gavin's father was right. The fault for his death lay at her feet. The sting of Ethan Kade's words rang through her mind with every bit as much clarity as when he first uttered them. *You killed my son. I will never forgive you. I hope you burn in hell for what you did.*

And she couldn't bear the pain on his mother's face when they found out the truth. She could still feel the burning in her legs as she had bolted out of the house that day, dashed down the concrete steps, and sprinted toward her car. She recalled Lucas was in hot pursuit, but she climbed behind the wheel before he could catch up, and tore out of the drive, hearing him call her name through closed windows and over the roaring of the engine. She hadn't laid eyes on him again until now.

And he wouldn't listen to reason. What she and Lucas did could never be forgiven. She couldn't understand why he couldn't see that. The sweltering desire she still had, and the way being near him muddled her brain and sent her heart racing, made it even worse. His having stormed back into her life proved she never got over losing him, even though she tricked herself into believing she had from time to time.

She almost hated him for showing up out of the blue and forcing her to confront those old feelings again.

The knock on the door startled her. She swallowed the lump in her throat and dried her tears. Then braced herself to deal with the man who caused her pulse to skyrocket a thousand times a day. She should lock him out and refuse to talk to him, at least for tonight. The respite would give her a chance to deal with the storm of emotions he evoked in her. But she couldn't help but feel bad. Gavin Kade happened to be his brother. And all the suffering she'd faced over the years because of his death, had to haunt him just as deeply.

"Come in," she said, without the heart to back up her words.

The door creaked open, and his presence filled the doorway. Without glancing in his direction, she sensed his attention sweeping over her. "Are you all right?" he finally said.

She stared at the floor and slowly nodded. "Sorry for the outburst," she admitted, still not raising her attention to him.

The sound of him shuffling into the room caused her heart to palpitate. He said, "You were right."

Now she glanced at him. He stood there hunched over, his eyes reflecting defeat. "Part of me came clean with my parents because I'd hoped it would prevent you from leaving. I thought if there was someone else to share the blame, the focus would be taken off you, and you might reconsider staying."

He wandered over and sat on the edge of the bed. After a moment of silence, he buried his head in his hands and said, "The other part knew I couldn't live with myself unless I did the right thing. There was no way in hell I could let you take full blame for something I caused."

"What are you talking about? What makes you think you caused Gavin to commit suicide?" She could hardly believe the words that came out of his mouth. She was the one who called off the wedding.

"It was me who came on to you."

"Oh no," she said, staring straight at him and willing him to acknowledge her. "I was already thinking about you in ways I shouldn't have. It started the day you picked me up at the airport. And a week later when you kissed me, I already made up my mind I was going to be with you."

When he finally graced her with his attention, a renewed sense of conquest burned in his eyes. "Why did you decide that?"

She shrank back, staring at him as if she'd missed something. "What do you mean?"

"You were engaged. Why did you make the choice to be with me?"

"Because I was attracted to you. And the chemistry between us was magnetic."

"And that was because…"

She shook her head. "I'm sorry. I'm not following."

"What was it you used to tell me all the time?"

"That I loved you?" *Did he have a point to make?*

He searched her eyes, and the glow in his softened at her admittance. "We both loved each other. That's why neither one of us could fight what was happening. We are not in control of who our hearts choose to love. Although you were engaged to someone else, he was not the person you were meant to spend the rest of your

Donnette Smith

life with. In the end you were honest with Gavin. Most people would not have had the courage to do that. But you didn't want to see him tied down to someone he was not meant to marry. You were never his destiny. This wasn't your fault."

She frowned, almost impressed with his effort. He pulled out all the stops this time. Anger welled deep inside her. "How can you say that? Your brother is dead because of me. I waited until our wedding day to tell him. How selfish can a person be? I don't think I cared about his reaction as much as I was concerned with my desperation to end the relationship. All I could think about was my lust for you."

"Lust, huh? Wow. That was cheap." Lucas stood and backed away from her. It appeared like he was doing his best to tamp down the resentment she saw pinching the corners of his face.

"I'm sorry," she blurted out. "That came out wrong."

"Did it?" he asked with cynicism. "Is that all I've ever been to you? A good fuck when you weren't getting what you wanted from my brother?"

"How dare you."

He pursed his lips and crossed his arms over his chest. "How dare I what, talk like that about my dead brother who you continue to worship despite the fact he took the easy way out and left you all alone to deal with the mess he'd made? It was me you came running to anytime you needed to talk. Remember? I did everything I could to comfort you. To be there for you. And you ran off and deserted me as if I never even mattered."

"That's not why I left."

"You can't even be honest with yourself, can you?"

She wagged a finger, the sting of outrage winding its way through her nervous system. "I left because everyone in the department made my life a living hell. Because your family hated me. Because—"

"Because I loved you and I offered to go anywhere with you that you wanted. Because you preferred to drown in guilt. And because if you chose me, that meant you would have been happy, and you wouldn't get to punish yourself like you've done every day for the last thirteen years."

"Stop it," she said, on the brink of tears.

"You need to face the truth. You can't continue to live in denial. Gavin Kade has been dead a long time. Did you ever stop to think my brother didn't love you as much as you think he did?"

"What?" she shot to her feet, floored he would say such a thing. "Why would he kill himself after I called off the wedding?"

"I think you give yourself far too much credit for his suicide. I'm doubtful it had as much to do with you as you want to think it did."

Flames engulfed her. The nerve of him. "You are delusional."

"Me," he accused, throwing his arms wide. "I'm not the one wearing an engagement ring, one a man who's been dead for more than a decade gave you, while ignoring the guy you vowed to love who is alive and standing right in front of you."

"Get out," she said, stabbing a finger at the door, holding on to control by a thread.

The expression chiseled into his face appeared to be a clear warning she stood on the threshold of crossing a line she could never walk back. "I won't take your dogged rejection much longer, Remi. If you keep pushing me away, I'll get out of your way for good. A man needs warmth and affection from the woman he loves, not resentment and avoidance."

With the shutting of the door, she slumped on the bed, curled into a ball, and cried the way she hadn't since Gavin hung himself.

****

Lucas would have considered himself lucky if he managed to catch a few hours sleep last night. Between the tossing and turning, and the interruption of Remi opening and shutting doors, as well as roaming through the house until the wee hours of the morning, he found it impossible to drift off.

He wasn't the only restless one in the house last night. The frank discussion he had with her in the bedroom must have gotten to her. He ran out of options to wake her up. She refused to see what lingered right in front of her face. Gavin's death was never her fault. And the more Lucas considered the drastic actions his brother took over the years, the more convinced he became he didn't commit suicide because his fiancé called off the wedding. Gavin could never be accused of being that impulsive.

Scrutinizing their relationship when he saw his brother and Remi together told him something crucial was missing all along. He'd gotten the feeling the couple merely fell into the mundane habit of being with each other. The spark between them didn't exist, no body language took place between the two that would have convinced him they were madly in love.

He stood over the stove and gave the eggs another

few seconds to fry, and then scooped them out of the skillet. After preparing the rest of the food, he laid everything out on the table. Remi's face when he glanced up to see her standing silently in the doorway, told him immediately she'd spent most of the night crying. A nuance of guilt passed through him. His harsh words upset her. But he became desperate for a way to break her out of this vicious cycle of self-punishment. She couldn't go on this way. They couldn't go on this way.

He gazed in the other direction, hardly able to stand the sight of her appearing so lost and burdened. If she would just allow him to wrap his arms around her right now, he'd shoulder all her pain, and kiss away her heartache. But she'd only run from him the way she'd been doing all along. Thoughts of comforting her were getting him nowhere.

"Can we call a truce," she said, in a voice that sounded every bit as exhausted as defeated. "I hate that we argue like this."

He clutched the back of the chair in front of him with both hands and hunched over it. "I don't think we're arguing. I think we're working this out, even if our emotions get out of control."

She gazed into the distance, as if she stared at nothing. "It doesn't feel like we're not arguing."

"Look at me."

When she did, it melted his heart. He'd give anything to take the pain out of her beautiful eyes. But he could only lead her so far before she'd have to go the rest of the distance by herself. "I see you suffering like this, and it tears me up because I know I'm partly to blame for it. The other, more selfish part of me wants you back. Not the woman who's gotten lost in grief and misery, but the woman who used to laugh at my stupid jokes. The one who didn't flinch when I touched her. If I didn't care so much about you, I wouldn't be trying so hard to resurrect her."

Her eyes softened at his words, and his heart fluttered. There were times he cursed the powerful hold she had on his emotions. "I can't just snap my fingers and be who you want me to be," she said. "I am trying. I...I—"

"What can I do?"

"I need some time to work through this."

He took one more, good glance at her, then lowered his head. "I don't think you know how hard it is for me to be in the same house with you and keep my distance. But I will be as patient as I know how to be."

"Thank you."

He shrank down into the chair and gestured for her to do the same. "I hope you like fried eggs, hashbrowns, and toast."

"It looks delicious and I'm starving." She joined him at the table, and took hold of the pitcher, pouring orange juice into her glass.

As he filled up his plate, and she busied herself with doing the same, she stared at the transiter radio sitting on the counter behind him. "You hear any news about us on that thing?"

He nodded. "It's the same regurgitated shit from yesterday. But I caught the weather forecast. A blizzard is expected to move in by tonight."

"Great. Just what we need on top of everything else."

He sliced off a chunk of egg and slid it into his

mouth, then went for the hashbrowns. "I expect the electricity will go out when the blizzard hits. I saw some kerosene lamps in the barn, but I didn't run across any kerosene. Do you know if there's any here?"

She shook her head, breaking off a piece of toast, and dipping it into the egg yolk. "If you didn't find it in the barn, more than likely there isn't any."

After swallowing a mouthful of food, he said, "That means we'll have to make a run into town. They should have it at the hardware store I stopped into yesterday. We're about to run out of firewood, so I'll get out there today and attempt to split some."

"The hell if you will." The expression on her face resembled a solid mask of refusal. "You're still healing, and all you'll do is make it worse. Besides, with your injuries I doubt you could even raise the axe above your head."

"I'm feeling better today," he argued. "I don't think my ribs are broken after all. Just bruised."

"And if you try to chop wood, you'll be back in the bed screaming in agony all over again."

He cocked an eyebrow. "I was screaming in agony?"

"Your injuries were pretty bad when I brought you here. Victor's men worked you over good. You were slipping in and out of unconsciousness. And yes, you made some less than desirable noises."

He frowned, taking another bite of egg. "Sorry about that."

"I was just relieved I found you alive in that warehouse."

"I was in capable hands. Thank you for taking care of me."

She sliced into her hashbrowns, and shoveled a forkful into her mouth, shrugging as if she considered helping him no big deal.

"I've been thinking," he said. "If we can get to Bain, we can find out what he knows."

"Didn't you say he was under police protection?"

"I know someone who may be able to get the intel on where they're keeping him. Then we can get him to admit who's behind all of this. I have a feeling it's more than Victor Craven behind the wheel."

She took a swallow of juice, and when she set the glass back down, she said, "What do you propose?"

"First we'll have to wait out the blizzard, of course, and then we're going to have to take a trip to Texas."

"What makes you think Bain is in Texas?"

"Hiding him out here would be too risky. Victor's men could get to him. They would have extradited him back home, and then put him up in a safehouse there."

After helping himself to a sip of juice, he frowned, and then stared at her as if considering the words about to come out of his mouth. "With all the miles on the Pontiac, I don't think it's capable of making a trip that far. And we can't take your car. They'll have an APB out for your license plate. We need another mode of transportation."

"What if I can get us fake IDs. We can fly out then, can't we?"

That would work. "Can you do that?"

She smiled, appearing as if acquiring fake IDs was as simple as taking a trip to the nearest department store. "I know a guy. I'll call him when we get to town."

What kind of shady shit was she into before he

came along? Didn't matter. He wouldn't question lady luck today. "Do you think he can get the job done before the blizzard sets in?"

"He's proficient. I think he can handle it."

"Well, eat up," he said, pointing his fork at her plate. "We've got a lot of preparations to make."

Chapter Seven

Lucas took note of the time when they finally arrived back at the cabin and swung the Pontiac into the garage. According to the radio, it was past three p.m. At least they accomplished everything they needed to do in town, including two brand new IDs with aliases stamped across the plastic.

"I guess we better get a move on. The blizzard will be here soon," Remi said after he killed the engine. "As soon as we get the stuff we bought into the house, I'll start splitting wood."

Somehow, accepting she had to do the heavy lifting—when it should have been his job—made him feel like less of a man. But letting her do the brunt of the work made the most sense. With his injuries, he'd find himself right back at square one if he took on anything strenuous. "I spotted a bucket of nails and a hammer in the barn last night. There are a few places around the cabin where I noticed the siding is loose and in need of repair. The blizzard is expected to bring in some high winds and I'm afraid if those spots aren't secured, we'll lose the siding."

She opened the car door and glanced back. "I've seen the areas you mentioned, and some of them are close to the roof. Climbing a ladder could make your injuries worse."

"Listen, sweetheart. I've already let you take the

axe from me. You're not getting the hammer and nails, too. This is not up for discussion."

She threw her hands up as if surrendering and climbed out of the car without another word.

Once everything was put away, he headed into the barn to fetch the tools he needed to mend the siding. The aluminum ladder was another matter entirely. It weighed enough that lugging the blasted thing to the front of the house put pressure on his ribcage, leaving him in pain and gasping for air. Even though he'd told Remi he doubted his ribs were cracked, he reassessed that statement at this point. But if they were injured as he assumed, there'd be nothing he could do other than to give them time to heal.

After setting the ladder down a few times to catch his breath, he'd pick it back up, and edge a few yards closer to his destination around the east side of the structure. By the time he stood in front of the cabin, he needed to brace his hand against the wooden post to regain his strength. He might have been a lot of things in his life, but useless was never one of them. And he refused to be helpless now. He pushed through the pain and discomfort and positioned the ladder in place. He set his sights on mending the siding, or he'd damn well die trying to complete the task.

The first strike of the hammer sent pain shooting through his abdomen. He gritted his teeth, telling himself it would get more tolerable as he went along. It didn't. And by the time he'd worked his way around the house and drove the last nail into the siding, he began to fear he wouldn't be able to move for a month. *Who the hell puts siding on the outside of a cabin anyhow?* Someone who didn't want to go out the expense of using logs, dummy.

He stumbled over to the stoop and let himself fall onto the bottom step. Sucking cold air into his lungs and clutching his side where the giant bruise covered his flesh, he could hardly believe the severity of the pain that sliced through him. Would he be able to make it into the house on his own?

A noise rustled in the distance, and before he fully considered the cause, Remi stood in front of him in her snow gear, the axe he bought hanging from her grip. "Are you an axe murderer coming to put me out of my misery?" he said, in between gasps, and grunts.

She tossed the tool on the porch, and then collected him by positioning his arm around her neck and helping to haul him to his feet. "I'd say I told you so, but with you, I'm afraid the point would get lost somewhere in that stubborn head of yours."

"Hush, woman. And help me into the house, will you?"

They trudged through the doorway and lumbered to the couch. Once he slouched onto the cushion, she unbuttoned his coat, and he shrugged out of the garment. Staring at her face the entire time, he noticed her 'all business' attitude as she lifted his shirt to examine the bandage. Her attention worked its way to his face, and without saying a word, she shook her head, her expressive eyes telling him only a complete idiot like him would push the boundaries of his injuries. She wasn't far off the mark, and he'd realized that an hour into his self-torture session on the ladder. But she had firewood to chop, and he refused to let her do everything that needed doing by herself.

She gently removed the blood-soaked gauze and

stood. "Don't move. I'll be right back."

"Yes, ma'am."

Having her fingers brush across his flesh made every ounce of the pain he suffered through well worth it. Imagining her touching him in more intimate places sent a flood of heat coursing through him. Even though he'd agreed to give her a little time to work through her emotions, the need to have her body wrapped around him was no less profound. Whether he could survive until she gave in—letting him do all the naughty things that ran amuck in his brain and kept him awake at night—appeared to be another matter entirely.

She strolled back into the room, all the necessary 'fix it' items in her hands. She knelt on the floor in front of him, and the instantaneous image of her loosening his belt, unzipping his pants, and wrapping her hands around his shaft crashed into his mind, and his breath caught in his chest.

"You okay?" she said, shattering the blissful illusion.

Being around her constantly and forced to ignore every instinct to throw her down and make sweet love to her affected him in the worst way. He took the bandage and peroxide from her, damn well knowing if she touched him one more time, he would throw all the rules out the window and make his move. And this time he wouldn't let her get away.

"I got this," he said, swallowing the rising desire blazing like Tonto's trail inside him. "Why don't you tend to the fire? It needs a few more logs."

She got up and sashayed away, and even the sight of that sent his heart into a fit of palpitations. He stood and staggered down the hall to the bathroom. He needed a shower, and if he knew what was good for him, he'd make it a cold one.

****

Remi swept her gaze away from the window when Lucas entered the room. Her pulse quickened like it did every time she feasted her eyes on him. She noticed he'd taken the time to blow dry his hair, and he appeared fresh and relaxed. She said, "The snow is really coming down and the wind is picking up."

As he advanced toward her, he glanced at the coffee table, and grinned. "You made sandwiches?"

She peered at the saucers of food then focused her attention on him again. "Sorry it isn't a hot meal, but it was getting late by the time I showered, and I was a little preoccupied with the coming blizzard."

"Ham and cheese, huh?" he said upon closer inspection.

"It's your favorite, isn't it?" She gestured toward the blanket and pillows she'd arranged around the fireplace. "I figured we could eat by the fire. With the way the wind is kicking up out there, it's going to get colder, and at least we can stay warm."

Lucas grabbed the plates off the table, carried them over to the fireplace, set them down, and settled himself in. He patted the spot next to him. "Hungry?"

In more ways than he knew. She sat beside him, snatched the bottle of wine out of the ice bucket, and filled the tumblers halfway. When she handed him the glass, he pursed his lips and cocked an eyebrow. "You plan to get me drunk and seduce me?"

"I'm just trying to get us drunk."

With a lopsided grin, he responded, "I'm more a fan of the seducing part."

So am I. "Sorry to disappoint you."

The expression on his face told her she'd been doing a lot of that.

She swept her gaze away, got to her feet, and placed another log on the fire. Then wandered back over and plopped down. After taking a bite of the sandwich, she picked up the glass and helped herself to a sip of wine. "You said something about being a broker for the *Infierno* Cartel. How did that come about?"

He held the sandwich close to his lips, then set it on his plate without taking a bite. "Dom knew some of the lower-level drug runners for the organization. Though he'd been involved in covert operations for some years, I was relatively new to the undercover unit but had never been a front runner in any of the operations. The DEA didn't have anyone else who was up for the challenge, so I took a few business courses in brokering, I set up shop in downtown Dallas and opened a mortgage firm. Since I minored in business and finance in college, it wasn't that hard."

Surprise lit her face. "You actually opened a firm?"

"The cartel always does its homework. If the business wasn't legit, they would have seen right through it."

That made sense. Although she'd worked in law enforcement for a while, back then she'd never encountered undercover work, so she couldn't be sure of the logistics involved.

"Dominick spread the word that I was really good at money laundering," he continued. "Before we knew it, Draco requested to meet with me while he was in Texas. I showed him what I could do, and they took me for a test run."

After finishing off the first half of her sandwich, she said, "They must have been impressed enough to hire you."

"Things were going so well with the brokerage firm in Texas, that after a few months, Victor invited me to his house in New York to meet with me. That's what brought me out here."

"Why get involved as a broker? Weren't there less complicated personas you could have undertaken?"

"The idea was to follow the money. Going after the narcotic shipments in Texas wasn't getting us anywhere. It became obvious these guys knew how to cover their tracks. So, the dirty money of the operation became the focus. And it would have worked—if my cover wasn't blown."

She finished off her glass of wine and poured another. When she threw her attention on him, he was watching her intently. "What?"

"You drank that pretty fast. You weren't lying when you said you intended to get drunk."

The last two days were a test on her resistance unlike any she'd ever known. Forced into close quarters made it a challenge to keep her distance when the idea of ripping his clothes off tempted her like nothing else. He wore her down, and tonight a premonition settled in the pit of her stomach if he made advances toward her, the only choice she'd be left with would be to give in at last. First, she'd need liquid courage. So, yeah. Getting hammered became a necessary task.

"You might want to slow down," he said, taking the last bite of his sandwich.

"And you might want to pick up the pace." She

gestured toward the snow coming down outside the window. "It's not like we have anywhere to go."

He stared at her as if she had a point. Then picked up his glass and chugged the rest of the alcohol. He handed her the empty tumbler. "Is that more to your liking?"

"Absolutely." She filled his cup, already feeling the effects of the wine. She couldn't remember the last time she set out to get tipsy. But she sensed a change in the air tonight. "So, tell me," she said, allowing the alcohol to heighten her bravery. "How was Miz Black Dress in the sack?"

He raised an eyebrow. "Why would you want to know?"

She shrugged, taking a healthy gulp from the glass. "C'mon. She's gorgeous. All the curves are in the right places. Legs up to her chin. She was sure staring at you as if she intended to devour you."

He frowned, propped his elbows against the pillows. "She's a beautiful woman."

The admission sent a wave of jealousy thundering through her. She'd been envious from the moment the long-legged redhead set her sights on Lucas. Watching that woman paw all over him made her sick to her stomach. And what she'd probably done with him after they left the ballroom together elevated her angst to a new and disturbing level. She wanted to rip a trail through the entire mansion, until she located the bitch's room and snatch her out of the bed she shared with Lucas.

She could tell by the way he stared at her right now he gauged her reaction to his earlier opinion of Lucy. She swallowed and glanced away, sorry she'd asked.

"Were you jealous of the attention she was giving me?"

His cocky attitude was like a slap in the face. "Why would I be envious? I was with someone too that night."

"Ahh, yes. Your little tryst with Victor Craven. How could I forget?"

"I already told you why I was with him. It had nothing to do with sexual attraction."

"The two of you seemed cozy."

"I couldn't very well act like I wasn't attracted to him, now, could I?"

"I saw the way he looked at you," he said. "A man doesn't look at a woman that way unless he has reason to believe she's into him."

The way I'm into you?

It occurred to her his little trick of merely digging for information had reared its head again. He asked how she felt about Victor the day he dropped her by the apartment on his way to the airport. She refused to answer him then. And she damn sure wouldn't appease his curiosity now. He'd been evasive where it concerned Lucy. Why would she offer information about her relationship with Craven?

"It's okay to admit it," he told her, lifting the glass to his lips. After taking a swallow, he said, "I was out of your life for a long time. It's not like I haven't been with other women."

He said that as if they were discussing how to cook a turkey. No emotion. No regrets. If sleeping with other people seemed like no big deal, why should the thought of another female exploring him intimately, and giving him pleasure drive her mad?

"So, were you?" he pressed.

She refused to acknowledge him, and instead grabbed the saucers and stood.

But he seized her by the wrist. "Answer the question."

She released the plates, shrank back, and sighed. "Victor was very good to me."

"That's not what I asked."

"Were you attracted to Lucy?"

"Stop deflecting and answer my question."

She finished off her second glass of wine and set the empty tumbler beside her, then cleared her throat. Why did she find herself putting such effort into being careful with her words? "We were a couple. And I'd be lying if I didn't say there were times I enjoyed being in his company."

Before she knew what hit her, she lay on her back, and he straddled her, trapping her arms above her head. The weight of his hips settled around her midsection, holding her in place like a prisoner. "There's no one here to save you, sweetheart. You're going to tell me the truth. And you're going to do that right now. I've waited long enough for an answer."

Between the effects of the wine slowing her response, and the lightheadedness, she could do little else than to surrender within his hold. His suffocating nearness cast a spell on her. "Yes," she said. "I was attracted to him. Is that what you want to hear?"

When he shifted position to lean closer, she became fearful the tingling sensations ripping through her would cause her to faint. "Do you love him?" he asked, the tone of his voice catching on a hoarse note.

She licked her lips, considering the consequence of

being honest with him more than lying. "I haven't loved anyone since you."

And instantly wanted to kick herself for her honesty.

His face hovered over hers for a few heart stopping moments, then he leaned in even closer, and she closed her eyes, waiting breathlessly for the pressure of his lips to crash down on hers.

But the kiss never came, and his weight lifted off her.

She lay there stunned, disappointed and humiliated. Out of all the advances he'd made toward her, this time she would have given herself to him, freely and completely. But it became clear, he only planned to toy with her. She couldn't believe he'd used such an underhanded tactic to get her to confess she'd never loved Craven.

He got up slowly, clearly favoring his side, gathered the saucers, and headed into the kitchen as if nothing had happened.

His footfalls padded back into the room. She snorted with an air of righteous dignity, swiped the bottle of wine from the bucket, snatched her empty glass, and got to her feet.

The expression on his face as she swept past him could have melted steel. "Where are you going?"

"Any place you're not."

****

Lucas' hand wrapped around the doorknob leading into her room, and every conscious fiber of his resistance fought against what he intended to do. He'd been the one chasing after her ever since she reentered his life. Until now, he'd only received one rebuff after another for his troubles. But he witnessed an expression of hunger in her eyes when he held her down earlier. And her admission that she didn't love Craven was the cherry on top. Judging by her pissed reaction when she swept past him and stormed into her room, she'd expected a kiss and became cross when he didn't deliver.

He had no intention of laying one on her. Seeing her respond with resentment when she didn't get what she wanted gave him vindication for all the hell she'd put him through. She needed to understand how it felt to want someone so much it hurt, only to be continuously spurned and left in the cold.

Before he could rethink confronting her, he knocked on the door, and when he didn't receive a response, swung it open.

A flashfire scorched a trail through his insides the second his attention collided with her. She stood beside the bed in her panties with both hands behind her back in an obvious attempt to unsnap her bra. He took in the sight of the nearly empty wine bottle sitting on the nightstand, and it told him all he needed to know about what she'd been doing in here.

She stared boldly into his eyes and completed the task of unfastening the bra as if no one interrupted her, then loosened the shoulder straps and let it slide from her body, laying bare her breasts for his view.

Over the years, the distinct shape of her breasts faded from his memory. But staring at her now reminded him in a heart-stopping instant how lovely they were as he took them in, in all their exquisiteness. Her small nipples were always such a turn on, and gazing at them now brought back the recollection of how they tasted as his tongue wound around them.

She blinked, hiccupped, and swayed, nearly losing her balance.

He could approach her right now, run a trail of kisses from the base of her neck, down to her midsection, then slide those white lace panties over her slender hips. She would let him fondle her in ways he'd been dreaming about since he first laid eyes on her after thirteen years of not knowing where she'd gone. The notion of laying her down on the bed, climbing on top of her, and burying himself so deep in her sheath of warmth he'd lose himself, caused his heart to pound, and his head to swim.

"Come and get me, Luc," she said, slurring her words enough to remind him she was drunk.

He stepped toward her slowly and easily. She blinked again, her expression changing from a teasing grin to a lustful stare the closer he got. When he stood a hairsbreadth from her, he slid his hand to the back of her neck, and gradually tugged her to him. She closed her eyes, and he held her steady as his mouth covered hers.

She shifted in rhythm with his ravenous kiss, and he slipped his tongue inside her mouth, tasting her sweetness. When he came up for air, her warm breath swept across his face, and she bit her bottom lip in such a way that told him she wanted more.

He gazed directly into her eyes as he slid his hand around to the front of her neck. She didn't move a muscle. He waited until her breathing became heavy, and her chin quivered with wanting, then he began the slow, torturous descent down her throat and across her collar bone.

He cupped her breast, his thumb fondling her hardened nipple. And her lips parted, a moan of pleasure spilling from them.

He inhaled deeply, doing his best to reign in the savage desire ripping a trail of destruction through him. Her skin was so malleable and warm under his caress, he wondered how much hotter her body would feel wrapped around his hardened shaft. But his inner voice reminded him of his intention tonight, and it had nothing to do with giving in to her. When she surrendered the next time, she'd be sober, and he planned to watch intensely as she took as much pleasure from their coupling as he would. Then she'd no longer question whether she belonged to him and no one else.

His hand skimmed over her stomach, and her muscles retracted. Then his fingertips brushed the hem of her panties and she spread her legs in preparation of his fondling. Gentle spasms of desire rocked her body, and her breaths came short and quick.

Only then did he work his way beneath the lacy material and stroke the wetness between her legs.

"Oh, God, Luc," she called, urging him on.

He leaned into her ear and whispered, "Do you like the way my fingers feel when I touch you there, baby?"

Heavy breathing and soft murmurs were her answer.

The moment he dove his fingers inside, he whispered again, "You have no idea how badly I've wanted inside you, Remi. But every time I get near, you push me away. You need to understand how it feels to be this close to what you want just to have it ripped away from you. That's what you do to me. Over. And.

Over. Again."

He let go of her, and when he backstepped his way toward the door, confusion reflected in her eyes. But as the seconds ticked by, her expression hardened into a mixture of hurt and anger.

He clutched the doorknob, saying, "You're drunk. Sleep it off."

****

Lucas took one more sip of his coffee, and set the mug down on the counter, then switched off the transistor radio. Thank God they didn't lose power last night, and the blizzard didn't turn out to be as severe as the weather forecaster predicted. He peered out the window above the kitchen sink and took note of the amount of snow covering the ground. Although they acquired more accumulation, the flurries slowed to a light dusting. And according to the broadcast, the weather should be clear for air travel by tomorrow.

He considered the news a tremendous relief. Not only did they need to hightail it back to Texas to move forward with the plan to locate Bain Delgado but being cramped in a small cabin with Remi and forced to recover from one heat stroke after another every time she got near was taking its toll.

Although he could have taken advantage of last night and satisfied his insatiable appetite to bury himself inside of her, come light of the early morning he would have regretted making love to her while she was bombed. They both deserved better than that after thirteen years apart.

As he roamed into the living room to stoke the fire, he wondered how she fared this morning. And how pissed she'd be because of his actions last night.

He didn't have to speculate long.

She stood by the fireplace when he entered the room, and he realized she'd already placed another log on top of the burning wood. "I would have done that."

She spun. Her attention settled on him. By all accounts she appeared fresh and ready to start her day. She wore a pair of designer jeans that showed off every curve and a white, turtleneck sweater. "I wanted to thank you for stopping me from making a fool of myself last night. I had a little too much to drink, and…"

A muscle tightened in his jaw, and he nodded perceptively. "So, that's what you're turning this into, huh? You were drunk and didn't know what you were doing."

She shook her head, "Lucas, I—"

"You what? Didn't have the guts to come on to me while you were sober, so you waited until you got inebriated. And because I didn't fuck you while you were in that condition, now you're going with the excuse you weren't in your right mind. How convenient."

She swallowed hard, and her face stiffened with reproach.

He'd hit a nerve.

"That's not true," she exploded. "You agreed to give me time."

He advanced on her with the speed of a lightning bolt and got in her face. "As I recall, you weren't asking for more time last night. You threw yourself at me and got pissed when I didn't take the bait."

She blinked away his words and took a few steps back, acting as if he'd lost his mind. "I didn't throw myself at you."

"Come and get me, Luc," he mimicked. "Do you recall that? Or were you too drunk to remember? Perhaps, you don't recollect stripping in front of me either."

She lowered her head and put even more distance between them by backing up. "The point is, I shouldn't have. I…I wasn't thinking clearly."

"Let me get this straight," he said, "you want me, but only when you're not in your right frame of mind. Why don't you just admit you don't have the courage to say how you really feel? Then we can get past the bullshit."

"I've told you how I feel. You don't listen."

A few quick steps carried him so close, he could see the trembling of her lips, and the quaking of her body. "The words coming out of your mouth," he said, running his thumb across her bottom lip, "are the opposite of what your eyes and your body are telling me. I know damn well you want me, sweetheart. I can feel the heat between us every time we get close. But I'm not so desperate to have you in my bed, I'm willing to settle for a drunk version of you."

He leaned in as if to kiss her but didn't. Instead, his intense gaze slid over every square inch of her face. "When you surrender to me, I want you sober, because I'm going to touch you in places you forgot you even had. And when you come, sweetheart, it's going to be my name pouring out of that delicious mouth of yours. So long as we understand each other."

He backed away, "But don't worry. I won't lay a hand on you unless you ask me to." Then he headed toward the door, saying over his shoulder, "We're catching a flight to Texas tomorrow. I'm going out to shovel the snow in front of the garage. Be ready to leave in the morning."

Chapter Eight

She hated Lucas Kade's guts.

He'd only shown himself to be the cocky son of a bitch she already figured him for. Being in close quarters with him for the last few days only proved nothing changed between them. She wanted him every bit as much now as she did back then. As much as she tried, there'd be no hiding her feelings from him. But he sure as hell didn't have to rub it in her face.

He couldn't give a good enough excuse for the way he handled her advances last night. She was vulnerable and invited him into her bed…into her heart. Then he spurned her efforts. And even worse, had treated her like some cheap floozy.

Resentment spurred her on as she swiped the duster across the blinds with more zeal than she would have had she not wanted to tear his head off. They were leaving tomorrow. The dust and cobwebs would only accumulate before anyone stepped foot in this place again. Performing chores here was a waste of time. But she had to do something with the nervous energy that zig zagged through her like a game of Centipede.

How could someone be so infuriatingly smug? He wasn't the boss of her or her emotions. She should tell him to go straight to hell.

She'd rather kiss him until she melted into a puddle.

Where the hell did that come from? She marched into the bedroom, with the sole purpose of making the bed, but stood in the doorway instead as if she had a brain freeze. He climbed into her head, and if she didn't pull it together, she would be so consumed with thoughts of him she wouldn't be able to concentrate on anything. Wasn't that already happening?

She sighed, bounded into the kitchen, and switched on the transistor radio. Some kind of noise to distract her was in order. After tuning the radio to a station with music, she headed back into the bedroom to make the bed.

Once she arranged the last pillow on top of the comforter, and finished straightening the room, she realized she could no longer ignore her growling stomach. It had to be after four in the afternoon. Having nothing to eat all day didn't do her any good.

After marching back into the kitchen, she opened the fridge to examine her options. Although dinner time wouldn't be for another hour or two, a sandwich didn't sound appealing. Cold cuts were on the menu last night before Lucas shredded her confidence like an Enron document. She needed a hardy meal, even if she had to eat alone.

She decided to start with a salad and grabbed a few tomatoes and a head of lettuce out of the crisper drawer. She carried them over to the counter, then gathered the rest of the ingredients needed.

As she sliced the vegetables and put them in the bowl, the front door creaked open. The person entering the house couldn't be anyone other than Lucas. A flash of heat wound through her, and the memory of his closeness and the candid words he spoke this morning came tumbling back. Now she'd have to get through another encounter with him without allowing his presence to scramble her brain and mangle her heart.

Footfalls echoed in the distance. They advanced into the kitchen and across the linoleum floor. When the music cut off in the middle of a song, she imagined he'd switched off the radio. She could feel him in the atmosphere as if he floated among the particles in the air she breathed into her lungs.

Bottles on the inside door of the fridge rattled, telling her he'd opened the refrigerator. Something slid across the shelf, and the door shut.

Movement swept past her, and the faucet turned on. A cabinet door creaked, and china clinging together made her aware he'd taken down a plate.

The next thing she knew, his body pressed against her backside, and she jumped, a gasp escaping her.

"You okay?" he said, his deep voice reverberating into her ear, causing a case of jitters. He placed a hand on her shoulder and extended his other arm above her head to fetch a glass out of the cupboard.

The asshole crowded her on purpose. Then the smell of him hit her. Fresh soap mixed with the scent of the outdoors. "You don't have to worry," he whispered, his lips no more than an inch away from her ear, "I'm only getting a glass. Besides, I don't bite."

Oh, he bit, all right. It just wasn't the kind of penetration that broke the skin. But he sure as hell sank a few fangs into her heart.

She stepped away shaken but managed to retrieve a block of cheese from the fridge and collected the grater from the drawer. As she threw her attention into tossing the salad, he floated around the kitchen, clanging pots, and opening cabinets and drawers.

She finally glanced at him as he stood over the stove, pouring oil into a pan, and tossing a mixture of flour and seasoning into a bowl. A package of pork chops sat on the counter at his elbow.

His actions reminded her of the first meal he'd ever cooked for her. Fried pork chops, baked potatoes with a side of vegetables. They had snuck off together and he'd taken her to his apartment. As she recalled, bringing her to his place was also another first. He'd snatched her off the couch after they'd finished dinner and carried her down the hallway to his room. That's when they became acquainted with each other on a new and sensual level.

Although that night was like a lifetime ago, his mannerisms as he seasoned the meat, and gently laid the portions into the frying pan, were the same now as they were then.

Fire engulfed her cheeks when he caught her staring. She quickly glanced away and cleared her throat. "I can put on some rice if you like."

"That sounds great," he said, arranging more pork chops into the skillet.

She grabbed the bag of rice out of the pantry, and when she spun around and took a step, she collided right into him. His hand wrapped around her waist to prevent her from falling. After a heart-stopping moment of silence, she straightened, and managed to regain her balance. "Sorry," she said, ducking out of his hold.

But as she strolled to the opposite side of the kitchen to grab a pot, her head swam from the contact, and her hands shook, making the task of opening the bag of rice a challenge.

"Maybe you should sit down," he said, taking the bag from her.

His skin touched hers, and the contact forced her to take a deep breath and relinquish the rice to his control.

Her rubbery legs somehow took her to the table, and she shrank into a chair. This was ridiculous. A grown woman shouldn't act like a teenager chasing after her first crush. Yet every time he touched her, she was like a love-struck kid standing by the lockers and zeroing in on the hot guy in school. He was the love of her life. They shared intimacies and secrets. And he became more familiar with every part of her than any other man.

She blushed when she should have been angry at his behavior earlier this morning. Wasn't she pissed about it most of the day? What, did he think he could simply show his face, invade her space, and she would magically forget the sting of his recent words?

Staying furious with him became a chore. It didn't seem to matter how atrocious his actions were, when he got within a few feet of her, she'd throw her indignance out the window and start panting like a female dog in heat.

Geez, maybe she should jump his bones and get it over with. *You tried that last night and look where it got you.*

Now that those feelings resurfaced, she refused to let him run her through another gamut of stormy emotions.

When he set the completed meal on the table and slid an empty plate in front of her, she did her best to keep her face void of expression. No more wearing her heart on her sleeve. Not another reaction to whatever phrase came tumbling out of his mouth. If he wanted to get a rise out of her, he'd have to work damn good and hard for it.

As she filled her plate, he sliced into his pork chop and slid a chunk into his mouth. "We didn't make plane reservations," she said, keeping her tone neutral.

He swallowed and stabbed a fork in his salad. "They'll put us on stand-by."

She chewed a small heap of rice. "That's risky, isn't it?"

"I've done this more than you know. Nine times out of ten, there's a few people who miss their flight or don't show up."

She shrugged and took a bite of her meat.

He gestured toward her plate. "How's the pork chop?"

She nodded, helping herself to another chunk. "It's really good."

"I'm glad you like it."

Of course, she did. She loved everything he cooked, always had.

She cleared her throat, reminding herself to hold her emotions at bay.

He leveled her with a grin, his expression telling her he remembered the first time he made pork chops for her.

She peered away and had to work hard at remaining indifferent.

"Have you packed what you're taking?"

"It wasn't much, since I had to leave all my stuff behind at the apartment," she said in between polishing off her salad. "Luckily I left some clothes here and they still fit."

"We can get you whatever you need." His long fingers wound around his glass, and he lifted the iced tea to his lips.

Those strong lips that kissed her in so many places last night. And those fingers that were… Oh, God. The unexpected blush she realized must be coloring her cheeks, forced her to glance away.

"What is it?" he asked, in a dark tone that said he knew more than just the warmth in the room had caused her face to redden.

Of course, he would notice the slightest change in her complexion. She cleared her throat, and said, "Nothing," although it came out more like a chirp. She gathered her wits. "The only thing I didn't already have here is my makeup."

He frowned. "You don't need any."

Another heat wave accosted her. "I feel naked without it."

"Makeup doesn't do you any justice. You're a beautiful woman."

"Like Lucy?" *Good God, why couldn't she keep her mouth shut?*

A slow grin spread across his face. "She doesn't hold a candle to you. And despite her long legs and sexy curves, she's nowhere near as hot in the sack as you are."

Those unexpected words sent her shooting out of her chair. "The stack of firewood on the porch is running low. There's a few more bundles by the barn. I'll bring the wheelbarrow over and gather them up."

He set his glass aside, folded his arms, and leaned back in his chair as if settling in for a long conversation. "Don't your legs ever get tired?"

She stared at him. "My legs are fine."

"You run away from me so often, I'm surprised you haven't worn them out by now."

Anger rushed back again. "Odd you should say that since I wasn't the one running last night."

****

Remi's gloved hands snatched the seasoned log on top of the wood pile sitting against the barn and flung it through the air like a torpedo. Luckily, the firewood hit its intended target and tumbled inside the wheelbarrow settling on top of the others. Although she realized stacking the wood in an orderly fashion would have made it possible to fit more logs into the wheelbarrow, the anger billowing inside of her caused her not to give a shit. Besides, chucking firewood as if it committed some offense against her, gave her an absurd sense of satisfaction after the way Lucas pushed her buttons.

The creep waiting on the front porch for her to wheel over the fourth load of firewood, so he could stack it in a neat pile, had the audacity to have acted surprised when she'd told him a few days ago she could split wood and cut down trees. Did he think a woman couldn't perform necessary tasks to take care of herself? What did females need men for anyhow when they weren't even useful for a good romp beneath the covers? Only he was, she'd remembered all too well. And he withheld that from her which chaffed her ass all day.

How did she go from denying him sex for days because of the tragedy that happened with Gavin, to being angry now that the shoe was on the other foot? If she were being honest with herself, she could sympathize with how he felt all those times she'd run

141

from him when he showed her affection. And she could understand how upset he must have been when he discovered she'd packed up and left Texas without a word. But she'd been so riddled with guilt and grief because of her part in Gavin's death, she had no choice other than to flee from the firestorm she created. As she recalled, Lucas didn't make it easy with the constant pressure he put on her to stay and ride out the storm with him.

Now that Gavin reentered her mind, she marveled at the fact the usual stab of intolerable pain she'd often experienced didn't slice through her heart the way it normally would have. Perhaps, after all this time she was healing from the past? Was there truth to Lucas' statement, that it wasn't her fault, and she couldn't control who she did and didn't love?

He'd asserted if she would have followed through with the wedding, it would have been unfair to Gavin to allow him to marry someone who didn't love him. It struck her as unbelievable, she now understood and accepted his words, although at first, she couldn't fathom how he could utter what she believed at the time to be nonsense.

But it wasn't nonsense. She knew couples who married for the sake of convenience, when years later they only grew to resent one another for the choice they made. If she did the same thing to Gavin, he would have hated her for it, and such an act would have undoubtedly stolen an opportunity from him to find that one person who was meant to love him unconditionally. It was never her, even if they both fell into the destructive pattern of pretending it was.

Yet, through Gavin Kade's action in the church

that day, he'd sent an undeniable message he ultimately thought she was the one. Or perhaps, Lucas was right and something else caused him to commit suicide the way he did.

As she loaded the last stick of firewood into the wheelbarrow, Lucas' words from this morning crashed into her brain like a seven-car pileup. *I'm not so desperate to have you in my bed, I'm willing to settle for a drunk version of you.* So what if her inebriated state went a little far last night? She still had full control of her faculties, didn't she? Her performance in bed wouldn't have been hampered by her drinking if that's what he worried about.

But that couldn't be the basis of his concern. She could see in his eyes he refused to settle for less of her in any capacity. And deep down she sensed her foolish pride suffered because of his rejection. If she allowed herself to put enough consideration into it, she'd have to admit she admired him for his ability to control his sexual impulses because he didn't want just a cheap lay.

But who said she had to put *that* much thought into it? Hmph. He certainly could have been more of a gentleman about turning her down instead of pointing out her drunken state and telling her to sleep it off after he'd purposely toyed with her.

The low rumbling of what sounded like a growl coming from behind stopped her dead in her tracks. Her hand, reaching for the handle of the wheelbarrow, froze in midair, and goosebumps rose on her skin, sending with it a riptide of fear snaking through her like a lit fuse. She waited, holding her breath, afraid to make a move.

The vicious snarling that followed the guttural

sounds made her blood run cold.

Then the sound of several canines howling and yapping told her more than one was present.

Panic set in like a fierce windstorm whipping around her. A pack of wolves descended on her. The location of the cabin was nestled far enough into the woods, wild animals roamed out here all the time. But why would they approach a human? Such a brazen attempt by a pack of wolves seemed unlikely. Unless they were scavenging for food and couldn't find any.

The growling became more intense, and she realized the beasts were closing in on her. She slowly braved a glance over her shoulder to find three gray wolves standing in her peripheral vision. Jesus, they were close enough if one of them lunged, they'd all be on her in an instant.

Barely aware of the shift in her movement, she spun full circle. She had no weapon to fend them off and her brain scrambled for a solution. As they inched forward, her shaking hand grabbed for a log on the stack beside her. She snatched the wood and aimed it at the animal closest.

The firewood flew through the air, only to roll to the ground a few inches from its target. The bold behavior only heightened the aggressiveness of the wolf standing in the center, as it snarled louder, its hackles raised, and its muzzle drawn back, showing off a mouth full of long, sharp teeth, dripping with saliva.

As the provoked creature stepped toward her, the rest of the pack—four in all—crowded in around her, getting into place to take her down. She had no means with which to defend herself, and if she turned and ran, they'd be on her before she could take five steps.

But her back was against the wall, and the overwhelming instinct to flee washed over her in the space of a heartbeat. She spun and took off in a blind panic, heading in the direction of the house, hoping she'd get close enough for Lucas to see her from his vantage point on the porch.

In her haste to escape, she didn't think to avoid the large, frozen puddle stretched across the ground in between the barn and the house, and the moment her feet pounded across it, the ice broke and she lost her balance, tumbling into the frigid water.

As she rolled over, she realized they were going to attack her. The sight of the wolf lunging overhead seemed like a dream. This couldn't be happening. She couldn't die like this.

Just as she braced herself for the attack, a loud noise rang out, and something struck the animal in midair. Blood spewed from the beast's gut, and a few crimson droplets landed on her cheek as the body of the injured wolf thudded to the ground. The thing howled and yelped, as the rest of the pack ran off.

Remi stared into the blue eyes of the suffering animal, and the sound of footsteps compacting the snow told her someone approached.

Lucas stood over the wolf, aimed a gun at its head, and buried a bullet in its skull.

****

A soaking Remi trembled in his arms as he helped her up the porch steps and shouldered her through the door. He carefully laid the handgun on the nearest end table and hustled her toward the fireplace. He snatched the blanket strewn over the couch and immediately wrapped her up in it.

With trembling, purplish lips, she stammered, "Is…is…th…that my g…gun you sh…shot that wolf with?"

"I found it in the dresser in the spare bedroom." Lucas scooted her closer to the warmth of the fire and ran his hands up and down her arms to help generate heat. "I've been carrying it around with me the whole time for protection."

"Wh…why didn't you tell me?"

"I don't know. It never occurred to me. Listen," he said, peeling back the blanket. "You're shivering. We've got to get these wet clothes off of you."

She didn't argue, and when she attempted to remove the jacket, her body shook so severely her fingers had difficulty gripping the zipper latch. He stayed her hand with his. "Let me, Remi. You're trembling too much."

She dropped her arms to her sides, as he freed the zipper, and tossed the soaking jacket to the floor. Judging by the condition of her drenched sweater, he imagined when she fell into the puddle, the water must have seeped in through the collar of her coat. "Lift your arms." He raised the hem of her blouse.

Once he removed the item of clothing from her body, his fingers worked to unsnap the button of her jeans. He tugged the drenched material down her legs, and she wiggled out of them.

She stood there with wet hair, arms hugging her quaking body. He wound his hands behind her for the clasp of her bra, and she stepped away, her eyes growing large with uncertainty.

"I'm not trying to seduce you. Your undergarments are saturated," he said, staring deeply into her eyes, as if to drive home the importance of his words. "I'm worried about hypothermia. We're going to remove all your clothes, and I'll warm you with my body. The same way you did for me when you brought me here and I was freezing to death, remember?"

She finally nodded and allowed him to step close and unfasten her bra. Next, he drew her panties down and laid them on top of the pile.

He couldn't take his eyes off her as he slipped his hand behind his back and tugged on his shirt to draw it over his head. She stood there trembling, and it dawned on him he ought to hurry and shed his jeans, but that task became nearly impossible when the urge to rake his eyes over her exquisite physique curve by sensuous curve overpowered him. It was so long since the last time he'd seen her completely naked, and his body reacted to the tantalizing view of her beautiful nudity, becoming rock hard.

He forced himself to turn away and threw his attention into removing the rest of his clothes, opting to leave his boxers on to hide his erection. After all, he vowed he wouldn't touch her unless he had her permission. And now was certainly not the time to reconsider his promise, even though he realized it would literally kill him to get close, wrap himself around her and not devour her.

By the observant expression on her face, he could tell she'd already feasted her eyes on the bulge in his undergarment as he stepped toward her. But thank God, she didn't say a word, and saved him the embarrassment of coming up with a lame excuse for the way he reacted to seeing her like this.

He collected the blanket off the floor, flipped it

around to the dry side, and draped it over her shoulders. Then he stepped in front of her, and gently guided her body against his.

Not a second ticked by before she latched onto him, wrapping her arms around his midriff, and laying her palms flat against his backside so her limbs could soak up his warmth.

The freezing condition of her skin as she molded herself against him shocked his system. He found himself resisting the urge to shrink back, and instead went headlong into the ice storm and circled his hands around her dainty waist, drawing her snugly against him and letting her absorb every ounce of heat he generated.

"I c...couldn't figure out w...why the wolves attacked me like that," she said, still shivering in his tight embrace.

He slid his hands up and down her arms, her back, and then molded them around her shapely ass. She didn't jerk away, which surprised him. He said, "I noticed a few dead rabbits just outside the barn when I went to fetch the hammer and nails the day I fixed the siding. I think that's what the wolves were after, and you got in the way of their meal."

"That makes s...sense. Thank G...God you came along w...with the gun. They would have t...tore me to shreds."

"Do you have a habit of hiding guns in different places, or was this a one-off situation?"

"I have a g...gun at my apartment t...too."

"I bet you do." Since she was ex-police, keeping guns stored in different locations wasn't an unusual practice. "Have you ever had to use it here at the cabin?" For thirteen years he wondered if she'd kept herself safe wherever she ended up.

"I honestly f…forgot I even had it."

"You have so many weapons laying around you lose track of them? Sounds like you were running from more than me, sweetheart."

Although he expected to hear a snide remark in response to that little dig, she didn't take the bait, only shrugged, and said, "I was d…dealing with some bad people. I had to do what I could to protect myself."

"Thank you for saving me," she said, unexpectedly.

An internal grin cropped up from his stomach, and he noticed her shivering abated. Thankfully, he managed to subdue her chills…and his own as hot blood raced through his veins at the sensation of her bare breasts lying flat against his chest. An image formed in his mind of his lips gliding across the arc of her neck, trailing over her collarbone in search of a voluptuous breast, and suckling the nipple while his hand slid past her bellybutton to the wetness that was hidden between her legs.

He swallowed the lump in his throat, and the overpowering urge to take her here and now, whether she permitted the advance or not. And the temptation only heightened when she rolled her head to the side and the intoxicating warmth of her breath fanned across his neck, causing goosebumps to flourish all over his body.

"Will you kiss me now, Luc?" she whispered, coming closer to his ear, her voice booming like a bullhorn through his head, shattering the last bit of resistance he clung to.

He closed his eyes, breathing heavily. "Don't play games, Remi," he said, his tone catching on a hoarse note. "Once I start touching you the way I want to, there will be no stopping me this time."

"I want you so bad it hurts," she confessed, taking his earlobe in between her teeth, and tugging gently.

Those words were his complete undoing, and he slid the cover off her shoulders, letting the blanket fall around her feet. His lips crashed down on hers, and he drank from her mouth like a man stumbling across the desert in search of water. It was a thousand kisses all in one. Every pang of agony he'd suffered when she fled from his life so quickly, every ounce of longing that burned in the bowels of his tortured soul night after night when the thought of making love to her became too much to bear, was tangled like a web in the pressure he applied to her lips.

And she rode the tidal wave with him, moving when he moved, and twirling her tongue around his in perfect rhythm.

She tasted more delicious than he remembered. There was no alcohol on her breath this time, just the pure, sweet nectar of Remi Shaw, the woman who owned his heart since the day he saw her coming down the escalator as he waited for her in the airport terminal. He lapped up every drop she gave until she broke free of the kiss, dragging her warm, supple lips to his chin, down further still to his neck, and across his chest, pausing to tease his nipple by circling the tip of her tongue around it.

His breath became trapped in his chest as her kisses burned a path over his abdomen, past his bellybutton, and halted just above the waistline of his boxers.

When she freed his erection, sending his undergarment sliding down his legs, a tingling sensation attacked his nerve endings, and his heart pounded like a stampede of wild animals tearing across the earth. Her hands molded around his shaft, and her tongue swirled around the head, causing a low groan to tear loose from his throat.

But when she took his full length inside her mouth, a burst of ecstasy ripped through him, stealing his breath once again, and sending his thoughts scattering across the four corners of the world. Her tongue twirled around the sensitive skin of his shaft, and she stroked him at a teasing pace. He found himself resisting the urge to mold his hands around her head and thrust himself deeper into the warm depths of her mouth. But more than anything, he wanted her to have full control to freely explore and pleasure him in whatever way she desired.

And when her foreplay nearly sent him spiraling over the edge, he lifted her up by her shoulders, cupped his palm against her cheek, sliding it to the back of her neck, and tugged her toward him, taking command of those incredible lips that pleasured him beyond logic.

While he kissed her, those magical hands of hers threaded through his hair, then skated down his neck and around to his shoulders, leaving a trail of searing heat in their wake. He worked his way toward her ear, and whispered deep and low, "It's my turn to touch you. Spread your legs for me, sweetheart. I want to feel your wetness between my fingers."

When she did as he wished, his fingers brushed a feathery path across her body, skimming over her nipple. He paid close attention to the way the contact made her gasp in anticipation. Then he continued with the maddening torture, drawing a circle around her navel, before guiding his hand to the tip of the small, shaved triangle of hair just above the area he was most interested in.

When his fingers at long last found her moistness, it instantly took her breath, and it aroused him even more to discover how wet she was. With his heart beating out of his chest, he stroked her clitoris, and her cries of pleasure drove him on. He slipped his fingers inside of her, gauging her reaction to every slow, meaningful thrust. An animalistic hunger glowed in her eyes, and she called out his name in a high-pitched tone of sweet surrender that had him fighting for control.

Power over his emotions ceased to exist in a world where Remi lived and breathed. From the moment he laid eyes on her, she would change his life forever. She crawled into his heart and took possession of his thoughts. For better or worse, he belonged to her, and there would be no escaping the everlasting prison she'd put him in.

But in this moment, he couldn't have been a more willing captive. And he had a few tricks of his own to make her succumb to his will. As he continued to fondle her, he leaned into her ear again, his voice cracking with raw emotion when he said, "How does it feel when I touch you this way?"

"Like Heaven," she answered breathlessly. "Please, don't stop."

"After today," he whispered, dropping a kiss into her ear, "No man will ever touch you like this other than me. Do we have an agreement?"

Her silence caused him to withdraw his hand. He

stared into the depths of her eyes, waiting for a response.

"You play dirty," came her winded reply.

"I'll take it any way I can get it, sweetheart. What's your answer?"

She trailed her gaze down the entire length of him, then swept it back up, appearing as helpless as anyone he'd ever seen. "I'd ask the same commitment from you."

"That's not something you'll ever have to worry about." *Because I love you and I have for longer than I wanted to admit, until now.* No other woman on the face of the earth affected him the way she did. He lived and breathed the scent, texture, and sounds of her as if he had no ambition in life other than to claim her as his own.

"Then, I'm all yours, Lucas Kade. Do with me what you will." The last part of her breathy declaration tumbled off her tongue as more of a plea to continue with his indulging caress, than it did a disappointing statement confirming she agreed to his terms.

A grin blossomed across his face now that he had her where he wanted her. He brushed his hand across her cheek, threaded her hair, and ended with twirling a red lock around his finger. Although he'd teased her into conformity, he needed more. "Before we go any further, I need to know if you'll be satisfied with just me."

"It's always been just you, Lucas."

The genuine emotion in her eyes when she said that struck a chord deep within him and his eyelids drifted shut for a moment, giving his tremulous heart time to digest the weight of her confession. It was obvious she'd always legitimately cared for him more than she cared for any other man.

And for now, it was enough. He stepped back and offered his hand, palm up. She slipped hers in his and allowed him to lead her to the bedroom.

Chapter Nine

Remi swore she'd never been so thoroughly loved in all her life. The mattress creaked under his weight as Lucas climbed on top of her, taking her face between his hands and staring intensely into her eyes. "I've missed this with you," he confessed, dropping a kiss on her lips.

His touch remained alive on her skin long after she'd made the devastating choice to abandon him. It was never more apparent than right now how much of a fool she had been to walk away from the only person who sparked life into her soul and made her feel as if she could conquer the world just by being his lover.

She didn't exaggerate when she admitted as they stood by the fire it was always him and no one else. Leaving him in Texas only put physical distance between them. He lived in her heart. And she saw him in every couple she'd seen holding hands and kissing, every lover's sentiment uttered in a public place, and every time she sat on a park bench watching a mother and father playing with their little one. She'd gone through the last thirteen years with an empty void in her soul, always wondering how different things would have been if she stayed. They could have married and had children together. The past would have been written with a much different ending.

She couldn't take it back. She could only throw

herself into the here and now and soak up the tantalizing sensation of his fingertips as they traced circles around her breast.

He leaned in and took her mound into his mouth, suckling her hardened nipple, and trailing his tongue maddeningly around it. He planted slow, agonizing kisses down the length of her body, leaving her with a burning need to feel his touch once again between her legs.

Her pulse thudded in her ears, and a lightning bolt of heat seared her flesh as his moist lips made their way to her pelvis. He ran his tongue across the sensitive skin down there, dropping soft kisses around the patch of hair. Then he parted her thighs, settled between her legs, and stroked her clitoris with his tongue.

An explosion of heightened pleasure rocked her body as he continued to lap her up. And she couldn't control the moans of hunger that tore loose from her throat any more than she could stop him from tasting her.

If her body was a roadmap, he damn well knew how to navigate it with perfect execution. Every flick of his tongue and path of his kisses sent her spinning into a world of ecstasy that she'd never find her way out of. Not that she ever wanted to.

Her hands curled around the bed sheets. Red-hot embers morphed into an inferno devouring her like wildfire sweeping across the forest, and if he stroked her one more time she would erupt into orgasmic spasms.

Before she knew what hit her, Lucas backed away. She imagined he must have read her body signals, realizing she was on the verge. "I told you," he said, an expression of heated desire burning in his eyes. "When you come I want to be inside you."

"But I'm afraid I'm going to need your help." A pang of discomfort flitted across his face. "My ribs are killing me."

She moved to get up. "Are you okay? Maybe we shouldn't—"

He laid a finger across her lips. "Trust me when I say quitting now will cause me a hell of a lot more pain than finishing what we started. There's only so many cold showers a man can take. Catch my drift?"

Thank God for that. Because if they were forced to stop now, she honestly feared she'd die from spontaneous combustion. She helped settle him onto the bed and then climbed on top of him. A groan pushed from his lips when she wrapped her hand around his shaft and guided him inside of her.

A prism of colors swirled behind her eyelids, exploding like fireworks, and the air in her lungs burst from her in a series of moans. "Oh, God, Lucas," she cried, losing sight of everything around her other than the breathtaking sensation of grinding down on him.

"Your body is so fucking hot, baby…so tight," he confessed, settling his hands around her waist gentle enough as to allow her to continue to ride him at her own pace.

"Open your eyes, Remi," he demanded, the tone of his voice drenched in desire. "I want you to see everything you're doing to me."

Her eyes flickered open, and his handsome face came into view, muscles tightening in his jaw as he now flexed his hips, moving deep inside of her. She noticed a light sheen of sweat glistening on his broad, muscular chest. He was the picture of a Greek God, and she couldn't resist touching him. His skin was like silk under her hands as they began their ascent from his forearms, around his shoulder blades and then to his abdomen. He briefly closed his eyes against the contact, a visible shiver running through him.

She noticed he'd removed the bandage from his injury, and she gently traced her fingers over the Y shaped scar. She lowered her head and placed a gentle kiss on the abrasion. Then, skimmed her lips across his broad chest until finding his mouth.

The pressure and mannerisms of his kiss left no doubt as to the immense pleasure he took as she moved over him with deliberate, tormenting strokes.

But their slow lovemaking tested her patience. She waited so long to have him inside her that her animalistic desire to devour every inch of him swept over her like a heatwave. But he was injured, and she didn't want to hurt him.

The effort wasn't lost on him, and he said, "Do you want more of me, Remi?"

She gazed into his eyes and nodded.

"Then say it," he ordered, his voice a low groan. "Tell me what you want."

"All of you, Luc. I want to fuck you hard and deep. But I don't want to hurt you."

"You're not going to hurt me. Take what you want, baby."

"Are you sure it won't make your injuries worse?"

"Don't make me beg, Remi. If you don't take what you want, I'm going to put you on your back and give it to you."

Judging by the reflection of unadulterated lust in

his eyes, he'd make good on his threat. From the moment his hands locked onto her shoulders, and the intensity in his eyes grew, penetrating her soul, she thrust herself down on him so hard and deep it took her breath.

She rode him at a furious pace until the only sound penetrating her ears was the slapping of flesh.

An intense orgasm gripped her, and she clung to him, calling out his name as spasm after glorious spasm caused her body to quake.

He rammed into her one last time, and she could tell by the intensity building in his eyes he had reached the pinnacle of their love making. "Fuck…baby," he groaned, holding her in place as his body tensed.

She collapsed onto the mattress, and he inched toward her, laying his head between her breasts. She threaded her fingers through his hair as her heart pounded. "Can we lay here for a while?" she whispered into the silence.

He didn't say a word, rose on his elbows, kissed her sweetly, then settled in beside her and collected her lovingly into his arms.

****

The fire crackled and popped as Lucas—in nothing more than his boxers—settled in beside Remi sitting in front of the hearth. The light from the fireplace created dancing shadows against her skin, making her cheek appear as smooth as porcelain. He couldn't resist lifting his hand and tucking a stray tendril of hair behind her ear.

Spending the day with her—snacking on leftovers only long enough to satisfy their growling stomachs in between making love—shaped up to be the most memorable day of his life. Now that nightfall descended upon them, the peace and tranquility that filled his soul was too good to be true. He'd gotten so used to having to fight for every ounce of submission from her. But the agony of being in her presence for so long and not having her blessing to explore her in the ways he so desired, was at last laid to rest and replaced with fulfilment. He was at ease in his own skin, and the burden that laid heavy on his heart caused by her constant avoidance of him, was lifted. At least for now.

She glanced at him, her expression telling him she took notice of something important in his eyes, and a peculiar smile pinched the corners of her lips. "What is it?"

"Everything," he responded, taking in the perfect image of her sitting there, wrapped in a bed sheet with the moonlight drifting in through the window casting its shimmering radiance against her bare shoulders. "It's how breathtaking you are. It's the many times I envisioned touching you, making love to you. It's just you, here with me right now."

She leaned against him, and he wrapped his arm around her. "Not a day went by I didn't think of you," she admitted. "I was an idiot for leaving the way I did. But after Gavin did what he did..." She cleared her throat, submerging herself in silence. And then, "I left because I couldn't escape the guilt of his death. Everyone hated me. Your father, the entire police force, and—"

"I never hated you, Remi. I loved you with all my heart. And when you left, it crushed me."

When she peered up, he could see she'd read in his eyes how profoundly her decision to disappear affected him. "I'm so sorry I did that to you. You deserved so much more from me. I honestly thought with the Godawful stigma surrounding me when word got around I was responsible for Gavin's death, you'd be better off not associating with me."

"I already spent half my days defending you against those assholes. If you stayed it wouldn't have made it any worse, believe me."

She inhaled sharply as if something occurred to her, then slipped out of his embrace. "Nobody on the force knew you were the one I'd been sleeping with, did they?"

He shook his head, lowering it. Her question brought back the burning regret that had eaten at him for the last thirteen years. "My father made me promise not to say anything to anyone on the force. I think his insistence I keep my mouth shut had more to do with saving himself the embarrassment of the department finding out his son was the sleazy son of a bitch partly to blame for Gavin's death, than it did saving me the ridicule I would have received from my fellow officers."

"So, none of them knew?"

"I was a coward," he said, with a crack in his voice. "I should have stood up for you more and told all of them the truth. But I knew it would only drag Dad's name through the mud. He took my brother's death so hard I just couldn't bring myself to heap more pain on him."

The expression in her eyes told him his statement blew her away. "You were not the coward in all this. You stood by my side and did your best to support me. I was the idiot who abandoned the only person who would have walked through fire for me."

"I was the coward," she said, barely above a whisper. "I convinced myself leaving was the only solution. I let Gavin's death drive everything meaningful out of my life because I held myself solely responsible for what he'd done."

"And now?" he wanted to know, lifting her chin, and searching her eyes.

"Now I think you might have been right. There was something more to his suicide. Although Gavin cared a great deal for me, it wasn't love."

"How do you know?" Although he knew the answer as sure as he existed, he wanted her to explain, in her own words, what brought her to that conclusion.

"I knew because me and Gavin didn't have what I had with you. All I needed to do was look at you across the room, and it would set my insides on fire. Every time you touched me, it was like you were reaching into my soul and making an everlasting impression."

"But when I touched Gavin," she continued, her shoulders quivering, as if when she spoke, the realization of the truth set in on her, decimating the whole core of what she once believed, "what I saw in his eyes couldn't compare to what I saw in yours every time we were together. He didn't long for me the way you did. There was no electrifying connection like that."

Now she peered down, hunching her shoulders as if to convey deep regrets. "I did everything I could to convince myself I should marry Gavin. The arrangements were already made. Everyone was expecting a wedding. But as I stood in the mirror staring at myself in my wedding dress, it hit me like a ton of bricks that after that day I would have to give you up forever."

A tear rolled down her cheek, and she sniffled. "God help me, I couldn't do it," she said, her voice weakening.

A pang of sympathy tugged at his heart for the tormenting battle she faced that day between a man she felt obligated to marry and a man she'd fallen in love with. To make matters even more impossible, they were brothers. Even if she ignored the fact one of them would get hurt, no matter what she chose, her decision would change the dynamics of a family forever. And that had to weigh on her like a death sentence.

He could never forget the way his heart had thudded in his chest, standing at the altar as the best man, and hoping and praying she would call the wedding off, even at the expense of destroying his brother's well laid plans.

"I'm not going to lie, Remi," he finally said, conviction in his tone. "I was relieved when you backed out of the wedding. It was pure hell being Gavin's best man, and wondering how the hell I was going to get through the ceremony knowing I was the one who loved you, and it should have been me in his place."

"I know," she said, wringing her hands in her lap. "I kept thinking it would have been the happiest day of my life if only it was you waiting for me at the altar. I was also relieved when I told Gavin the truth. And the damnedest thing, even though he was upset, he didn't seem devastated. It was as if he expected it."

"Before the wedding I spent enough time with my brother to know he didn't talk like a man who was on the verge of marrying the girl of his dreams. It was odd behavior, and I just couldn't figure out why he barely mentioned you in any of our conversations. He didn't bring up plans the two of you might have had, or even any expectations of how his life would have been with you as his wife."

"Then why did he commit suicide after I told him the truth?"

Lucas didn't have an answer. But he sensed with everything in his gut Remi had nothing to do with his brother's choice. "I know what it's like when a man falls in love with a woman, because I was head over heels for you. Gavin did not display those sentiments. We may never know why he chose to end his life that day, but I don't believe it was because you called off the wedding. And my only hope for you has always been you would one day absolve yourself from the responsibility of his actions. None of it was your fault."

He lifted his hand and gently wiped his thumb across the wetness glistening beneath her eye. Then he tugged her toward him and planted a kiss where the trail of tears once streaked down her cheek. "As awful as this sounds because of what happened, I'd be a liar if I didn't say I'm not relieved you decided you couldn't let me go forever. When you left, I was beginning to think I didn't mean as much to you as I thought I did."

"Don't you know?" she said, staring at him as if he missed the boat.

"Know what?"

"I've only ever loved you, Lucas Kade."

His pulse picked up, and a powerful sense of exhilaration swept over him. He hoped she still felt the same way about him as she did years ago. As much as he loved her, he had no idea what he planned to do with these overpowering emotions if it turned out she didn't love him anymore.

He closed his eyes, and allowed the staggering fear she may not have reciprocated his feelings to pass. And when he opened them again, she stared at him, the biggest, bluest eyes penetrating his soul as if they were connected. "I love you so much I would lay down my life for you," he confessed, damn well knowing uttering those words gave her the power to destroy him if she so chose. All he had was blind faith she wouldn't.

Tears flowed from her eyes, and in that moment it became clear she truly loved him.

****

Lucas swung the Pontiac into the convenience store and killed the engine. His gaze brushed across Remi sitting in the passenger's seat, her hair swept up in a neat ponytail, and a pair of shades covering her eyes. With the inconspicuous way they were dressed, no one at the airport would recognize them as being the wanted fugitives splashed all over the news. With any luck, once they located Bain Delgado and forced the truth out of him, they'd bust this cover up wide open, and then go back to being ordinary citizens. They'd stop looking over their shoulders for the next cartel member or law enforcement agent hiding in the shadows to take them down.

Thankfully the store wasn't that busy. Only a few stray customers shuffled about. He slipped on his shades, and said, "I'll only be long enough to use the phone and get hold of my contact. You need anything in here?"

When she threw her attention on him, her expression appeared void of emotion. She sat ramrod straight, appearing as solemn as an undercover agent on an assignment. She gave one, quick nod, then faced the windshield saying, "hurry," so abruptly it became difficult to tell if her lips even moved.

He'd worked in law enforcement long enough to know the signs. She was in full-fledged cop mode. It would be all business until they touched down in Texas and tucked themselves behind closed doors. Good. She still had her touch from the old days of working in the force. They were going to have to rely on that kind of experienced training to get through the next several hours.

As he shuffled from the car, he considered his next move. Each step felt like lead weights anchored around his ankles. When he'd mentioned at the cabin, he may know someone in Texas who could help them get the intel they needed on Bain's location, he'd purposely kept that person's identity under his hat. If she knew who it was, she would have flat out refused to go along with the plan. And he had to admit, he'd rather jump from the highest bridge in New York city and plunge headlong into freezing water than reach out to the one person he needed to contact. But given the situation they were in, there simply was no one else who had the capability to get them the information they needed.

As he shoved open the door, a chime rang out, alerting the cashier another customer entered the store. The ringing sound brought a chilling reminder of the reality he faced, and that he stood on the threshold of doing the one thing he didn't want to do.

He lumbered over to the cash register, grabbed a bag of seasoned peanuts from the display in front of the counter, and tossed them onto the stand, knowing if he purchased something, the cashier would be more inclined to let him use her phone.

The young girl with diamond stud earrings, freckles, and honey colored hair who couldn't be more than twenty-one, rang up his purchase. After telling him the amount, he plunged his hand into his pocket and came out with a fistful of bills. He threw a wrinkled five dollars on the counter, and she collected the money, punched open the register, and counted out his change.

"Say, I've misplaced my phone," he said, as she dropped a few coins in his palm. "I'm on my way to the airport and I need to make an important call. Do you think I can use your phone. It will only take a second. I promise."

She took her time sizing him up and munching on her lip. Then he took note of the change in her expression, and realized she'd come to a decision. She ducked under the counter and popped up with her phone in hand. "Make it quick, mister," she said, handing it out.

Lucas stepped to the side and punched in the digits he remembered from long ago. With any luck, the person he needed to reach still had the same number.

"Hello."

The sound of the man's voice brought back a rush of memories buried in the deepest recesses of his mind. He fought the urge to end the call and slink back to the Pontiac empty handed. But he couldn't do that. His and Remi's freedom depended on it.

"Who is this?"

"It's Roger, your next-door neighbor," Lucas said, hoping the man would recognize his voice, and catch on to the fact it wasn't Roger, since no one by that name lived next door. He couldn't very well give away his identity in the event the authorities were waiting for him to make this call. "You remember, don't you? My boy used to play with your sons when they were little."

Silence, and then, "What is it I can help you with, Roger?"

Lucas swallowed a wave of relief. His plan had worked. "My lawnmower broke down. My in-laws are coming tomorrow, and I was hoping I could borrow yours. I could be over there to get it in about five hours," he said, feeling out the situation to see if it was safe to come to his house.

"It'll be here waiting for you. I'll leave the garage door open."

"Great," he said, blowing out a sigh. "I'll see you in a bit."

As he carried the phone back to the cashier, dread filled his gut. He honestly didn't know if Remi would ever forgive him for the shitstorm he was about to bring into her life.

****

Once on the ground in Dallas, Remi sat in the back of the taxi, exhausted from the long flight and more than ready to get to their destination so she could take off these damn sunglasses, let down her guard, and relax a little.

Lucas smiled from his position across the seat from her, but she could tell he'd been on edge since he strolled out of the convenience store where he'd made contact with this friend who agreed to help them.

According to him, she didn't know this acquaintance. But she couldn't shake the feeling he'd left a few details out. Even though he played everything off as if he had things under control, and the plan was going forward as expected, something didn't add up. She didn't know how big or little of a concern what he didn't tell her should be. But at least she could rest assured knowing he would never put her in harm's way. Whatever it was he didn't want to reveal, he'd tell her in good time. She trusted him, and never doubted he had their best interest at heart.

They finally exited the highway, and she noticed the change of landscape a few miles into the ride. They were headed into a subdivision with neatly trimmed hedge bushes, and two-story, brick homes. They passed a church on the right side of the road with a huge steeple, surrounded by a wrought iron fence. The building appeared eerily familiar.

Her attention swung toward Lucas. He sat as unmoved as a statue, his eyes glued to the back of the driver's seat, hands clasped together and thumbs twiddling in his lap. The hairs on the nape of her neck stood on end, and the churning in her gut told her something wasn't right. Exactly where were they headed? The houses, trees, and bushes seemed somehow memorable. It reminded her of the strangest déjà vu she could ever recall experiencing.

The taxi slowed its pace, and before she knew it, the car stopped in front of a two-story home with its garage door standing open. She stepped out of the vehicle, while the shuffling of Lucas striding around to the trunk, and gathering their luggage echoed in the background.

The shutting of the trunk, and the crunching of gravel told her he was on the move again. Words exchanged between him and the driver, and the taxi drove off, leaving her with an unblemished view of the residence looming in the distance. The full force of where they were, hit her like a punch to the gut, and she instantly realized why the address Lucas rambled to the driver when they'd settled into the backseat sounded so familiar. Hell would freeze over before she'd ever step foot in that house again. What hairbrained idiocy caused him to bring her here?

He stepped toward her, luggage in hand, and she stared at him as if he'd lost his mind. She took a few steps back, her mind reeling with disbelief.

"Remi," he called, the sound of his voice muffled by the blood rushing to her head, causing an instant pounding in her ears. "We had nowhere else to go."

"No," she said, shaking her head in absolute refusal. She spun on her heels and headed in the opposite direction, the shock of his actions leaving her numb with outrage.

"Where are you going?"

She kept walking, her mind not able to process the full weight of what just happened. But one thing was for sure, Lucas Kade could go straight to hell if he ever thought she'd darken the doorway of that house again.

"Our faces are all over every television around," he called out to her retreating back. "How far do you think you'll get before they catch you and bring you in?"

She stopped, knowing he was damn well right, and hating herself for admitting it. Footfalls approached from behind, and she spun full circle, stabbing out her hand, an unmistakable message he'd better not come an inch closer.

He stood there, shoulders slouching, and he

dropped the luggage in his hands. "I'm sorry I couldn't tell you. I knew you never would have gotten into the taxi if you knew the truth."

Her hand trembled with fury as she lifted a finger, wagging it. "Your father made it very clear he wished I'd dropped dead the last time I saw him. There's no way I can face him, and you knew that bringing me here."

"He doesn't particularly like me either."

"You're his son. It's different with you. He'd be more prone to forgive you than me. He blames me more than anyone for Gavin's death."

He ran his fingers through his hair, appearing as if he'd rather throw himself in front of a fast-moving locomotive than have this conversation with her. She was sorry for his bad luck. "If there was anyone else I could have turned to," he said, throwing out his hands in exasperation, "we wouldn't be standing out in the street in front of my father's house having this discussion."

She marched toward him, arms stiff at her sides until a stray branch in the road tripped her, and nearly sent her sprawling across the asphalt. She regained her footing while red hot pokers of anger enflamed her flesh. As if she needed the embarrassment of practically falling flat on her face while intending to bring the wrath of God down on his head.

To make matters even more intolerable, he stood there with that lopsided grin etched into his face at her misstep. She'd ignore it for now, because if she didn't, she'd tear off that display of amusement with the nine-inch claws that were about to come out. "You mean to tell me you don't know anyone else in all of Texas we could have turned to?"

"Oh, I know plenty, but since they all work in law enforcement and are presently hunting us down, I figured my pissed off father would be the safer option. Besides," he said, his eyes burning into her with a loud and clear message her explosive reaction came off as unreasonable, "we're going to need Dad's contacts within the department to pinpoint Bain's location."

The wind was knocked out of her sails...a little. Despite her welling fury for his inconsiderate actions, he did have a point. "You could have at least warned me, you jerk," she shot back, not quite ready to give up her anger just yet.

"I already told you. If I said anything, you would have never climbed into the taxi."

"Is this what I have to look forward to with you? Withholding information from me when you suspect I won't react the way you want me to?"

She could swear his eyeballs were about to explode out of his skull. "Don't be ridiculous!" He snatched up the handles of the luggage. "This situation was a little different. Our freedom depended on you coming here with me. I had no choice."

"Well, I have a choice," someone said, approaching the road where they argued. "And that woman is not stepping foot in my house."

Remi's attention swung toward the voice. A clearly agitated, middle-aged man with salt and pepper hair, directed his fury on her. If it weren't for the similarity in the eyes, she never would have recognized Ethan Kade. Jesus, how the last thirteen years had aged Lucas' father.

No one uttered a word as they all stood there,

squaring off at one another. Then Lucas broke the silence. "Hello, Dad."

"Hello Dad, my ass," the older man grumbled, turning his anger on his son. "I haven't seen you in years, and you have the audacity to show up? With *her*?"

"She's being framed—just like me," Lucas told him. "And we both need your help."

Ethan didn't appear to give a shit. "You're welcome to come inside, but she's got to go."

"If she goes, then so do I."

Mr. Kade threw up his hands and waved them erratically, as if he didn't need this crap. "Suit yourself," he said, spinning on one heel and sprinting toward the house.

"Like it or not, I'm the only family you have left," Lucas called after him. "If you send me away now when I need you the most, I won't ever come back."

The man slowly came to a halt. He stared at the sky, then braced his hands on his hips, not bothering to turn around.

"Look, Dad, I really need your help. I didn't do what they think I did. And if I don't clear my name, they're going to lock me away for murder and throw away the key. You of all people know they won't stop until they find me. I'm begging you. I have nowhere else to go."

Ethan stood silent for a moment, not moving a muscle. Then he let out a groan, glanced over his shoulder. "Bring the luggage into the den. I don't know what's going on between you two after all this time, but you won't disgrace the memory of my dead son by sleeping together under my roof."

Chapter Ten

As the trio sat around the kitchen table eating sandwiches, tension cloaked the room like blinding fog. His father stared off into the distance, as if the guests in his house were total strangers. Since more than enough time had elapsed since the last time they'd laid eyes on one another, that assessment wasn't too far off the mark.

Lucas asked the first question that had weighed on his mind since he saw the initial TV coverage of the warehouse horror show. "Has the DEA come to see you, Dad?"

"They were here," Ethan confirmed, then took another bite of his sandwich.

He waited for his father to elaborate. When he didn't, he asked, "Are they—"

"They won't be coming back. I told them we haven't spoken in years, and I doubted you'd ever come back here again."

Although his answer gave Lucas some comfort, the way Ethan's expression hardened on that last remark left no doubt the man still harbored pent-up resentment for the way things went down between the two of them that dreadful day they laid his mother to rest.

"So, who shot Dominick Barlow?" his dad wanted to know, ignoring the bigger elephant in the room.

"Victor Craven," Lucas said. "I saw the whole

174

thing go down." He took a gulp of tea and set the glass back on the table. "They brought me to the warehouse under the guise I was to meet a banker who had money laundering prospects."

The expression in his father's dead eyes told Lucas to hit the pause button on what he'd planned to say. "Money laundering prospects? Is that what you were doing for them? Laundering money?"

"I was working undercover as a broker for the cartel. The objective was to follow the trail of money. The DEA felt that would make more of a solid case against them after the big bust."

His father propped his elbows on the table and tucked his fist under his chin. "Go on."

"I realized too late that it was a set up. They were waiting for me in the back room of the packing plant. They'd already made me, and they had Barlow tied up in a chair. Craven shot my partner in the chest, then they all beat the living shit out of me. Remi came in and dragged me out of there before they set the warehouse on fire. After the fact, they made it look like I perpetrated the whole thing."

Ethan's attention floated toward Remi who sat there, eyeballing her sandwich as if her stomach couldn't handle a single bite. "According to news reports, she," he said, pointing an accusing finger at her, "was sleeping with this Craven character."

Judging by the look on Remi's face, she used incredible restraint by not leaping across the table and throttling the old man. "You don't know anything about what was going on, Mister Kade. And if you're getting your information from the media, it's little wonder you're so clueless."

"Then perhaps, you can explain it. Just make sure to do a better job than you did explaining to me how you killed my son!"

She shot up from her chair, wild eyed, and trembling. With one jerk of her head, she fixed the full brunt of her emotions on Lucas. "I told you I couldn't come here. Now do you see?"

"You weren't invited if that's any indication," his father retorted.

"That's enough," Lucas stood and stared pointedly at his father. "Do you think what you're doing is helping?"

"Outside you said you needed my help," the man reminded him impatiently, moving on from his outburst as if it hadn't happened. "What is it you think I can do for you?"

Lucas trained his attention toward the Heavens, doing all he could to reign in the irritation boiling inside for his father's unpredictable behavior. He shoved one fist into his pocket, and the other hand gripped the back of the chair. He leaned forward and said in as calm a voice as possible, "The authorities have the informant, Bain Delgado, hidden away somewhere in a safe house. He's covering for the cartel by claiming I was the one who shot Barlow and set the place on fire. I need to know his whereabouts so I can bleed the truth out of him."

"And how do you suppose I can help with that?"

Lucas frowned as if to say, *we both know the answer to that*.

Taking the hint, Ethan broke eye contact, then lowered his head. "I retired from the force how many years ago? What makes you think they'd give me that information?"

"You know people in the DEA, Dad. Hell, it was your recommendation that got me the job." When his father's head jerked up in shock, Lucas went on. "You think I didn't know about that? The director, Andrew Webber, told me if it wasn't for the good word from you, they wouldn't have hired me."

"I told him not to say anything," Ethan complained. "You and I weren't exactly on speaking terms. But I knew you'd make a damn good agent. So, when I found out you planned to interview for a job over there, I put the word in."

Lucas shrank down into the chair. "You didn't have to do that, but I'm glad you did. Thank you."

The annoyance pinching the corners of his dad's eyes eased a bit. "You're welcome."

Even though his father's grudging acknowledgement wouldn't erase the years of animosity between them, the stab at being cordial presented a promising start. He cleared his throat and motioned for Remi to have a seat.

Even though she appeared as if she cared nothing about complying, when she sat back down, he supposed she'd done it for argument's sake. "As for Remi's involvement with Craven, her nephew went missing. He was a small-time drug dealer for the *Infierno* Cartel. She infiltrated his organization in the hopes of discovering what they'd done with Natty. She has a suspicion the boy's disappearance has everything to do with the involvement of dirty cops in the Dallas PD."

Ethan briefly eyeballed Remi, picked up his sandwich, and took a bite as if he had nothing more to say on the subject. At least he refrained from going postal and causing another scene with Remi—who appeared to be in a mood to strike back. Lucas could be grateful for that.

After polishing off the remainder of his sandwich, Ethan wiped the crumbs from his mouth, stood, and carried his saucer to the sink. "I'll give Webber a call and make arrangements to meet with him for lunch tomorrow. We usually have lunch once a month, so he won't suspect anything fishy. I can't make any promises," he added, tossing a cautioning glance in Lucas' direction, "but I'll do what I can to get the information you need."

Remi stood to clear the table, and Lucas stopped her by grabbing her wrist. "It's okay, babe. I got this. Why don't you relax on the back porch while me and Dad clean up?"

She snatched her hand away, the expression in her eyes making it crystal clear he wasn't out of the woods with her. "I don't need your help," she insisted, plucking a plate off the table. "The last time I let you handle things for me, you tricked me and brought me to the one place I'm most unwelcome in the whole entire world."

As she stomped away toward the other end of the kitchen, Lucas' attention fell on his father who stood by the sink. Ethan shook his head.

****

Fatigue settled into Lucas' bones. He suffered from a sleepless night due to the fact he found himself tucked away in the one place he never wanted to lay eyes on again. But the tension between his father and the woman he loved ticked like a time bomb. One false move or careless word would have thrust the two of them into World War II territory.

And of course, Remi Shaw hated his guts all over again.

He stepped out onto the back porch. Even with the temperature at forty-five degrees, the afternoon sun broke through the winter sky radiating its warmth and making it bearable to stay outside. The truth was, he could have had the run of the house if he wanted to stay indoors. She'd been holed up in her room all day, resurfacing twice. Once to use the bathroom, and another time to grab a cup of coffee and a muffin. She'd avoided him like the plague both times. But he couldn't stand roaming around this big house by himself. Too many memories of his mother's big personality and infectious laugh haunted every room. God, how he missed her, and being here among her memories, and some of her things that his father never packed away caused an aching in his heart he wasn't ready to face.

And Remi's aloofness made everything less tolerable. So much for the honeymoon period he expected to experience now that they'd rediscovered one another. *You knew damn well once you brought her here, she'd be pissed as hell.* Honestly, it amazed him she hadn't used his head as target practice for every piece of china in the house.

If he were in her shoes, he would have.

He blew out a sigh of distress and wandered over to a lounge chair situated at the far end of the porch. Before he could sit down, the door opened, and Remi stepped out. She headed toward the railing overlooking the rolling backyard. He realized instantly she didn't know he was there. And he remained in place for a moment, just watching as she took in the scenery.

"You remember the volleyball tournaments we used to have right there in between the little red tool shed and the firepit?" he finally said, not sure if revealing himself would send her scurrying away.

She gasped in surprise and spun to face him.

He grinned and took a few steps toward her. "You and Mom used to team up against me and Dad." Her eyes followed him as he made his way to the railing, and stood beside her, staring out at the winter lawn, his mind's eye picturing the sagging volleyball net that once stretched across the ground. There was still evidence of sand visible through blades of grass.

"Gavin was never one for sports," she said, turning back toward the yard beyond the railing.

It struck him as odd that hearing his brother's name didn't cause an instant pang of regret and heartbreak as it did over the years every time Gavin was mentioned. Perhaps, being open with Remi and discussing his emotions regarding his deceased sibling during their last day at the cabin in New York afforded him the opportunity to heal and begin to bury the grief he faced as part of that devastating loss. It occurred to him he stubbornly held on to it for too long.

He chuckled and shook his head. "That's because he was a poor sport. He'd rather not participate than run the risk of losing."

"You're kidding?" she said, staring at him in genuine surprise.

"He played baseball as a teenager. But if he didn't get a decent hit or got sent to the outfield, he'd sulk for days. It got to the point he refused to pick up a bat because he couldn't tolerate the thought of losing a game."

She pursed her lips, awareness lighting her eyes. "I could see that about him. Remember when he got on that detective kick?"

"You mean when he put in for a transfer to Homicide?"

She nodded. "You wouldn't believe the fit he threw when the chief told him he wasn't quite ready. He was inconsolable for a week. It took me two days to get him to eat."

"My little brother was a ball of fire. He set high standards for himself, and when he couldn't live up to them—"

"His entire world would come crashing down in one day." She laughed and brushed her hair away from her face. "That was Gavin Kade, all right. But you took a much different approach."

Lucas raised an eyebrow, becoming intrigued by what she could have meant by her statement. "And what different approach would that be?"

When the amusement died down, she cleared her throat and glanced away. He could sense discomfort rolling off her in waves. "You'd patiently wait and strategize. And before anyone realized what happened, whatever it was you wanted would be putty in your hands."

"You got it all wrong," he confessed, leaning into her ear. "It was me who was putty in your hands. And it had nothing to do with strategizing and everything to do with fate."

"I believe you're right, Lucas," she said to his surprise. "But the thing you're missing is when two people love each other, they also trust one another enough to be honest, even if they can't predict how the other person will take the truth. They don't hide information from the one they love. They make decisions together, as one." With that, she spun on her heels and strolled away.

"Remi," he called, as she sashayed across the porch.

She didn't turn back, only stopped walking.

"For the record, I'm sorry I didn't tell you about coming here. I didn't see any other way for us, and I knew you'd refuse."

"And for the record, you didn't even give me the opportunity to refuse."

Ethan stepped out onto the porch just before Remi reached the door. He held up a piece of paper in one hand. "This is Bain's location, but we need to talk." Lucas followed close behind Remi as the three of them marched into the house and gathered around the kitchen table. His father laid the paper on the table. "Delgado is holed up in the safehouse with his girlfriend, a twenty-year-old blonde by the name of Tish. They send an agent from time to time to check on them. The DEA is there right now. And I've been informed they won't clear out until the morning. So, you'll have to wait until tomorrow to drive out there."

Then, his dad settled his focus on Remi. "The Dallas PD has your nephew in police custody."

"Oh my God," Remi sputtered, the expression on her face making it clear she didn't know whether to be relieved or concerned.

Lucas' father hardly waited for that shocking news to sink in before he plunged into his next statement. "Nathaniel Shaw has been working with internal affairs. An investigation has been going on for some time."

"Natty told me corrupt cops were involved with the cartel," Remi added, pounding her fist against the table as if to say she'd known it all along. "But he was afraid to tell me who they were because he worried about my safety if I knew."

It appeared as if Ethan read in Remi's eyes the question of who the dirty cops were. He shook his head. "The department is tight lipped about the identity of these cops. If you ask me, the only ones who have any idea at all are Internal Affairs themselves. And they sure as hell aren't saying."

His father sat back against his chair, his guarded mannerisms telling Lucas he had more news. Why did he get the feeling he wouldn't like it? While staring at the table, Ethan said, "There's a corrupt DEA agent working for the cartel."

And just like that an overwhelming sense of chilling awareness crawled up Lucas' spine. That was the missing peace to the puzzle, and the whole reason they set him up at the warehouse. They were framing him to take the fall as the dirty DEA agent. He frowned, hiding the brunt of his fury behind a controlled grin. "How long have they suspected this?"

"Pretty much from the beginning of the undercover operation," Ethan said, a hint of sympathy lingering in his eyes. "Listen, son," the man said, doing his best to sound optimistic. "We're going to do whatever is needed to prove your innocence. It's obvious these sons of bitches set you up from the beginning to take the fall to conceal the identity of the agent involved. You have my word we're going to find out who that is, and we're going to take the bastard down."

"You're damn right we are." But even as the words

tumbled out of his mouth, Lucas' common sense warned him they weren't playing with amateurs. It wasn't just the cartel he had to worry about. A gang of dirty cops, and some unidentified agent working on the inside at the DEA, had colluded to bring him down. No matter which way he sliced it, proving his innocence would pose a challenge with this many corrupt officials working in cahoots to frame him for a murder he didn't commit. He needed to identify the corrupt agent. But it didn't seem to matter how many of his coworkers' faces flashed before his eyes, not one of them stood out as suspicious. But someone was behind all of this.

Now Lucas glanced down at the address in front of him, carefully examining the location where authorities were keeping Bain. "We'll head out to this address," he said, his eyes roving across the cursive writing scrawled on the paper, "at noon tomorrow. By then the agents who are with Bain right now, should have cleared out."

"You know where this is?" he asked his father, sliding the paper toward him.

The old man grinned. "I used to duck hunt in this area years ago. If memory serves correct," he added, gazing off into the distance as if to conjure an image of the area in his mind. "It's a cabin me and my hunting buddies stumbled across deep in the woods. I'd imagine the acreage surrounding the place is still undeveloped land, since the DEA wouldn't have used anything other than a secluded spot for a safehouse."

Ethan wasted no time marching over to the bank of cabinets closest to the stove and yanking open the bottom drawer. Lucas recognized that particular drawer to be the spot where everything in the household that didn't have a place ended up. In his mother's famous words, 'the junk drawer'. His father rummaged around and drew out what appeared to be a folded map and carried it over to the table. Once he cleared a few objects out of his way, he spread it out, ran his finger down a trail, and then tapped on a location. "Here," he said, seriousness chiseled into his face. "The cabin I saw that day is in this area. It couldn't have been more than an eight of a mile away from the path we were taking. I remember seeing the structure from the trail. We hiked over to it more out of curiosity than anything else. It was abandoned at the time. Lots of high weeds and heavy growth. But there was a white rock driveway in front."

His father traced his finger across a red line on the map. Upon closer inspection, Lucas realized the name of the street Ethan showed them was Burnt Hickory Road. And when he glanced down at the writing on the paper his dad gave him earlier, it dawned on him the address matched. "What's the most inconspicuous way to get to Burnt Hickory Road?"

Ethan grinned. "There isn't one. You're going to take Silo Road to the cabin." He pointed to a spot on the map. "It's where we used to park our cars when we hunted these woods."

"Then we take the same trail you took the day you ran across the safehouse," Remi piped up and added.

Ethan's reaction to the sound of her voice as the muscles in his face drew taut with annoyance, was an unmistakable sign his tolerance for her existence in his house remained just as short-fused as it did yesterday. The man came across like Jekyll and Hyde, speaking calmly to her one moment, and then turning on her the next. He didn't glance her way when he said, tightly,

"This isn't some detective novel for your amusement." Now he stared her dead in the eyes, contempt sprouting from his. "Personally, I could give a damn less what happens to you, but it's my son's ass on the line if you mess around and get captured."

She blinked passively, displaying indifference to his crass words. "Thanks for the enlightenment. Me and your *son* have only been running and hiding from the police and a ruthless drug cartel for the last week without getting noticed by any of them once. We've managed to board a flight from New York to Texas without raising the slightest bit of suspicion or attention even though every Joe has seen our faces plastered all over their television sets. But I honestly had no idea the situation was this serious."

Lucas siffled a laugh. For a minute there, he figured he'd have to stand up and defend her, but with the way she put his father in his place, it appeared his services on that front would not be needed.

"By the way," she threw in for good measure. "I prefer true crime documentaries over fiction, thank you very much."

Ethan swung his head in Lucas' direction, affixing his berating eyes directly on his son in reaction to the clear amusement splashed across Lucas' face regarding Remi's bold retort. And even though the man's pupils were dilated in anger, there existed a hidden respect buried deep within them for the way she'd handled his belittling efforts.

His dad snapped his attention away, still pissed, and snatched the map off the table in one, quick swipe. He folded it haphazardly and tossed it onto the counter as if he could give a shit less if it landed in the middle of the floor. "You'll take my car tomorrow," he grumbled. "I'm going outside to replace the damaged shingles on the barn. That's what I was doing before you showed up here with her," he said, turning his head and stabbing an irritable glance in Lucas' direction.

"Do you want my help, Dad?" Lucas offered, already knowing his father would turn him down.

The man didn't want his help to nail down shingles, or to complete any other task around his house. He sought the opportunity to justify to anyone who would listen, the resentment he'd built up in his heart for a woman he blamed for killing his son. Only Remi wasn't to blame for Gavin's death. Gavin himself was. And somewhere deep inside, Ethan Kade knew it. But blaming her for so long kept him from facing the heartbreaking reality of his youngest son singlehandedly making a decision to end his life, and in doing so, punishing everyone who loved him.

"The only thing I want," Ethan snapped, collecting his jacket from around the backrest of the chair and slipping into it, "is for the two of you to gather whatever evidence you need to clear your names." He strode toward the door and flung it open. "And then get the hell out of my house." The door slammed on that final word.

****

The only light in the room came from the infrared digits on the alarm clock, letting him know it was ten minutes past midnight. Lucas let out a sigh, climbed from beneath the covers, and grabbed his pants off the floor, not bothering to dig around in the darkness to locate his shirt. After donning his jeans, he ran his fingers through his hair and rubbed his face. He'd lain awake for the past few hours, and he couldn't stand waiting for the clock to tick out another thirty minutes. Perhaps, he'd stumble into the kitchen for a glass of milk and wait for exhaustion to overcome him.

The whole day was the worst one he'd had in years. None of the occupants in the house were on speaking terms. The silence hanging over them resembled a dark, angry cloud. He couldn't help but wonder when the rain would come pouring down, washing away any chance they might have had to reconcile. As if that was even possible.

He stepped down the hallway and let the light that spilled out from the half-open bathroom door lead him into the living room. From the time he'd been little, his parents kept the door cracked and that light on for years, worried he or his brother would stumble in the event they got out of bed in the middle of the night and had to use the restroom. Some things never changed.

It didn't surprise him his dad hadn't redecorated, or even rearranged any of the furnishings in the house since the time his mother passed away. All the same family portraits still adorned the walls. Every owl nick-nack his mother collected over the years still sat on the same glass shelves. From the time he walked back through the door, everything appeared as his mom left it, even down to the placemats on the table, and the throw rugs covering the floor. Adeline Kade became such a fixture in this house, he imagined her husband couldn't bear the thought of altering anything she'd touched. Too bad he didn't cherish the memories of his older son, as much as he did his wife and younger son.

"I gather you couldn't sleep either," a voice said, stopping Lucas before he reached the fridge.

He glanced over his shoulder at the kitchen table. Ethan leaned back in the chair, his legs crossed and resting on the seat of another, a half empty glass of milk sitting in front of him. Then it clicked in Lucas' mind he must have gotten his craving for milk in the middle of the night from his father. He hadn't realized that until now.

"I can see you know how it is," he told his dad, continuing his trek to the refrigerator, and fetching the gallon of milk. He plodded across the floor to retrieve a glass out of the cupboard. The only light in the room radiated from a small bulb tucked underneath the vent-a-hood.

"I hope I didn't wake you with the noise I was making out here," Ethan said, apologetically.

"Naw," Lucas placed the jug back inside the fridge, and joined his father at the table. "I didn't even know you were up."

"Your mother used to hate it when I got up in the middle of the night. It interrupted her sleep. She used to call my name nonstop until I came back to bed."

"I remember. She'd always wake you up if you fell asleep in the recliner too." Lucas took a gulp of milk, wiped his mouth with the back of his hand, and then frowned. "Have you dated anyone since Mom passed away?"

The man peered down at the table and fiddled with the napkin ring. No doubt, Lucas brought up a sore subject. "I don't need another woman coming in here and bossing me around. I'm an old man set in my ways. No one would put up with me like your mother did, anyhow."

"I'm sorry, Dad," Lucas said. "I know how hard it

was losing Gavin, and then Mom."

The expression on his face froze. Then, slowly, his muscles relaxed, and he appeared vulnerable. Lucas had to admit he'd never witnessed such a weak emotion coming from his father. "Didn't your brother's death mean anything to you?"

The man just blurted it out like that. It didn't matter when he planned to mention it, Lucas realized the subject of him supposedly stabbing his brother in the back had been on Ethan's mind since he led him into the house.

Lucas averted his attention, running his fingers up and down the condensation accumulating outside of his glass. The point his father struggled to make was, why in the world would he opt to be with the woman responsible for Gavin's death? "She wasn't the reason Gavin committed suicide."

A hint of anger played across the contours of Ethan's face. He uncrossed his legs and slid them off the chair. "How can you say that when you know it's not true?"

"Do you think Gavin was in love with Remi?"

His expression hardened. "What are you saying?"

"It's a simple question. Give me an honest answer."

"Of course, he was."

"You sure about that?"

The reflection in Ethan's eyes told Lucas he thought his question outrageous.

"Okay," Lucas said, settling in for the long haul. "Tell me this then. Did the two of them ever act the way you and Mom did when you guys first met?"

To begin with, Ethan appeared stunned, then his

attention bounced around the room, as if he'd find the answer hiding in the crevice of a wall somewhere.

"Anything," Lucas said, in an attempt to conjure an answer. "Chemistry between them when they looked at each other across the room? An undeniable attraction when they touched…kissed?"

Ethan crossed his arms, leaned back in the chair again, and munched on his lip. After a long moment, he said, "What me and your mother had was different."

"In what way, Dad?"

"Well, when I ran into your mother that day outside of the bakery, when she tripped coming out the door and I caught her, I looked into her eyes, and I just knew she was the woman I was going to marry. I don't know how to describe it, but I could see a reflection of myself in her eyes." He took a breath and drew a circle on the table with the bottom of his glass. "When you meet the person you're meant to spend the rest of your life with, you know. What more do you want me to say?"

"You and Mom were married for thirty-five years. And I know ever since I was old enough to understand affection, the way you looked at her was something else. There was admiration, pride, and love in your eyes. She hung the moon and that never changed between the two of you."

Now Ethan stared at the table, his hands nervously flattening out the placemat. "I'm sorry, son. But I'm not following."

Lucas realized his father knew very well what he meant. "Let me spell it out for you. My brother never once looked at Remi the way you looked at Mom."

"But I already told you. What me and your mother

had was different."

"No," Lucas said, and shook his head to further drive home the fact he didn't buy his father's weak stab at convincing him he was right. "What you felt for Mom was no different than what anyone else experiences when they fall in love with someone."

"How do you know?" his dad demanded, becoming impatient and angry.

"I know because I looked at Remi the same way you looked at Mom. And I still do."

"I can never understand how you could have stolen your brother's fiancé away from him without so much of a thought as to the damage your actions would cause this family."

Lucas took notice of the anger and hurt building like the crest of a wave in Ethan's eyes. But he plowed forward, realizing someone had to get through to the man. If he continued to hold on to the bitterness of the past, and refused to let go of the belief someone else was to blame for that tragedy, it would eat him alive until nothing remained. "You can't steal something away from someone they never had to begin with."

"What do you mean? They were engaged."

It occurred to Lucas it was going to take an act of congress to get him to understand the reality of the situation. But he wouldn't give up. "I know in my heart Gavin never loved Remi. But I think what drove my brother to the impulsive decision to propose to her, was because he knew you and Mom loved the idea of them together."

"So, now this was mine and your mother's fault?" Ethan shook his head in disbelief and gazed up at the Heavens as if he couldn't believe how disillusioned his son was.

"You know Gavin couldn't stand to lose, and when he saw how happy he and Remi made you and Mom, it felt like winning to him. And Remi didn't have much of a family left after her parents died. When the Kade's welcomed her into their circle, it felt real enough to her she managed to convince herself for a time, agreeing to marry Gavin gave her all the things she missed in life, except for the person she was meant to be with."

"Let me guess," his dad said, frowning derisively. "That's you. The love of Remi Shaw's life."

"It wasn't my brother, and I think we can both admit that. Gavin ignored her. When he made plans to go somewhere or do something, none of those plans included her. Did you know the night before the wedding, he came to me and asked if he was making a huge mistake by marrying her? He went on and on about how much you and Mom liked her. I think he knew what was expected of him, but he was burdened by the thought of marrying someone he didn't love to make others happy."

His father tore his attention away from Lucas with the snap of his head, making it obvious he understood 'others' to mean him and his deceased wife. "Just because they didn't love each other the way me and your mother did, doesn't mean they couldn't have had a good life together."

The man's response should have shocked him, but it didn't. Ethan would have been content allowing his son to wed not out of love, but to satisfy his own desire to have Gavin marry a girl he, himself, approved of, at least at the time. So much for wanting the best for your children, like the opportunity for them to marry the one person in the world they love and want to spend the rest of their life with.

He stared at his father sitting across the table from him, appearing vulnerable and broken. In that moment Ethan Kade became a person whose mistakes and regrets were catching up to him, someone going down on a sinking ship still stubbornly clutching onto thirteen years of bitter emotions and self-inflicted suffering as if it was a life raft.

Lucas' eyes softened when he said, "I know growing up, I was a lot more rebellious than Gavin. I insisted on doing my own thing and doing it my way regardless of the heavy price I might have paid when it turned out to be the wrong decision. My little brother was much more susceptible to influence. When you told him which decisions to make and which paths to take, he obeyed because gaining your approval somehow became more important than his own wants and desires."

The expression in Ethan's eyes told him his statement hit home. "But," he continued, not letting up on getting his point across, "you never stopped to consider you didn't get to choose who Gavin loved and who he didn't love. You and I both know Remi was not the woman for him. And if she didn't make the decision to confront him about it before it was too late, Gavin would have been miserable, and that marriage would have ended in disaster. After a while, even Mom understood forcing two people to be together when they don't love each other can never work."

His father shook his head adamantly. "No. That was you doing all you could to convince her those two didn't love each other." In a fit of anger, he scraped his chair back, stood up and wagged a finger in Lucas' face. "You drove her crazy with that kind of talk. She became someone I didn't recognize. Always running around telling me what a big mistake I made and insisting I give that woman," he said, stabbing a finger in the direction of the guest room where Remi lay sleeping, "another chance. That none of this was her fault. But I knew better. Your mother would never listen to reason."

"It was Mom who came to me," Lucas said, raising his voice and exploding out of his own chair. "I did not approach her with this. She wanted the truth, and I gave it to her."

"And what truth was that?" Ethan wanted to know, his eyes wide with anger.

"You already know because she obviously brought it to your attention time and time again. But you, being the stubborn son-of-a-bitch you are, refused to listen to her. Instead, you used Remi as a scapegoat to blame for Gavin's death, when the fact is, if you didn't push so hard for the two of them to marry, none of this would have happened." His heart pounded, and his body shook. He couldn't believe those words flew out of his mouth, even if they were long overdue. If he'd been smart, he would have confronted his father about this a long time ago, not held it back for so long, afraid of how he would take it.

His father shook with rage. "Don't you dare turn this around on me. All of this was her fault. She came into our lives and tore all of us apart."

"The same way I tore you and Mom apart by answering her questions? Didn't you blame me for her death? You stood right there in this kitchen the day of her funeral," he said, stomping toward the sink and pounding his fist against the counter next to the spot he stood that day when he and his father got into a heated argument, "and told me I killed her because I was the one sleeping with the woman who was responsible for Gavin's death, because I convinced her me and Remi couldn't help the way we felt about each other."

"Mom had a mind of her own," he continued, staring at his dad as fire consumed his insides. For the first time in his life, he became empowered. And standing here right now, even with a thousand volatile emotions exploding through him, he truly understood the meaning of the words, *the truth will set you free.* "She came to that conclusion because it was the truth. It's funny how there's always someone else to blame for the tragedy in your life besides yourself, isn't it, Dad?"

A slight movement caught Lucas' attention, and his eyes zeroed in on the dark shadow lurking in the doorway of the kitchen. The silhouette slowly approached until the form took shape as Remi. She stood arms-length from him now, in a white, silk nightdress that shimmered in the soft glow of the room. The material was as short as a miniskirt, showing off the lean shape of her legs. The sight of her sensual body scantily dressed, sent an instant flashback tumbling through his mind of his hand as it skated up the creamy flesh of her thigh, worked its way around the dainty curve of her hip, and molded around her breast.

Expressionless, she said in a whisper, "Why didn't you tell me Gavin came to you with reservations about marrying me the night before the wedding?"

His mind reeled with uncertainty. How long was

she hiding in the darkness, listening to their conversation? He carefully examined every facet of her face, hoping to identify a single emotion that would tell him how she felt, and what she thought. She displayed no anger, yet buried in the depths of those blue eyes he sensed an overwhelming sentiment of pain, distrust, and disappointment. Christ, he couldn't win for losing. "I wasn't trying to hide it from you, I...I was just—"

"Hiding it from me."

He lowered his head. She was right. He'd purposely kept that information from her. "I just didn't see any reason to hurt you like that," he said, now braving a glance at her, hoping she'd see the sincerely in his eyes.

"Hurting me?" she said, backing away from him in disbelief. "You could have told me before the wedding, couldn't you? At least I would have known he felt the same way as me before I told him I couldn't go through with it."

"I didn't want to influence your decision." He took a few steps toward her, but she continued to back away from him. "I couldn't be sure not marrying my brother was what you truly wanted."

"What do you mean you couldn't be sure?" It came across as more a statement of outrage than a question. "How much clearer could it have been I'd given you my heart? You knew how much I agonized over telling Gavin getting married wasn't the right thing for us, yet you withheld from me the fact he told you he felt that way too."

"Listen to me," he said, grabbing her by the wrists, his heart pounding with the fear he would lose her forever. He hunched his shoulders, towering over her until their gazes locked. "Part of me didn't know if I would be enough for you. This was your future and your decision. If you called the wedding off because I told you what Gavin said to me in confidence, then I would have spent the last thirteen years of my life wondering if I caused you to make the worst mistake of your life. I loved you too much to persuade your decision."

She shook her head and wrestled out of his hold. "You're wrong. This was our future and our decision. Not just mine. I waited for you to make it with me. But that time never came. And before I knew it, there I was, standing in the church, in Gavin's dressing room, and telling him I was in love with someone else. So, I guess, in the end, you were saved the uncertainty of whether you were enough for me."

When she stalked off, it was like watching his whole world slip away with her.

Chapter Eleven

As Lucas drove Ethan's car out of the subdivision and headed toward the highway, Remi shifted uncomfortably in the passenger seat. "Don't look at me like that."

Her nerves were already on edge knowing they would soon be plunged into a confrontation with Bain Delgado and his girlfriend. She had no idea how the duo would react when she and Lucas converged on them. According to the information provided by Mr. Kade, the rogue informant wasn't given a weapon to protect himself. They should be easy to approach and subdue, especially since she and Lucas were both armed. But in her experience working for the police department, and later infiltrating a dangerous drug cartel, there'd be no telling what a desperate person was capable of doing when pushed into a corner.

"I just want to talk," Lucas said, shooting her another harmless glance. "

"As far as I'm concerned, you've already said enough. We're about to walk into a dangerous situation. We need to prepare ourselves and stay focused."

"There's no reason we can't do both."

She blew out a sigh of irritation, her attention drifting toward the window on her side of the car. Why couldn't he ever let anything go? "I'm here for this mission. Nothing else."

"Remi, goddamn it, don't do this."

"Stop," she demanded, swinging her head in his direction, and shooting him one of those, don't push my buttons today, pal, expressions. "I don't want to get into this with you."

"I can see that. But it's not going to make me shut up about it."

She groaned. "God, you infuriate the hell out of me."

He frowned, and gave a curt nod, as if he agreed with her. "Good. Because I'm going to do a lot of that, and you will as well. That's what two people who refuse to give up on each other do. They piss one another off."

Okay. She'd play this game since he was so hell bent on playing it, right now, while they were on their way to take the bastard down who wreaked havoc on their lives for the past week and a half. Fuck it. If he continued with his persistence, she'd dish it out. "You want to know what I think of you?"

"Please."

You asked for it, asshole. "You are the single most self-righteous, insufferable, jerk I've ever met in all my life. You have the nerve to talk to me about how we promised we'd always be honest with one another. Then you lied through your teeth when you told me I didn't know who your contact in Texas was, when it was your father all along. You left me in the dark and dragged me to his house, damn well knowing I had no time to prepare for that encounter."

"I'm sorry for that. But it had to be done. And I'm glad it's behind us."

"Shut it," she demanded. "I'm not finished yet."

"By all means."

The blood pumping through her veins boiled like a pressure cooker before she could get one word out. But determination to let it fly overshadowed good sense. "Even though you knew Gavin was having second thoughts about going through with the wedding, you hid it from me, and let me go through hell imagining how I was going to tell him we weren't right for one another."

"But you told him."

"That is so not the point." If she had the strength in her small body to strangle the life out of him, she would have clasped her hands around his neck and watched him struggle for air. It didn't even matter that such an act would cause him to crash the car with her in it.

"I'm sorry."

"Stop apologizing."

"You're right. I've been a dick."

Is that all he had to say for himself? "I'm afraid that response isn't going to cut it." After all, he'd only sent her world careening off its axis over the span of two days. She deserved a hell of a lot more than a simple admittance he was a dick.

He took a huge breath before he said, "Even though I told you I didn't mention we were going to Dad's house because I was afraid you wouldn't go, and we needed his help to discover where the DEA was keeping Bain, that wasn't the only reason I wanted you to go there with me."

He closed his eyes for a second, and when he opened them, she could tell by the expression on his face whatever he wanted to say wasn't going to be easy. "I knew I needed to confront my father. He's the only family I have left, and I was afraid I wouldn't get through it without you by my side for support. And, more importantly, I wanted him to see you're not the monster he's made you out to be. I thought if he let down his guard long enough to pay attention, he would realize you're an incredible, selfless, beautiful woman. You are my future, and I wanted him to know that, and to understand how I could have fallen so completely in love with you."

Her heart skipped a beat, and a compassionate, warm emotion replaced the anger that once raged inside of her. "Why didn't you tell me you needed my support? I wouldn't have jumped for joy at the prospect of facing your father again. But if I would have known you wanted me there to help you through the difficulty of confronting him, I would have agreed to do it."

That brought a hint of a grin to his face. "Would you have?"

"All you had to do was ask."

Now, he appeared as if asking for her help to stand beside him to face his father, knowing the way the man regarded her, would have been a possibility. She kept telling him when two people love each other, they work things out together. She was hopeful that message was getting through.

He cleared his throat and tightened his hands on the steering wheel. "I wish I could take back not telling you about Gavin. Even though I had this overwhelming fear you would ultimately choose him over me, I thought if I'd made you aware of what he shared with me, and that ended up being the reason you changed your mind, then it wouldn't have been because you loved me at all. I couldn't stand the thought of you making the decision to be with me without wholeheartedly wanting to."

She was floored. "What made you think I would have gone through with the wedding?"

His long fingers massaged his chin, and he appeared lost in thought. As she studied the profile of his face, a cascade of warmth twisted through her, and she was sure a blush reddened her cheeks. He was heart stopping gorgeous. Any time she stared at him too long, it weakened her knees and sent euphoria rushing to her head. The spinetingling way he caressed her in a thousand different places that last night at the cabin awakened that part of her that ached for the feel of his touch once more.

He opened his mouth to speak, shut it, then opened it again. He glanced at her with uncertainty in his eyes. "Look, my brother was always the one to follow the rules. He had a plan. I knew he could offer you a stable, secure future." He shook his head. "But me, I was—"

"Willing to take risks," she chimed in. "Not afraid to let your heart lead you where it may. Loved deeply and was always wise enough to rely on your instincts. Those noble characteristics really turned me off, I must say."

He grinned that irresistible, lopsided grin of his. "That wasn't exactly what I was going to say, but I like your version of me a lot better."

"That's because my version is the real one. I forgot to add humble, because you never give yourself credit for the admirable man you are. That's the guy I fell in love with. And once I experienced what life could be like with you, there was no way I could have gone through with that wedding."

When he stared at her, she swore she'd never

witnessed so much profound emotion in his eyes. He picked up her hand, laced his fingers through hers, and lifted it to his lips, placing a soft kiss on the back of it. Although he didn't respond with words, her heart was content enough to know he didn't have to. "Just promise me, no more dishonesty. No more hiding things from each other."

"You have my word."

"So, I'm your future, huh?" she asked, sheepishly, referring to his earlier statement.

His raised eyebrows spoke volumes. Then he frowned as if to say she ought to know what she meant to him. "The question is, am I your future."

"Of course," she said, instead of, just propose to me, you fool, and our futures will be locked together forever.

When he added nothing more than a smile, she gave one in return, even though disappointment settled into her heart. Although he loved her, she wondered if he loved her enough to give her his last name, and make a commitment to navigate the sometimes turbulent, sometimes wonderful trials of life with her. She was never more ready to take that plunge with him than she was right now.

****

Lucas slowly trained the lens of the binoculars on the rear of the house from his position behind a giant oak tree situated a good distance from the residence where Bain could be found. He signaled to Remi standing directly behind him that he witnessed movement in the backyard. "Didn't Dad say this Tish person has blonde hair?"

"I think so," Remi answered, keeping her voice at a

minimum, and remaining as still as a statue.

"Well, there's a blonde hanging clothes on the line about ten feet from the sliding glass doors."

"She alone?"

"Bain isn't anywhere in sight." He glanced at his watch, noting it was two-fifteen p.m., and then situated the binoculars back against his face. "Doesn't the football game kick off at two?"

Her silence told Lucas she probably wondered why on earth he mentioned sports when they were in the middle of a mission. "I wouldn't know," she finally answered, curiosity in her voice. "I'm not a fan."

"Well, he is," Lucas said, holding out the binoculars toward the cabin to insinuate he meant the informant tucked away inside. "He never missed a game if he could help it. I'm guessing his ass is parked on the couch in front of the living room television drinking a beer."

"So, we approach the girl first."

"I'm not exactly sure of the details regarding Delgado's involvement in this cover up, or what kind of deal he struck with Victor enabling him to keep his head intact, but I'd bet he's skating on thin ice. He'll be fearful someone might track him down here. So, he'd take precautions and lock all the doors and windows."

"Obviously, the sliding glass door in the back is unlocked, since that would have been Tish's way out of the house."

Lucas handed her the binoculars, and she immediately began her surveillance of the light-haired woman. He said, "We're not getting to that door without alerting her. She's positioned too close to it."

Remi handed back the binoculars and shrugged.

"Then we take her hostage and get her to lead us straight to Bain. But we need to hurry though, she's hanging sheets, and we can use the linens as cover to sneak up on her."

They both crept through the tall weeds, closing in on her as quickly as possible.

Lucas edged to the other side of the sheet and had the small woman in a headlock with one hand over her mouth before she had an opportunity to flinch.

Remi stepped around in front of her, raised her weapon on Tish's head, and clicked back the hammer. "You move, you die," she warned, not batting an eyelash.

Tish stopped bucking and squirming. Her muffled cries died in her throat, but Lucas could still feel her trembling. He leaned into her ear and said, "I'm going to ask you a series of questions. You're going to shake your head for no, and nod for yes. Do you understand?"

When she nodded, he said, "Is Bain in the house?"

She nodded again.

Remi asked, "Is he in the living room watching TV?"

Tish indicated he was. "I'm going to remove my hand," Lucas told her. "If you scream, Remi here will bury a slug in your forehead. Got it?" She nodded one last time, and he slowly slid his hand from her mouth, but kept a tight grip on her. "Where's the living room?"

"R...right through those d...doors," she answered, in a shaky voice that told Lucas she was subject to piss her pants at any time.

"Is the couch facing toward or away from the door?" Remi asked.

"A...a...away."

Lucas said, "I'm going to cover your mouth again, and we're all going to take a little walk through the door."

She remained silent and all three of them headed in that direction.

Remi slid the door open and stepped aside for Lucas and the hostage to enter.

An open floor plan made Bain easy to spot. Lucas zeroed in on the back of his head resting against the cushion of the couch. The television blared in the background, as the sports commentator relayed his analysis of the latest play. "Hey, honey," Bain hollered, obviously having heard the door open. "Would you bring me another beer?"

Lucas placed his gun to the side of Bain's head, clicked back the hammer and said, "Don't fucking move."

The man froze. After a few seconds, Delgado closed his eyes briefly, and without even turning his head to identify who held him captive, said, "How the hell did you find me, Kade?"

"You framed me for murder. Did you honestly think I was just going to let that go?"

"What have you done with Tish?"

"She's still alive," Lucas told him. "Whether she remains that way depends on you and what you have to tell me."

Maintaining a tight grip on Tish, gun trained on her, Remi stepped in front of Delgado. Tish stared wide-eyed at the man, trembling from head to toe. "Y…you said there w…was no chance they'd f…find us here."

Lucas grinned. "Surprise, surprise."

"What do you want?"

Lucas detected undertones of irritation in the informant's voice. Like being confronted for ruining innocent people's lives was a huge inconvenience. Too bad; the man could cry him a river some other day. "C'mon, man. You're smarter than that. What do you think I want?"

"Listen, god dammit, I don't know anything."

Lucas clucked his tongue, and peered at Remi, who slouched her shoulders in pretend disappointment. "Well, damn," she said, frowning. "Guess we should leave now. He doesn't know anything."

"Maybe I can jog his memory." Lucas slammed the butt of the gun against Delgado's head hard enough to rattle his brain.

"Owe!" The guy rubbed his noggin. "That shit hurts, asshole."

"It only gets worse with each lie you tell."

"You know I can't tell you anything. They'll kill me."

"I'm seriously considering taking care of that for them." Lucas warned, shoving the barrel of the weapon against his head again.

"I'm sorry, man," Delgado spat, shaking his head with determination. "I'd rather have you blow my brains out right now. Because what they'll do if they catch me is a whole lot worse."

So, he wanted to play it that way. Lucas locked eyes with Remi, and the expression on her face told him she was growing bored with this. The time came to advance to phase two. He nodded, and she swung into action.

She tightened the headlock on Tish, and holstered

her weapon, then with the sweep of her leg, sent the woman tumbling to the ground. She wrestled with the girl on the floor to get her into a sitting position, then she laid Tish's hand flat against the glass coffee table and whipped out the switchblade in her pocket, yanking it open. After positioning the knife against the woman's finger, she said, "Which one should I slice off first, pinky or index?

Lucas pursed his lips for show. "I'd go with the pinky. We have plenty of fingers left and we haven't even started on his yet." He tapped the muzzle of the gun against Bain's head.

"Fuck you, Kade!" Spittle dripped from Delgado's lip. "You won't do it. You're cops."

"I left the police force thirteen years ago," Remi snarled, keeping pressure on Tish's pinky finger. "He may work in law enforcement," she pointed out with a nod toward Lucas. "But he's not the one holding the knife."

Bain shook his head stubbornly. "There's no way you mother fuckers are gonna cut off her finger."

Remi stared at Lucas and munched on her lip. "I think I'm going with the index finger." When she applied enough pressure to send a few trickles of blood spilling from the woman's flesh, Tish began screaming as if an axe murderer was attacking her.

Bain's girlfriend jerked erratically, her eyes as large as saucers. "Jesus Christ!" she bellowed. "Don't let them cut my finger off, Bain! Do something."

"All right, all right," Delgado finally said. "I'll tell you what you want to know. Just please, don't hurt her anymore."

"See, that wasn't so difficult," Lucas said, as Remi

removed the blade from Tish's hand. The woman breathed a huge sigh of relief. "Who's the dirty agent I'm taking the fall for?"

Lucas needed to get down to business and put this shitshow behind him. When Delgado didn't respond, Lucas told Remi, "Go ahead. Slice off the rest of the finger."

"Okay! I'll tell you! Just give me a minute, man."

"Now works better for me," Lucas told him while Remi reapplied pressure to Tish's finger.

"It's Dominick Barlow," Bain blurted out.

The scrawny mother fucker was playing games. "Victor shot Barlow in the chest. I saw it."

"You only saw what they wanted you to see."

Lucas' mind wandered back to the scene that unfolded in the packing plant after they shuffled him into the back room and forced him to confront his worst fear. He witnessed his partner strapped to a chair. Victor lifted the gun to his chest and shot him point blank in the heart. No one walks away from that.

Anger boiled inside his gut for the lies the informant spouted in an obvious effort to cover for the real corrupt DEA agent behind this whole thing. He took the front of the man's shirt in one fist and with a swift jerk, lifted the skinny son-of-a-bitch over the back of the couch, and threw him onto the floor like a sack of potatoes. Christ, that hurt. He wanted to recoil in pain, but revealing the slightest indication of weakness would only encourage the informant to fight back. He couldn't take that risk.

When Bain landed on his back with a thud, he struggled to catch his breath as he writhed on the ground.

Lucas bit back the pain shooting through his abdomen and grabbed him, clasping one hand around his throat, and holding the firearm snugly against the side of his skull with the other. "You're going to tell me who the hell set me up, or I swear to God your girlfriend will be mopping your brains off the floor with no fucking fingers. You feel me?"

"He's telling the truth," Tish hollered, then busted out in uncontrollable sobs.

Lucas eased up on choking the scumbag long enough to stare at his girlfriend.

The woman sucked air into her lungs and fought to gain control of her emotions. "It was fake. The gun. The blood. All of it."

"What the fuck is she talking about?" Lucas said, staring down into Delgado's eyes, his own reflecting a warning if he lied, he wouldn't hesitate to finish him off.

Bain swallowed hard and said in a hoarse voice, "Victor got his hands on a prop firearm. You know, like the ones they use on movie sets. The blood you saw wasn't real. It came from a pouch inside Barlow's shirt."

"No way." Remi shook her head, completely dismissing Bain's statement. "I saw Dominick's body when I pulled you out of there," she said, staring dead at Lucas. "His face looked like someone took a meat clever to it."

"That was makeup," Delgado insisted. "Victor knows someone who works as a makeup artist. How do you think he got the fake gun and blood?"

Remi said, "It was at least an hour before I got to you, Luc. They left your partner sitting in that chair, dead. There's no way that wasn't real."

"I told you," the informant maintained. "You only saw what they wanted you to see."

Lucas hauled Delgado up by his shirt into a sitting position. "Why would Dominick set me up?"

"My back is fuckin killing me, man. Help me over to the couch, make her take that damn knife away from Tish, and I'll tell you everything. You have my word."

****

"Let me get this straight," Lucas said, pacing in front of the couch where Bain and his girlfriend sat while Remi kept a gun trained on the two lovebirds. "You're telling me my partner, Dominick Barlow is the DEA agent who's working with the cartel?"

"The internal investigation was putting heat on him," Delgado admitted. "Someone from the Dallas PD suspected a few of the cops were running drugs and money for the cartel. A few of the corrupt officers were brought in for questioning. And from what I was told, one of them started singing like a robin in a pear tree. When Barlow's name came up, Victor formulated a plan to make it look like you killed Dominick. That would take him out of the equation and put you in the hot seat as the dirty DEA agent."

The more Lucas listened to Bain talk, the more he realized how elaborate this whole set up was. Jesus, his own partner sold him out for exactly how much? He didn't even know what role Barlow played in the cartel, let alone how much money he raked in due to his involvement. Based on how many times they'd worked together on assignments, he assumed the guy must have been paid quite well to have been willing to go along with the plan to frame him for murder. During this entire undercover sting he never had a clue his partner was stabbing him in the back. How do you work alongside someone in such close quarters and not suspect they're up to no good?

And Remi was simply a loose end that needed to be tied up.

"Who's burnt body did they pull out of the warehouse, then?" Remi asked, appearing skeptical about this whole thing.

Lucas couldn't blame her for being unconvinced. The tale Bain spun seemed far-fetched and hard to swallow. But it made perfect sense Barlow was the dirty agent involved. He'd been on the inside of the investigations into the cartel. They could never get the goods on Craven, even though they'd been on his ass for years. Dominick Barlow was the reason the slimy bastard slipped through the cracks time and time again.

"I don't know," Delgado said in answer to Remi's question.

The guy ran his fingers through his hair, while Tish gazed into the distance, as if her life was over. The expression on both of their faces reminded Lucas of criminals who were busted in the act. They found themselves at the end of the road. They had nowhere to turn.

"It was some small-time drug dealer who worked for the cartel. The poor bastard had no family. No one to answer to." This time when the informant spoke, the tone of his voice displayed hopelessness. "He had a great physical likeness to Barlow. About the same height. The same weight. That's why Victor chose him to use as Dom's dead body."

People like Craven had no limit to the despicable

acts they were willing to commit. They'd take anyone out and never think twice about it. Lucas squared his eyes on Delgado. "You were supposed to be working for the agency, but you were working for the cartel. So, you knew about Dominick all along?"

Bain shook his head as if to immediately dispel the accusation. "It wasn't like that, man. I had no clue Barlow was playing the other side until Victor came to me and offered an ultimatum. Either I could go along with them and help them out, or they'd slit my throat right then and there. They needed an eyewitness who was willing to say they saw you kill Dominick. It's not like they gave me a choice."

"So, where is Barlow now? Lucas wanted to know.

"Where do you think?" Bain said, cocking his head. "He sure as hell ain't chillin at his apartment in Dallas."

It took less than a second for the whereabouts of his supposed dead partner to click. Lucas frowned, already formulating a plan to extract Dominick from Craven's house before his next statement reached his lips. "Is Victor there with him or is he away on business?"

"Doesn't matter," Bain answered, "You know as well as I do, nobody's going near Craven's house without getting blown to smithereens."

Lucas produced a small recording device from the pocket of his coat, held it up, and said, "You just cleared my name. Thank you."

Fear washed over Delgado's face in the space of a heartbeat. "And you just signed my death warrant, man. When Victor gets wind I spilled the beans, he'll come for my head.

Lucas dug in his coat pocket again, this time coming out with a roll of duct tape. He tossed it on the coffee table and fixed his attention on Remi as she stood there, not flinching, steadily training her weapon on the duo. She reminded him of a police officer on official business. All she needed was the uniform. It instantly roused memories of the good old days. And he wondered if she'd ever go back to the job she once loved.

"Hey, Remi?"

Her gaze flicked up to him, and she winked. He grinned. "You mind securing these two. I have a phone call to make?"

Bain spoke up and said, "Thanks to you, I'd be safer in prison than I would out on the streets. There's no need to tie me up. It's not like I'm going anywhere."

Lucas shrugged while Remi lowered the weapon. "Guess you got a point. In light of your present situation, maybe we can make a deal."

Chapter Twelve

Lucas carefully examined the facial expressions of Frank Tolliver, the special agent in charge of the DEA's Special Operation Division, as the man sat in a chair in the living room of the cabin where Remi and Lucas had confronted Delgado. Tolliver's feet were planted firmly on the ground, and his fist tucked under his chin as he listened to the voices coming from the handheld tape recorder.

Once the recording reached its end, Lucas clicked the stop button. Everyone in attendance remained silent as the SAC zeroed in on Bain Delgado. "The DEA is willing to offer you immunity for your cooperation in the capture of Agent Dominick Barlow."

Shock registered in Bain's eyes as he stared at Tolliver for a moment, then settled his attention on Lucas. "Man, you know I'm dead after this. I've already said too much."

"Is it protection you want?" Tolliver countered.

"There's not enough protection in the world to keep Craven away from me." The informant shivered, obviously thinking about what the drug lord planned to do to him when he found out he'd snitched.

The SAC shook his head. "The DEA has powerful resources. If we want you hid, the US president won't even be able to find you. Of course, you'll have to agree to relocate to a different state, and we'll have to

216

change your name, social security number, you catch my drift."

"What about Tish?" Delgado asked and offered his lady love a look of adoration.

Tolliver pursed his lips. "We'll extend the protection to her. But you both need to understand you can never again contact acquaintances, family, or anyone else from your past. At least not until we have Victor Craven and his men behind bars. And—you'll have to agree to testify against them in court."

A slight tremble moved across Bain's lips.

Tish placed her hand on his shoulder and squeezed. "It'll be all right, babe. We need to take this deal. I don't want you to go back to prison. This is our only way out."

"If it makes you feel any better," Tolliver offered, "we've never lost anyone through the witness protection program."

"Your girlfriend's right," Lucas added. "This is your only chance at a fresh start. Craven will never find you. He's going to prison for a long time."

After searching Lucas' eyes for a solid minute, Delgado relented, averted his attention, and bobbed his head. "Okay." Then he stared at Tolliver. "What do you want me to do?"

"I think if we play our cards right," Lucas said, "we can get a drop on the next narcotics shipment."

Tolliver stood and snapped his fingers. "Exactly what I'm thinking."

"Whoa." Delgado put his hand up in the universal stop gesture. "No way I'm gathering that intel. That's not part of the deal we just made."

After standing silently through the whole

conversation, Remi said, "That'll be Dominick Barlow's job."

"What do you mean?" Delgado asked, still visibly shaken by the idea of betraying Victor.

"I have an idea," she said, as Lucas and the rest of the crew stared at her curiously. "You're going to get Barlow on the phone." She pointed at Delgado, shaking her finger as if she'd had an epiphany. "And I know exactly what you're going to tell him."

****

Lucas strolled into the kitchen of the cabin, grabbed a glass from the cupboard, and stepped over to the sink for some water. As everyone in the living room busied themselves with the preparations for Bain to make that call to Dom, he took a much-needed moment to collect himself. He had at last cleared his name. But even as relief washed over him for that accomplishment, he couldn't relax yet. More work required his attention before the bastard responsible for setting him up would be locked behind prison bars where he damn well belonged. Out of all the people he might have suspected was behind this effort to frame him, he would have never guessed it would have been his partner. So much for thinking you knew someone. At least Dominick Barlow would get what's coming to him.

Someone cleared their throat, and his attention swung in the direction of the noise. His father stepped into the room, moseyed over to the counter next to Lucas, and leaned against it, staring at the wall opposite his son. Lucas closed his eyes and said, "Did I thank you for calling Tolliver and convincing him to come out here?"

"I don't need thanks," Ethan said.

Immediately after he placed that call to his dad, the guy swung into action. He contacted the SAC, let him know what went down at the cabin, and convinced him to accompany him there. Ethan never gave himself credit for the good things he did in life. Lucas imagined he'd acquired that trait from his old man, too. At least, according to Remi, he did. Until this moment, he'd never really considered how much he had in common with his father.

"Well, this is me thanking you," he said with a half grin. "Because you didn't have to help me and Remi the way you did."

"You're right about me, you know," Ethan said out of the blue.

Lucas set down the glass in his hand, and stared at him, unsure what he meant.

"What you said back at the house. How I always felt the need to control your brother's life."

Hell would have frozen over before he'd ever dreamed those words would spill from his father's mouth. "It's true." Ethan sighed, now staring at the floor. "I put pressure on your brother to propose to Remi. I never considered he might not have wanted that."

Lucas fought the urge to respond. Something told him his dad wasn't quite finished. "And I ignored your mother when she tried to make me see what an unreasonable bastard I was being."

"Dad, I—"

"No. I blamed you for your mother's death. And I shouldn't have done that."

Vindication was a funny thing. Although he waited

years for his father to realize what he did, now that it happened, it didn't feel the way he imagined it would. There was no long-awaited emotion of satisfaction, no, I told you so reactions running through his mind, only sadness and regret for the many years that were waisted, and a feeling of great loss for a father/son relationship that could have healed much sooner.

"It's okay," he told Ethan. "Life doesn't come with an instruction manual. We're all just a bunch of idiots stumbling our way through it and hoping for the best."

"Well, I'm sorry I allowed my grief to grow into anger, and then I turned in on you. I can only hope you'll forgive an old, stupid man for putting you through that."

Knowing his father the way he did, Lucas understood the courage it took for him to admit his wrongdoing and apologize. He clapped him on the shoulder and said, "I already have."

Ethan grabbed onto him and took him into an embrace. "I love you, son. And I'm glad you came home."

Forgiveness and love overflowed from Lucas' heart in that moment, and he tightened the hold his dad had on him, a tear rolling down his face. Although he'd known what the pain of losing loved ones felt like because of his mom and brother, this was the experience of regaining someone you lost.

"I love you too, Dad. And I'm more thankful for your help than you'll ever know."

The shuffling of feet told Lucas someone entered the room. He broke the embrace and caught a glimpse of Remi standing as still as a statue just inside the entrance. She lowered her gaze as if realizing she'd interrupted something important. After a moment, she pointed toward the living room. "Everyone's ready."

Not as ready as him to put this whole nightmare behind them. Once Bain made contact with Dom, they'd all agreed everything would go according to the plan Remi came up with. The time had come to get the ball rolling and put the criminals who set him up away for a long, long time.

Lucas straightened, focused his attention in the other direction to discreetly swipe the tear from his eye, then nodded at Remi as if to signal his eagerness to go in there and lay a trap for a partner who intended to send him down the river so the man could continue his criminal activities.

Remi offered her hand. He took it and they strolled into the living room together, Ethan close on their heels.

Delgado peered up at him and Remi from his position on the couch. Sweat dotted the man's forehead and dripped from the tip of his nose despite the comfortable temperature inside the cabin. The informant's attention darted from one person to the other, and his Adam's apple bobbed with each swallow he took.

"Hey, Bain," Lucas said. "What you're about to do is no different than what you've been doing in this undercover operation all along. You've been playing a role. This is just more acting. You know how to do this."

Bain finally nodded, took a deep breath, and snatched up the burner phone from the coffee table.

Before he could finish punching in the digits, Tolliver said, "Remember, if he asks why you have the phone on speaker, tell him there's a malfunction with the device, and that's the only way you can hear him."

"Got it." He continued making the call.

Dominick Barlow picked up on the third ring. *"Why are you calling me?"* he barked, *"Victor told you not to call unless it was a life and death."*

"I thought you'd want to know Lucas and Remi stopped by looking for you."

Everyone in the room held their breath. And then Barlow said, *"How the fuck is that possible?"*

"Seems your boy, Draco Vargas, spilled the beans you're still alive and working for the cartel."

"That son-of-a-bitch! I knew I couldn't trust him."

Lucas grinned at how easy it was to get criminals to turn on each other. But at the same time the familiar sound of Barlow's voice sent a chilling reminder that this man was never his friend. How many times had he trusted Dom and never gave the man's intentions a second thought? It chilled him to the bone Dom could be this calculated and corrupt. Worse, Lucas had played right into his hands.

"They offered Vargas immunity to cough up your name, man," Bain said, staring at Lucas.

"Do they know I'm at Victor's?"

"Obviously not, or they wouldn't have come here looking for you."

"You didn't tell them?"

Lucas picked up a note of panic in Dom's voice. Evidently, the trouble the bastard found himself in was sinking in right about now. Good, he hoped the scumbag's heart was beating out of his chest, and he was sweating a big enough puddle to fill a horse's trough.

"Dude, there's no way in hell I'd cross Victor ever again. I'm lucky he let me live the first time."

"Wait, have you got me on speaker? I'm hearing an echo."

Bain's attention immediately swept toward Tolliver, and the agent nodded, signaling for the informant to spill the excuse they rehearsed before he'd made the call. When he did, a long minute of silence came from Dom. Delgado took the initiative to plow right into his next statement. "Listen, man. I heard them talking when they were on the porch. The window was cracked, and I'm pretty sure they didn't know I could hear them."

"What did they say?" It became apparent Barlow would have grasped onto the slightest indication there still existed a chance he could get out of this unscathed. Unbeknownst to him, his freedom ticked away like the hands of an alarm clock winding down to its end. Lucas could hardly wait to see his face when he confronted him.

"They think you're still in New York, and they're catching a flight out tonight. They said something about going back to Remi's apartment. She has some weapons and ammo there. You need to get your ass over there and wait. It's the only way to get the jump on them."

"Should I tell Victor?" From the tone of his voice, Lucas imagined his old partner quaking in his shoes right about now. A thousand disturbing scenarios must be running through his mind. And things were only going to get worse from here on out for the dirty agent.

Bain's attention drifted over to Tish, and she nodded her encouragement. *You're doing great, babe,*

223

she mouthed.

He closed his eyes for a moment, then continued. "Once Victor finds out you've been compromised, he'll kill your ass just to save himself the trouble of dealing with this situation. The fact Lucas Kade knows you're alive could bring a shit ton of heat down on Craven and his whole operation. You know how ruthless that motherfucker can be. You need to take care of this yourself."

"Why are you doing this, man?" Barlow asked. *"It's not like you owe me anything. You informed for the DEA. If Victor hadn't confronted you and forced you to help him out, you'd still be working for them."*

As Bain sat there, obviously considering what believable excuse he could offer in return, Lucas couldn't help but notice the confidence the man now exhibited, from the determined way he held himself, to the stiff set of his jaw. Tish's small gesture of support must have done the trick. The informant's reaction to his girl's sentiments made Bain Delgado a little more human in Lucas' eyes.

Now when Delgado spoke, he did it with conviction. "Listen, I lied to the authorities here, man. I've been playing them this whole time to cover you and Victor's asses. If they find out about that, I'm never getting out of prison. You understand? So, it's best for all of us if you take Lucas Kade and Remi Shaw out of the picture. This is your only chance."

A long sigh, and then, *"Okay. I'll be there waiting for them."*

As soon as Bain ended the call, cheers erupted throughout the room. Lucas clapped Delgado on the shoulder, and a lopsided grin developed across the guy's face.

"Well done," Tolliver said, and then directed his attention toward Lucas. "It's time for me to contact the authorities in New York and get them in place to capture Barlow when he enters the apartment."

Butterflies danced in Lucas' stomach. If all went as planned, in a few hours, his corrupt partner would be taken into custody by the NYPD, and then extradited back to Texas where Lucas would come face-to-face with him on his turf. And then he would be one step closer to closing out the biggest bust of his career.

****

"You look good for a dead man," Lucas told Dominick Barlow, as he strolled into the interrogation room inside the Dallas DEA headquarters.

It took a bit of bureaucratic muscle, and some high-level officials willing to twist some arms and make some deals to get the dirty agent on a plane bound to Texas tonight. Lucas now stood staring at Dom. And when he took in the man's discomfort, sitting there, the shackles around his wrists chained to a heavy-duty eye bolt affixed to the metal table, he had to admit, it was worth the wait. The guy's face twisted in what Lucas could only define as agony. It must have been a real bitch sitting on the opposite side of the interrogation table. He recalled the many times Barlow himself assisted in cross-examinations. Those days were over. The best the guy could hope for now would be to steer clear of any violent criminals in a maximum security facility who might decide they wanted his cornbread in the chow hall.

Miles Daxton, the special agent seated across the table from his dirty ex-partner took his cue, scraped back his chair, and stood. "It's nice to have you back, man," he said, greeting Lucas at the door.

Lucas nodded his appreciation for the kind words and stepped out of the way for the agent to leave the room. Hinges creaked behind him alerting him Daxton shut the door. He stared at Dominick, and from the appearance of things, the man wouldn't be hard to crack.

The first words bursting out of Barlow's mouth were, "I didn't have a choice. You know how dangerous Victor is. If I didn't go along with him, he would have killed me."

Lucas frowned as he sat in the chair Daxton abandoned. Warmth still generated from the seat, inviting him to settle in and get comfortable. "We all have a choice," he replied, in a dangerously calm voice. "You chose to double cross me."

"As I recall," Lucas continued, leaning across the table to stare with intensity into Dominick's soulless eyes, "You sat there in that chair in the packing plant all dolled up in your Hollywood makeup, and your pretend black eye, and watched them beat the living shit out of me. Is that how you remember it? Because even though Victor's dog kicked me in the head so hard it knocked me out, I still can't seem to shake that memory from my mind."

"Listen, man, I'm sorry. I didn't know Craven would go that far. I told him not to involve you in this. There were other agents who could have taken the fall, but—"

"Other agents?" Lucas' calm disposition vanished in an instant. A knot of repulsion twisted in his gut for the blatant disregard this low life had for innocent lives.

It didn't seem to matter who got caught in the crossfire, just so long as the bastard could save his own hide. "So, if it wouldn't have been me, it would have been some other unfortunate soul you planned to destroy? You worked alongside these people, yet you were willing to frame them for a crime they didn't commit?"

Barlow lowered his head and shrugged his shoulders. "Things got out of hand. You don't know how many times I wanted to walk away. But Victor would have never let me do that."

"So, Craven paid you to keep the heat off of him all these years?"

"It started out that way. But he became more demanding. The truth is," he admitted, "I took the money and did whatever Victor asked me. It was either I do that, or I'd end up like all the other people who crossed him." Dominick appeared upset. But Lucas read his emotions like a book. He had no remorse for the people he'd hurt. The motherfucker regretted getting caught.

Lucas reflected on his intentions before he entered the room. He'd planned to punch Dom's lights out, then spit in his face. The scumbag deserved all that and more. But it was clear karma already caught up with him. And although he'd love nothing more than to bring the full weight of the law down on Craven and his allies, the desire for vengeance had to go onto the back burner while he got down to the business of being an agent.

"The prosecution is willing to offer you a lesser prison sentence if you turn Victor over to the authorities."

Examining Dom's face told Lucas he expected

such an offer. No surprise there. Barlow worked in law enforcement long enough to know the logistics of these deals. Hell, he even orchestrated a few himself. "What do you want me to do?"

"We want intel on Craven's next drug shipment."

"What makes you think I know that information?"

"If you don't, you're going to get it."

Now the man's eyes glazed over with confidence, as if to remind Lucas not to underestimate his intelligence. "I want immunity like you offered to Draco."

Lucas grinned when he said, "There is no immunity deal for Draco, because he was never involved."

The cocky expression on Barlow's face slowly melted away. The burning realization he'd been duped took its place. He cleared his throat and averted his attention. "So, Bain lied to me when he said Vargas gave me up."

"You can't really blame the guy," Lucas said, enjoying the way the tide had turned. "We gave him immunity to reel you in."

"You gave him immunity?" Dominick's lips couldn't have stretched any tighter across his face, showing his profound displeasure at falling for their trickery.

"Of course, we did. You were the bigger target. You know how this works. There was a time when you would have been sitting in the chair I am now, and you would have cut the same deal. Isn't that right?"

Judging from the way his ex-partner shifted uncomfortably in his seat, Lucas had no doubt he despised being reminded of the way things were when he was an agent working for the DEA. The thought probably made him sick to his stomach considering the situation he now found himself in.

The chains connected to the shackles around Dominick's wrists rattled as he leaned back in his chair. "I knew the minute those cops converged on me when I entered Remi's apartment, Bain was working for the DEA again. That scrawny son-of-a-bitch not only set me up, but he set you up. And here you are willing to forgive him and offer him immunity."

"It was a wise move, don't you think? After all, it was his cooperation that led you straight into an ambush. Without his assistance, we wouldn't be sitting here enjoying each other's company right now." Lucas frowned, giving off the impression he had complete control of his emotions, and Barlow didn't have a chance in hell of breaking through that barrier. "Me and Delgado have worked through our issues. Besides he's small potatoes compared to you, isn't that right?"

"I want immunity or I'm not doing shit for you!"

Lucas couldn't have been more amused at Barlow's loss of control. Watching everything in the man's world crumble around his shackled ankles pleased him to no end. "You're a sworn DEA agent, working for the drug cartel. You tried to set another agent up to keep the authorities from discovering your involvement. Then there's the little matter of a dead guy everyone thought was you. That's a murder charge."

"I didn't kill that man. Victor took care of that."

"You'll go down for accessory to murder, my friend, along with a shitload of additional charges the DA is chomping at the bit to charge you with. You can either rot in prison until the day you die, or you can get out in twenty years, lay low, and live the rest of your miserable life as a free man. You know you're going down for this. How long depends on what you decide right now."

Dominick huffed and puffed, wiggled around in his chair, and stomped his foot like a six-year-old. The tantrum revealed a side of Barlow he'd never seen before. But then again, there obviously existed a lot about the man he didn't know.

"Fine!" The fire shooting from his ex-partner's eyes could have melted steel. "There's a shipment all right. It's the biggest one yet. But before I agree to help with the bust, I want a deal with the DA in writing. Then and only then," he said, lifting his manacled hand and pointing at Lucas, as if he had some clout when it came to deciding his fate, "will I do what you want me to do."

Lucas shuffled out of his chair, snatched up the notepad the previous investigator left sitting on the table, and grinned down at the asshole who did everything in his power to hang him out to dry. "I'll talk to Tolliver and see what he can do."

When he approached the door, an idea struck him, and he turned back toward Dominick. "You look thirsty, man. Do you want a coke or something?"

The man stopped sulking long enough to say, "That would be nice."

"Well, fuck you. You're not getting one." With that, he strolled out of the room and slammed the door.

Chapter Thirteen

Lucas stared at Remi as she slept peacefully in his bed. Her legs were tangled in his sheets with her back exposed to the sunlight drifting in through the window down to her hips. He wandered into the room to wake her, but now that he found her this way, the temptation to simply stand there and take her in, laying there on her stomach, her red hair spilling across her shoulder, swept over him like a heatwave.

He sat down in the lounge chair close to his bed, glanced at his watch, and then crossed one leg on top of the other knee. He still had a few minutes to spare before he'd have to rouse her awake so they would make it to the surveillance van where Tolliver and other DEA agents waited to intercept the conversation between Barlow and Craven as the two traveled to the shipping sight.

Over the past week, while they waited for specifics on the date of Craven's next shipment, he failed to take time to reflect on having his old life back—or having the woman he loved in his house. He made up for it in this moment. As he sat there, staring at Remi, it occurred to him he did have a future.

And he would spend the rest of his days with the woman he always loved.

With that in mind, he slipped his hand into his pocket and produced the velvet covered box he'd carried for the last two days. He opened it and stared at the diamond engagement ring nestled inside. Victor asked for her hand in marriage once and offered a much bigger ring. But Lucas could not forget the crestfallen expression in her eyes when the man presented it to her, and the way she did her best to hide her true feelings.

Would he see that same reflection on her face when he asked her to marry him? Would the simple life he could offer her be enough? Thirteen years ago, the lack of confidence he could provide for her kept him from coming clean about Gavin, and how he was having second thoughts about their marriage. And the fact one of the wealthiest men he knew proposed to her—albeit he was a drug lord—did nothing to boost his confidence.

When she began to stir, he slipped the box back into his pocket. Her eyes flickered open and zeroed in on him as a smile lifted her lips.

She sat up, bunching the sheet around her chest. "Good morning."

A lopsided grin developed across his face. "You hiding them from me now?" he said, referring to her breasts.

She let loose a snort. "Something tells me it's necessary, since I'm guessing I don't have much time for a shower."

She was right. Seeing her naked body would instantly cause a certain part of his to harden, and they'd never make it to the meet up on time. "All right," he said, standing up and ambling toward her. He ran his fingers through her morning hair until he cradled the back of her head, and leaned in to kiss her in a slow, seductive movement.

When he stepped away, she licked her lips, a soft and yielding expression glowing in her eyes. And he said in a hoarse voice, "As long as I can have a raincheck." Then he slipped his hand beneath the sheet and molded it around her breast, fondling her.

When he stepped away, she said before he got to the door, "You are nothing but a tease, sir."

He grinned and gazed back at her, winking. "No, that was just a small sample of what I plan to do to you later." Then he exited the room and strolled down the hall.

His phone rang as he entered the living room. He snatched it out of his pocket and recognized his father's number. "Good morning," he said, sitting down onto the sofa.

"I was calling to wish you luck on the big bust today," Ethan said.

"You're going to be there, right?"

"Of course. I just don't know how much I trust Barlow to do the right thing."

"Don't start having second thoughts now, Dad."

Although Lucas would be an idiot not to have considered the same scenario. After what his ex-partner did, he couldn't trust him as far as he could throw him. But they'd had enough agents on Barlow's tail, surveilling his every move, and intercepting all his conversations, it would have been challenging for the bastard to plan an escape or tip Craven off to their intentions. And with the vast number of law enforcement hidden in the shadows, Lucas couldn't imagine Dominick having any chance to get away. Besides, this wasn't the same shipping plant as the one he'd been lured to in New York. There was only one road leading out of this one—and would be heavily guarded by the SWAT and DEA.

"Don't worry," Lucas said, shaking his head to dispel his own misgivings. "We're going to get these bastards today. Then we can put this behind us."

"You're right. We've been as thorough as we can be putting this raid together. Everything's going to go according to plan."

"Sure, it is." Now if Lucas could only convince himself of that.

"All right, son. I'll see you there."

When the call ended, he stood, and slipped his phone back into his pocket, wanting to kick himself for letting doubt cloud the confidence he'd worked so hard to build. Everything would go off without a hitch. It had to.

****

Remi glanced back at the trail she and Lucas had hiked for the last twenty minutes. After loosening the knot of the bandana around her neck, she used the material to pat the sweat along the back of her neck. "We're almost there," Lucas said, out of breath, as he plodded along beside her, and pointed toward the black surveillance van sitting off in the distance.

She zeroed in on the outline of the vehicle nestled in between high weeds and dense shrubbery. She'd already been briefed on the location the team chose to set up surveillance. The spot was hidden from sight, yet close enough to the shipping plant when Lucas needed to hightail it to the scene, he could arrive by foot within a few minutes.

Lucas threw open the back door of the van, and the attention of those huddling inside focused on them in a flash. Tolliver grinned from his post seated in front of a large screen and slid the headphones from his ears to rest around his neck. "Right on time," he said, motioning for them to climb inside.

A tall, slender woman in a DEA windbreaker stared into his eyes for a minute too long before she handed him a set of headphones. "This thing you got going on," she said, stepping back and summing up his new style of hair, "different than what I'm used to but…" She pursed her lips as if to indicate she liked what she saw. "I love the black color. It looks good on you, Kade."

Lucas cleared his throat, stabbing his eyes in the opposite direction. And within a second it hit Remi he'd been intimate with this woman at one time.

She did her best to shake off the instant pang of jealousy and reminded herself they'd been apart for thirteen years. Besides, he wasn't the only one who'd had a sexual relationship in that time. She'd like to take up the defense that Lucas didn't come face to face with her past lovers. But since he'd been in Victor's mansion while she slept in Craven's bed, that assertion didn't hold water.

"Thanks, Cat," he said, appearing as comfortable as a lamb stumbling into a lion's den.

Cat, huh? Was that the short version of the woman's name? If it was, he sure seemed familiar enough to use it.

He peered at Remi, grinned proudly, and slipped a hand around her waist to give it a squeeze. "This is my girlfriend, Remi," he said, leaning over and placing a soft kiss on her cheek. "She has some mean beautician skills."

"Oh," the woman said, her attention raking her up and down. "I'm Catherine. Nice to meet you. Me and Lucas worked together quite a bit."

"Yes," Remi responded, satisfied with the way Lucas handled the situation. "I gathered that."

Catherine lost her smile, cleared her throat, and then stepped away, fiddling with some equipment knobs while Lucas grabbed another set of headphones and handed them to Remi.

Tolliver waved them over to the audio track he'd been monitoring. "Barlow's traveling with Craven. They're headed to the shipping plant. We're intercepting the conversation."

As soon as Remi situated the headphones against her ears, she picked up Victor's voice immediately. *"Things didn't work out too well for the Kade brothers, did they?"*

Cracking came over the recording; she imagined it was the effect of Dominick moving around or shuffling the listening device. *"What do you mean?"*

"You really don't know, do you?" Victor laughed. *"Remember when Gavin Kade hung himself inside the chapel the day he and Remi were supposed to be married?"*

"I was there when they buried him," Barlow responded. *"I didn't know Lucas too well at the time, but his whole family looked pretty devastated. If I can recall, Remi never even showed her face at the funeral."*

Craven chuckled derisively. *"Can you blame her? That whole family and half the police force held her responsible for his death. Those stupid motherfuckers. They harassed her so badly, she had to leave town.*

Start over somewhere else."

The memories crashed over Remi, pelting her like an unforgiving hailstorm. Victor was right. They persecuted her mercilessly and held her up as the person solely responsible for the untimely death of a good officer and noble man. Their ruthless attacks on her integrity forced her to hightail it out of this town, and never look back.

She peered over at Lucas, and he stared dead at her, sorrow and understanding etched into those beautiful, chocolate eyes. He mouthed, *I love you,* and just like that, those torturous emotions from long ago melted away. He was her saving grace, and the one person who remained faithfully in her corner. In that moment, she instantly regretted it took her thirteen years to figure that out.

"I have to admit though," Craven's voice broke her thoughts. *"it broke my heart I couldn't be honest with her. I knew she'd go crazy if I told her the truth. I do love her, you know. That's the bitch about this whole thing."*

More astonishing than the fact he claimed he loved her, was his mentioning he couldn't tell her the truth. *What truth was he talking about?*

Craven let out a long sigh, then admitted, *"She left me no choice dragging her in the middle of the set up with Lucas. She hid the fact from me that she knew the asshole. Granted, I already knew he was an undercover agent. But still, she didn't have enough loyalty to tell me the truth. If Kade had gotten away with taking me down, she would have sat back and let him do it."*

As Dominick voiced his approval of the drug lord's sentiments, Remi wondered how she could have ever come to care one iota for Victor Craven. At one point, she went so far as to allow herself to believe he wanted the best for her, that he'd have her back no matter what. Now, she couldn't tell whether she'd gotten so wrapped up in the illusion her undercover persona created, or if the yearning for her broken heart to have a love like Lucas' drove her to believe Craven actually cared for her. But he was right about one thing. If it came to saving Lucas Kade, she would have thrown Victor to the wolves without a second thought.

"I have to ask myself sometimes," Craven said, a poignant tone in his voice. *"Was it all a farce? Did she ever care about me at all? I gave her the world and treated her like a queen."*

"Maybe she loved the guy," Barlow told him. *"You know. Never got over him."*

"I know exactly how that feels, because despite what she did to me, I still love her."

How noble. Remi couldn't help the anger that welled inside her. Despite the fact he framed her for aiding in a murder, he claimed he loved her. The son-of-a-bitch wouldn't know the first thing about love if it paraded in front of him and gave him a lap dance. Yeah, asshole, I knew about them too.

Dominick said, *"You mentioned something that if she ever found out the truth, she'd go crazy? What were you talking about?"*

After a minute of silence that seemed to stretch on forever, Victor said, *"Gavin Kade didn't kill himself. Mendoza snuck into his dressing room and hung him with his own belt."*

****

As that shock penetrated Remi's skull, Barlow

squawked, *"Wait a minute, are you talking about Miguel Mendoza? Isn't he one of the cops being investigated by internal affairs right now?"*

"The very one," Victor confirmed.

This time, when Remi focused on Lucas, his jaw went rock stiff and his eyes filled with rage. Scanning the faces of everyone in attendance inside the cramped surveillance van instantly told her she wasn't the only one stunned beyond belief.

"Gavin couldn't keep his mouth shut," Craven said. *"He was being paid to look the other way while Mendoza and a few of the others conducted business for me. Then he grew a conscience. Tried to convince a few of his buddies at the PD, also on my payroll, they should come clean. Tell the captain what was going on."*

The more Remi considered Victor's unbelievable tale, the more clearly she recalled the extra money Gavin seemed to snatch out of thin air. The expensive gifts he showered her, the gold watch he bought for himself, and the willingness to pick up the tab when they were out with friends. Craven paid Gavin to turn the other cheek while corrupt cops did the cartel's dirty deeds.

And the whole time, while the guilt of Gavin's suicide ate at her, Victor knew the truth, and let her suffer.

"That stupid son-of-a-bitch," Craven said. *"Going to the authorities meant Gavin would have been locked up himself. The apple didn't fall far from that tree, huh?"*

"What does that mean?" Barlow asked.

"It means his father and older brother are so

committed to serving justice, they can't see the forest for the trees. You know, the money they could have made by working for me. Gavin wouldn't be persuaded to bring his family in on our little business deals. Things would have gone much smoother if I'd had all the Kade's in my pocket. But Gavin suffered from a guilty conscience. And in the end, integrity got him killed."

Remi swallowed hard, knowing that calling off the wedding gave Craven the perfect cover to commit murder. The way Gavin died led everyone to believe he committed suicide because she dumped him at the altar. That's why no one questioned his death.

Ultimately, she helped them kill Gavin.

As that particular horror sunk in, she slid the headphones from her head and let them fall to the workstation. She backstepped toward the rear doors until her ass thudded against the hard metal, then spun around, tugged on the handle, and stumbled outside.

Someone called her name, but she raced forward as if in a trance, tears streaming down her face.

Then warm arms wrapped her up from behind, and before she knew it, a familiar, tender voice whispered in her ear. "Hey, Gavin's death was not your fault. Don't you dare start blaming yourself again. Do you hear me?"

She could have broken free of Lucas' hold without much effort. But the love and warmth flowing from his body instantly convinced her she belonged in the salvation of his arms.

"I know it's a shock," he said, resting his chin on her shoulder. "But now that we know my brother was murdered, the person responsible will be held to account. This is not your cross to bear any longer. You were just the girl who cared enough to tell the truth. And I, for one, love you for your bleeding heart. I always have."

Jesus, he was right. She could have taken the coward's way out and married a man that not only did she not love, but one that didn't love her in return. It just happened to be an unimaginable twist of fate someone planned to murder Gavin on the day she confronted him with what they both already knew: That they didn't love each other, and she saw it in his eyes that day. Call what happened to Gavin a tragic coincidence or the crimes he'd committed finally catching up with him. Either way, it was high time to absolve herself from the responsibility the actions his choices caused.

She sniffled, swiped the tears from her face, and twisted in Luc's embrace. The moment she glared into those warm, understanding eyes, she couldn't deny Lucas Kade was her forever home, and she laid her head on his shoulder. "I'm sorry," she whispered against his neck. "Gavin was your brother, and it must have been horrible to discover the crimes he'd committed, and what happened to him. Especially that way."

He took her face in his hands, forced her attention on him, and then planted a soft kiss on her forehead. When he was eye-level with her once again, he said, "Don't you know? I can get through anything as long as you're standing beside me."

She no sooner got the words, *I love you,* out of her mouth, that his lips captured hers in a slow, meaningful kiss. And she melted like she always did when he touched her.

Remi became so wrapped up in the sensation of his skilled mouth moving over hers, she almost didn't hear the noise coming from behind Lucas. Then someone cleared their throat, and the spell of the kiss broke at last. She peered over Lucas' shoulder to see Ethan standing there, appearing out of place and as fidgety as a getaway driver in a bank heist.

"Sorry to interrupt," the man said, staring at the ground. "But I need to have a word with Remi."

A hardened expression took shape on Lucas' face. And he said, tightly, "Dad, Remi has been through enough, and I'm not about to let you—"

"It's not what you think, son."

At that, he faced his father, examining him for a long, hard minute. Then he lowered his head and sighed, obviously coming to a decision. "Okay. But make it fast. We have a drug bust in operation."

When he strode away, Ethan took a few steps toward her. He directed his stare off into the distance and admitted, "This isn't going to be easy for me. I'm not good at this sort of thing."

She could tell by his uneasy stance whatever was about to tumble out of his mouth, was something she'd probably never hear again in a million years. He took a deep breath, leveled her with determined eyes, and said, "I owe you an apology for the way I've treated you. My behavior toward you was cruel and unforgiving. You didn't deserve that."

Before she could respond, he raised one hand and plowed on. "I'm not just saying this because of what I found out in there." He pointed toward the surveillance van. And when he refocused his attention on her, the pain of finding out someone murdered his son reflected in his eyes. None of this could have been easy for him.

"The problem has been me all along." He said that as if it took a chunk out of his heart. "It was never you. I was so wrapped up in my grief, I didn't want to admit you and Gavin were never right for one another. But you knew. And…"

"It's all right," she said, unable to watch him torture himself any longer. She forgave him after the first word.

He shook his head with dogged determination. "I came out here to say something, and I'm going to say it."

She threw up her hands, knowing that Kade stubbornness reared its head again and even a brick wall couldn't stop it. "Okay."

"You did the right thing by calling off the wedding. My wife tried to tell me that, but I never would listen to her."

"I'm sorry about Gavin. And I hate you had to find out this way."

"Well," he said, peering away. His jaw stiffened and his body language revealed the anger coiling inside him. "The bastard who killed Gavin is going to pay. You can take that to the bank."

"You're damn right he is."

To that, his muscles relaxed a bit, and he unflexed the fists at his side. "You're a good person, Shaw. And I'm glad my son has you. That's all I wanted to say."

Thank God. She didn't know how much more of this sentimental talk she could handle from Ethan Kade. Heart to heart speeches coming from a hard man like him seemed about as normal as a linebacker breaking down into tears after sacking the quarterback. But she realized how difficult it was to tell her these things, and she appreciated it more than he would ever know. "Thank you. Can we go back now?"

He appeared relieved to hear her say that. Then he swiveled and marched back in the direction of the van.

Remi approached the cargo area of the surveillance vehicle and wrenched open the doors to find agent Tolliver towering above her, holding out what appeared to be his personal cell phone. The inviting grin spreading across his face told her he was pleased with whatever news he had in store. "Here," he said, sticking out his arm, and helping her into the van. "Someone wants to talk to you."

She stared at him curiously, then hesitantly took the phone and placed it against her ear. "Hello."

"Aunt Remi?"

"Oh, my God," she uttered, instantly recognizing the voice. "Nathanial. Are you okay?" Since the time Ethan explained The Dallas PD had her nephew in protective custody, and he was helping authorities take down the corrupt cops involved, she'd wondered how he was holding up.

The sound of his chuckle immediately lightened her heart. "I'm fine. They're treating me well." A pause and then, "I've missed you."

"I miss you, too. I've been so worried about you."

"I'm sorry. They told me I couldn't contact you. But I wanted to."

She closed her eyes and breathed a sigh of relief, clasping a hand to her chest to still her pounding heart. Tears streaked down her cheeks as she considered all those sleepless nights she'd spent sick with worry, praying to God he was still alive, somewhere. "I can't tell you how good it is to hear your voice."

"I heard about what happened. Leave it to my crazy aunt to infiltrate one of the most dangerous drug cartels and try and find me."

She laughed through her tears. "Well, the two of us are all we have left." A memory burst into her mind. How many times did she recite that line to him after his mother passed away?

"From what I've been told, I'm not the only one in your life nowadays."

So much for thinking her love life could remain a private affair. "I guess a girl just can't keep a secret around these folks."

"As if it ever was a secret."

What exactly did he mean by that?

"C'mon, Aunt Remi. Even as a kid I knew you had the hots for Lucas."

Good grief. Was it that obvious or was he just that intuitive? It didn't matter. He slipped back into his annoying habit of being a wise ass, as usual. How she missed his playful sarcasm. "Hey, Natty?"

"Um-huh?"

"When do you think they'll let you come home?"

"Where exactly is home? You're not living in New York anymore, are you?"

A lot had changed since that dreadful day her nephew came up missing. Life as she knew it ceased to exist. The years following led her into the arms of a drug lord on her dangerous quest to find him. And then, miraculously, the man she loved appeared on her doorstep. Home existed wherever Lucas happened to be. That much she could be sure of. "Right now, I'm staying with Lucas in Texas. But I know he would welcome you into his house with open arms."

"I was thinking of joining the police academy when this is all over."

Joy and pride welled up from inside her. He'd gone through so much to come out on the other side with hopes and ambitions. His mother would be smiling down on him. "I think that's a wise and mature decision, Nathaniel."

"Well, I'm not a kid anymore, Aunt Remi."

"No, you're not." He had grown into a young man while he was away. She became regretful she didn't get the chance to see it.

Someone placed a hand on her shoulder. She glanced over to see Lucas standing next to her. He said, "I've got to go, Remi. The team is in place."

She swiped a tear from her eye and focused her attention back on the phone gripped in her hand. "I've got to go, Natty. But I love you so much and I can't wait to see you."

"I love you too. I hope to see you soon."

With that, she slid her finger across the screen, and handed the phone to Tolliver's outstretched hand. "Give me a gun," she told Lucas, staring boldly into his eyes. "I'm going with you."

His attention floated towards the Heavens. "We've been over this, Remi. You know I can't let you do that."

"This is ridiculous," she spat, crossing her arms in front of her in a stubborn gesture. "I have enough law enforcement experience. You know I can handle it."

He tucked a tendril of hair behind her ear, and took her chin in between his fingers, forcing her to stare at him. "That's not the issue. You haven't been on active duty in over thirteen years. If something went wrong out there," he said, glancing in the direction of the scene soon to unfold at the shipping plant, "it's my neck on the line. They'd can my ass for dragging you into the middle of a raid."

She jerked her chin out of his grasp and squared her shoulders. It was obvious her stab at convincing him she deserved to be there earned her no brownie points. "You didn't seem to have a problem with my help confronting Delgado, remember?"

His shoulders sagged, and he leaned against the wall of the van. "It's not like I even need to say this, because I know you're smarter than this, but we were not working in an official capacity. This is different. As an ex-police officer, you're aware of the trouble I can get into for letting you come with me."

She couldn't wholeheartedly deny the reasoning of his argument. Bringing up the situation with Bain was a desperate attempt to win a fight she'd already lost.

He ambled toward her, and when he stood in front of her, he slid both hands to the back of her neck, drew her close and said, "I love you. And I have to go."

Before she could think clearly enough to raise another protest, his lips were on hers, and she had no choice than to surrender to his persuasive kiss.

When he backed away and headed toward the rear door of the van, she called to him one last time, dread rising in her chest. "You don't know Victor Craven like I do. He's done things to his enemies you couldn't imagine. He has no conscience and no fear. A man like him is dangerous. What if he kills you?"

He swiveled to stare at her. There, in his dark eyes existed evidence he finally understood why she wanted to go so badly. "What do you think you can do, protect me from Craven?"

She lowered her head, knowing she'd officially lost the battle, and it wouldn't have mattered how hard she fought to convince him the monster he'd soon be dealing with always got his revenge. He wouldn't hear her. "It's going to be him that needs protection from me," he said, a bit peeved. The shutting of the door behind him slammed through her like a bullet.

Chapter Fourteen

SWAT stormed the inside of the warehouse like a swarm of hornets. The uniformed officers scattered, subduing their targets with trained ease. Lucas hadn't seen anything like it since that massive takedown of the Lombardi Mafia ten years earlier.

These men were the best of the best, and pride filled his chest to participate in a raid with them. But he wasn't looking to take out a lowly employee of the head honcho. He wanted Victor Craven himself. Nothing would have satisfied him more than to tackle the bastard to the ground, slap a set of cuffs on him, and read him his rights. Craven ordered a hit on his brother, and now, with all the atrocities the prick committed, it became personal. He had a score to settle. And bringing Victor in was the only way to call it even.

But as he scanned the faces of the men in the warehouse, no trace of the asshole could be found. What if he escaped? Not on his watch, Lucas decided, determined to check every crevice of this building to locate him.

His phone rang and he snatched it out of his pocket. Tolliver's number popped up, and he slid his finger across the screen, placing the device to his ear. Why did he have the feeling he wasn't going to like what the agent had to tell him? "Hey," he said, hoping he was wrong.

"She's gone."

He knew exactly who Tolliver referred to. An instant panic swept over him. "What do you mean she's gone?"

"She snuck out of the van without anyone noticing."

She planned to get to Craven before he could. The words she'd uttered during their disagreement right before he left, came crashing into his brain. *You don't know Victor like I do. What if he kills you?*

Had she lost her freaking mind? She'd put the whole operation in jeopardy because she thought the drug lord could beat him.

"That's not all," Tolliver warned. "My gun was laying on the table beside me. It's gone."

If he had any doubts before, Tolliver's words assured him Remi planned to go after Craven and eliminate him before the two of them ran across each other. He ended the call and slipped the phone back in his pocket. Fear for her safety, as much as anger for her reckless behavior washed over him. She worked in law enforcement and knew if things were going smoothly, you did not interrupt protocol. How could she throw a wrench in their plan?

When she first admitted she was afraid the drug lord would take him out, he didn't take it seriously. She evidently did. He should have heeded the warning flashing in her eyes enough to realize she'd make a move like this.

As he took off, rounding corners, and searching every place he imaged she might be, it struck him with the might of a hurricane. She'd already caught up to Victor. And he had her in his clutches. That's why neither one of them could be found. Jesus, how foolish could she be?

The chances of her being outside were slim to

none. Law enforcement crawled all over the place out there. If Craven had her as he suspected, there'd be no way he could get past the security, especially with Remi in tow.

His mind reflected on the planning they'd put into raiding the warehouse. As he and the experts examined the blueprints for this building, they'd gotten familiar with every facet of this place. But in his need to locate Remi, he'd neglected to check the rooftop. The area was nothing more than a flat, open landscape. One ladder led to the top and could only be accessed from the outside. How would Victor have gotten Remi up there without being seen? It didn't matter. Before he could eliminate the top of the warehouse as a possible escape route, he'd have to check it out.

His heart leaped into his throat as he made a mad dash for the ladder leading to the rooftop. He wanted more than anything to deny Craven took Remi hostage, but his detective instincts refused to allow him to ignore the truth.

After approaching the bottom step, he scaled the rest of the rungs two at a time in his haste to get to the top. And the second his eyes scanned the area, he spotted a police force issued helicopter perched in the center. But before his mind could decipher who ordered the use of a chopper, someone dressed in SWAT gear hauled Remi across the roof toward the waiting bird. She kicked and bucked wildly.

With blood pumping like a fire hydrant through his veins, he scrambled the rest of the way to the top and drew his weapon. Unless the guy was an officer gone rogue—highly doubtful—he sure as hell wasn't Victor and he didn't belong to the SWAT unit either. "Hey, asshole! Move away from the girl and put your hands above your head."

The identity of the guy holding Remi hostage became clear the minute he spun around to stare at Lucas. Dominick Barlow had the nerve to smile as if a good friend addressed him. "Well, well, if it isn't agent Kade come to rescue the damsel in distress." He placed the barrel of his pistol against the side of Remi's skull, cocked it, and said, "I'm afraid you're a day late and a dollar short, though, pal. In fact, if you don't drop your weapon, I'm going to do something rash, and you can collect her dead body after we leave."

We? Of course. He'd obviously struck a deal with Craven for his freedom. And the drug lord, no doubt, hid inside the chopper. "I think I'd rather take her alive and drop you where you stand. How does that sound?"

Barlow frowned and shrugged his shoulder. "You'll probably hit your target, but then, so will I," he said, gesturing toward the gun he held snugly against Remi's head. "Is killing me worth her life?"

Since he was in no position to force Barlow to drop his gun, perhaps convincing him to reconsider the DA's deal might be the only way out of this. "There's still time to change your mind," Lucas said. "Take the deal the DA is offering. You and I both know this won't last long with Craven. The minute he's through with you, he'll leave you dead in a dumpster somewhere. You read the file on him before we launched Operation Snowflakes. He's a cold-blooded killer and he'll stick a knife in your back the minute you're not looking."

"Listen, Kade," he said, losing the relaxed, arrogant demeanor he displayed a moment ago. An emotion much weaker and more desperate passed through his eyes. "I can't go to prison for twenty years. You know what will happen to me in there."

Should have thought about that before you decided to conspire with the cartel and frame me for murder. Even though an image of his former partner locked behind bars and getting the shit kicked out of him daily brought immense pleasure to Lucas—since Dom was more than willing to watch the same thing happen to him—sharing those sentiments with Barlow would have defeated his chances of convincing him to accept the sentence and surrender. Remi's wellbeing hung in the balance, and he'd use any tactic he could that would return her to safety.

"What if I guarantee they won't put you in the general population? You can serve out your time without the threat from other inmates."

Just when the slightest sign appeared in the guy's eyes, he might consider Lucas' offer, the door of the helicopter popped open, and Victor hopped onto the rooftop, dressed in the same SWAT gear as Dom wore. That's how they'd made it to the rooftop without raising suspicion. They'd evidently planned to have the helicopter waiting here to make their hasty escape.

"She's mine," Craven said, stepping over to Remi, and wrenching her away from Dom's hold. As the drug lord wrapped his arm possessively around her, Barlow, having snapped out of the lure of Lucas' attempt to reel him in, trained his gun on Lucas. "I'm sorry, man," he uttered, giving a smile that appeared anything but confident. "This is the way it has to be."

In a move Lucas didn't anticipate, Victor whipped out his gun, pointed it at Barlow's head, and squeezed the trigger. Blood splattered across Remi's face and she let out an ear-splitting scream. His ex-partner hit the floor with a thud.

"Does that solve the issue of going to prison?" Victor said, leaning in and pressing his lips against Remi's blood-streaked cheek. She recoiled but he held her firm. "C'mon, angel," he said, wiping Dom's blood from his mouth with the back of his hand. "He was a spineless coward. The world will be better off without him."

He nonchalantly raised the barrel of his gun to her head and clicked back the hammer as if doing so was as normal as an everyday chore. He then directed his gaze toward Lucas. "As I was saying. Remi here, accepted my proposal of marriage. So, that makes her mine."

"I don't think she's interested in marrying you anymore." If Lucas could keep him busy for a few more minutes, an opportunity might arise to get a shot off without the risk of hitting Remi. "Women," Victor said, shrugging. "Do they ever really know what they want? One day it's me, the next day it's you." "The difference is," the drug lord pointed out, resting his head against the side of Remi's face the same way a lover might do to show their affection. "I love her enough I proposed to her. Did you propose to her, Kade?"

For a fleeting moment Lucas caught a glimpse of disappointment in Remi's eyes. This whole ordeal came across as surreal. No way did she take the words of a madman to heart. He loved her as deeply as any man could love a woman. She knew that, didn't she? Besides, the diamond engagement ring he planned to present to her burned a hole in his pocket right at this moment.

"I risked it all to come back for her," Craven said,

pouring it on thick. "Do you think I would have shown my face at a drug raid if it hadn't been for her? Love makes a man do crazy shit, am I right?"

The rotten bastard didn't love her. A man like him wasn't capable of love. *Why are you letting anything this asshole says bother you? Snap out of it.* He came here to save Remi. That's where his focus needed to stay.

"Get in the chopper, Remi," Victor snapped. "We're leaving now."

The minute Craven removed the gun from the side of her head, she swung into action, plucked the knife from her ankle holster and sank the blade into his chest.

The guy stumbled back, and his firearm slipped from his hand. Lucas saw his chance, aimed his gun, and took the shot.

Unbelievably, it missed its mark. The slug pierced his shoulder, and before Lucas could fire another round, the son-of-a-bitch jumped into the helicopter and started it up.

Remi scrambled away from the whirling blades of the chopper, and Lucas let the bullets fly, hoping to pierce the window and stop Craven before he made his escape.

Horror settled into his gut as the bird lifted off the ground and took off with Victor inside.

****

Lucas stood off to the side of Tolliver's office, taking up a position flat against the wall that ensured no one inside the room could see him. He peeked through the glass door, examining Remi as she sat giving her statement. At times he noticed her moving her hands as a means of expression, but given the calm demeanor of her face, it would appear to any observer, she remained in control of her emotions. But the way she twirled a lock of hair occasionally while leaning to one side with her elbow propped against the arm of the chair told him her nerves bounced around like a ping pong ball.

Realizing he could decipher her feelings so easily based on her habits struck a chord. In that moment he'd made an astounding discovery. He knew her better than anyone. And the time had come to toss his doubts aside about how she'd receive him if he were to propose and do something about it.

Tolliver rose from behind his desk and crossed the room. Lucas cleared his throat, spun on one heel and headed in the opposite direction so his superior wouldn't know he'd been spying. The creaking of hinges signaled the man swung the door open, and Lucas stopped in his tracks as he called his name.

He faced Tolliver just as Remi stepped out. The haunting expression in her beautiful eyes caused his breath to catch. Her level of despondence rose higher than he expected. He read her mind as if she'd spoken to him. She placed the blame for Barlow's death, and Craven's escape completely on herself. He'd worked so hard when she blamed herself for what she thought to be Gavin's suicide, to get her to see it wasn't her fault. Now, she stood on the threshold once again of holding herself responsible for the actions of others.

Instinctively, he opened his mouth but Tolliver spoke first. "Lucas. Can I see you in my office?"

With that, her attention swept away, and she continued down the hall. He expelled the breath he'd been holding in his chest, unaware, and headed in the direction of the man's office. The door shut behind him, and he stepped over to the chair in front of the desk and sank down.

The minute Tolliver settled in across from him, the agent let out a deep sigh, as if the weight of the world saddled around his shoulders. "You're the only one who knows she took my gun while we were in the van. Judging by the conversation the two of you had before you stepped outside, I gathered she was worried for your safety, and that's what caused her to snatch my weapon and sneak off to the shipping plant. You'll be happy to know there will be no charges pressed against Ms. Shaw for her actions."

Relief rolled off Lucas in a wave. What his boss planned to do in retribution for Remi stealing his firearm, had been a nagging concern since they'd wrapped up the scene. "I'm sorry I let Victor Craven get away."

Tolliver shook his head, dismissing Lucas' apology with a shrug of his shoulders. "You didn't let anyone escape. No one even knew he'd gone to the roof. You're the only one besides Remi who was smart enough to figure it out."

What did he mean Remi figured it out? Although he'd found her on the rooftop with Dom and Victor, he assumed Barlow found her and dragged her up there.

"We know Barlow and Craven planned this all along," his superior continued. "They killed two SWAT agents, hid their bodies behind a stack of furniture in the storage room, and stole their uniforms. That's how they managed to slip past a warehouse full of law enforcement without being detected."

"You're saying Remi knew they were on the rooftop and went after them up there?"

He nodded, saying, "She'd make a good DEA agent. We should probably give her a gun so she wouldn't have to steal mine."

Even though his boss jested about the situation, Lucas couldn't help but wonder how Remi managed to figure out Craven's moves, when no one else did.

Tolliver said, "She's spent enough time with Victor she knows how he thinks. She figured he planned to make his escape from the one place no one would have expected."

"She wasn't supposed to be there." Lucas' head reeled as the truth smacked him in the face. "So, she couldn't ask for anyone's help. She thought she had no choice than to go up there and stop him herself."

"Barlow surprised her as she headed toward the chopper. He was hiding behind the ventilation unit."

Craven said he wouldn't have been there if it wasn't for her. He anticipated her moves. He knew she'd come because she felt she was the only one who could stop him. Him and Barlow set a trap for her. Lucas couldn't have been more grateful their plan to kidnap her didn't work. Neither one of them expected he'd figure out where they'd gone and that they had Remi before they got a chance to escape. "How'd they get their hands on a police helicopter?"

"None of our guys questioned the fact it was on the roof. It was one of ours, so the agents on the ground assumed someone called in for it." Tolliver plucked a pencil from the canister on his desk and rolled it between his fingers. Lucas recognized the action as something someone would do to kickstart their brain. "Of course, now we know, being that the bird was ours, Victor was counting on the fact no one would question it. A chopper went missing from the hanger this morning. But no one appears to know how that happened."

"I'm calling bullshit. It's a chopper for God's sake. Something like that doesn't go missing without someone noticing it."

"We're looking into it. Trust me. It could be a case of the left hand not knowing what the right hand was doing." He slipped the pencil back into the canister and cleared his throat. "On another note, we've notified the hospitals to be on the lookout for someone stumbling through their doors matching Craven's description. He's got a bullet injury and a knife wound. He'll have to seek treatment somewhere. We also have a chopper out searching for him."

"I'm afraid he's long gone by now. He has connections and he can get medical care off the grid. Wherever he is, it won't be where you can find him."

Tolliver's frown told him he knew that to be the case as well. "Dominick Barlow's wife has been notified of his death."

Even though his partner went rogue, and helped to set him up for a murder he didn't commit, there existed a small part of him that remembered the man for who he was while working alongside of him. The pain of that would never go away. "If we're done," he said, rising from the chair with an air of determination, "I'd like to go find Remi and propose to her." It suddenly dawned on him, if he didn't do it now, he may never get another chance.

That caught Tolliver off guard. "You're going to ask her to marry you...now?"

"You're damn right I am."

The man sat back in his chair, a wide grin spreading across his face. "It's about time. But you better hurry. She planned to grab a cup of coffee before leaving here, and then she mentioned something about heading to a motel. She didn't say it, but I could tell she figured you didn't want anything more to do with her after what she pulled today."

Geez, how many times did he need to pound into her stubborn head he loved her unconditionally? It'd take a hell of a lot more than an attempt to sacrifice her life to try and save his, to cause him to turn away from her. In fact, as he stood here now, he couldn't think of a single thing she could do that would make him abandon her. It took him thirteen years to find her again, and he wasn't about to let her slip through his fingers a second time.

He rushed from Tolliver's office with his heart beating out of his chest and made a beeline for the coffee station tucked into a small nook of the building. He rounded the corner so quickly, his feet nearly slipped out from under him when he hit a slick spot in the tiles.

Scanning the area produced no signs of Remi. A coffee stirrer lay on the counter, spots of dark liquid surrounding it, along with a scattering of creamer, and four or five empty sugar packets torn open and resting beside it. The evidence of someone making a cup of coffee could have been left by anyone. But sharing his mornings with her for the last few weeks, whether it be at the cabin in New York, or at his house here in Texas, he recognized her less than tidy coffee making habits immediately. No one made this much of a mess with creamer and sugar other than Remi Shaw.

He headed toward the front doors of the building. How much time did he spend in Tolliver's office? His heart sank the more he realized he'd chatted with his boss long enough for her to grab a cup of coffee and depart. There'd be no way of knowing which hotel she planned to stay at. A shit ton of them were scattered throughout the Dallas area. And since laws prevented hotels from disclosing the name of their guests, the only way to obtain that information would be to utilize police resources. He didn't want to picture that conversation with Tolliver. *Say, boss, you mind if we bend the law a little and use our intelligence to run down a woman I was stupid enough to let slip away?*

He'd rather pick cactus needles out of his hide than to go there with Tolliver. The man was a stickler for the rules, and if he asked for such a favor, it would only make him appear desperate and reckless in the guy's eyes. He was both at the moment.

When he neared the exit doors, he scanned the faces of everyone within eyeshot. No Remi. Shit. He'd missed his chance with her again. Why didn't he talk to her right after Craven made his getaway? He had to have known how she must have felt…that she blamed her intervention as the reason the capture of Victor Craven was fumbled so badly. But what she didn't realize was if she didn't show up and seek him out, no one would have ever guessed the drug lord planned his escape from the rooftop.

Someone clapped Lucas on the shoulder as he stood in the lobby, staring off into the distance as if gazing into the abyss. He glanced over to find Chuck Huxley, who worked in the tactical intelligence division, "It's a bitch about Craven," the guy said, shaking his head.

Word got around quick, didn't it?

Lucas averted his attention away from the glaring sunlight streaming in through the glass plated front doors—where he pictured Remi standing on the other side—and lowered his head. "Next time," he said, referring to what would happen if he ever crossed paths with the criminal again.

The jarring sound of the squeaky hinges on the nearby bathroom door as someone opened it, shot right through him in his agitated state. The damned things needed oiling for as long as he could remember. Why couldn't someone do their job and take care of the maintenance around here?

Then he recognized the face of the person stepping out of the restroom. The minute Remi's eyes connected with his, a transformation of her expression going from blank to emotional, sent hot blood pumping through his veins. Her mouth twitched as if she wanted to speak but nothing came out. And then, a mask of sadness fell over her, and she glanced away, sweeping past him.

At first, he struggled to understand why she'd simply leave him standing there like that. But then it occurred to him how well he knew her. She was running away again. It didn't matter if doing so ripped her heart out. She'd walk away, go home, and cry herself to sleep, all because she thought she'd wronged him in some way that could not be forgiven.

"Hey," he hollered to her retreating back. "You walked away from me once before, Remi Shaw. I swore I'd never let you do it again."

She stopped in her tracks, not turning around, and his pulse hammered in anticipation of her next move. If she refused to face him, he'd lay it on the line either way, and he didn't give a damn who heard it. "You were right to go after Craven. I was an idiot for stopping you."

She raised her head and her shoulders sagged. But she still stood there, facing the door.

"You knew him better than anyone. Including me. I was afraid he'd hurt you. That's why I didn't want you to go."

That prompted her to spin on her heels and stare at him, finally. With tears streaming down her face, she said, "It wasn't my welfare I was worried about. I figured Victor wouldn't kill me. But I knew he would you."

"I should have listened. And I'm sorry."

"It's my fault a man lost his life."

He took easy steps toward her, doing his best not to send her scurrying toward the door. "Barlow tried to kidnap you, Remi. He put himself in that position. That's what got him killed. I need you to understand that."

"But if I hadn't shown up—"

"You heard Victor," he said, now standing in front of her. His body trembled when he lifted a hand and wiped away a tear from her face. "He came to get you. He wouldn't have left without you. If you hadn't shown up, he would have gotten to you some other way. You know that."

He cupped her face in his hands and forced her to stare into his eyes. "When you blame yourself unnecessarily like this, it tears one helluva hole in my heart. These past few weeks, I have fought like hell for the woman I fell in love with thirteen years ago. The one with a carefree spirit, the one who refused to let anyone bring her down. You promised me you'd love me forever. I battled ghosts from the past to get you back, and now I refuse to accept I've lost you again."

"You haven't lost me," she confessed, gazing into his eyes with the most profound love and warmth that melted his heart on the spot. "In all my life, my heart has never belonged to anyone else. You could never lose me."

He plunged his hand into his pocket, produced the velvet box, opened it, and held it out. Putting his heart on the line like this meant she had the power to crush him. "I'm going out on a limb here and asking you to be my wife right here and right now. Stay with me forever, Remi. I'll give you everything I have, and what I don't have, I'll move heaven and earth to get for you."

"Oh, Lucas," she said, fresh tears glistening in her eyes. "All I ever wanted was your heart."

"Since the day you found me waiting for you at the airport, you have owned my heart. So, is that a yes?"

"A thousand times, yes!"

Applause and whistles broke out around them as he plucked the ring from the box and slid it on her finger. Then he wrapped her in his arms and took her lips in a slow, sultry kiss.

Someone hollered, "Get a room!"

"I knew you had it in you," He recognized Tolliver's voice as the man clapped him on the back. "All right, everyone," his boss announced, "The party's over. Get back to work."

The bitching and complaining of everyone standing around melted into the background as he drew the love of his life closer against him and continued to ravage her lips. A quote he'd once heard popped into his mind. *Life begins at the point you meet the one you're meant to walk through life with.*

Although he'd spent the last thirteen years pining after a girl he figured he could never have, now that he had her, life was just beginning.

A word about the author…

Although not a native Texan, Donnette Smith has spent more than half her life living in the Lone Star State. She is an entrepreneur and former business owner of Tailor Maid Services LLC. After spending a few years working as a journalist for the Blue Ridge Tribune, she realized her love for writing romantic detective novels. Her stories cover a wide range of genres, from horror, time travel, mystery, fantasy, paranormal, and thriller. But one theme stays the same, there is always a hot detective solving a crime, and a gorgeous victim he would lay down his life to protect. Donnette's biggest fascination is with forensic science and crime scene investigations.

www.donnettesmith.com

Thank you for purchasing
this publication of The Wild Rose Press, Inc.

For questions or more information
contact us at
info@thewildrosepress.com.

The Wild Rose Press, Inc.
www.thewildrosepress.com